A WIFE'S BETRAYAL

LIZ HARRIS

B

Boldwood

First published in 2020 as *The Flame Within*. This edition published in Great Britain in 2026 by Boldwood Books Ltd.

Cover Design by JD Smith Design Ltd.

Cover Images: Shutterstock

A CIP catalogue record for this book is available from the British Library.

Paperback ISBN 978-1-80703-094-0

Large Print ISBN 978-1-80703-096-4

Hardback ISBN 978-1-80703-093-3

Trade Paperback ISBN 978-1-80703-095-7

Ebook ISBN 978-1-80703-097-1

Kindle ISBN 978-1-80703-098-8

Audio CD ISBN 978-1-80703-088-9

MP3 CD ISBN 978-1-80703-089-6

Digital audio download ISBN 978-1-80703-090-2

This book is printed on certified sustainable paper. Boldwood Books is dedicated to putting sustainability at the heart of our business. For more information please visit https://www.boldwoodbooks.com/about-us/sustainability/

Boldwood Books Ltd, 23 Bowerdean Street, London, SW6 3TN

www.boldwoodbooks.com

PROLOGUE

BELSIZE PARK, LONDON

July 1923

A brown leather bag in each hand, Alice stood on the pavement and stared up the drive to the large Victorian house set back from the road – the house that was to be her new home.

Despite its imposing size, it looked warm and friendly, she thought with relief.

But it wasn't *her* house. It belonged to someone else – a Mrs Violet Osborne. A woman, who was no more than a name at the end of the advertisement for a companion that had caught her eye three weeks earlier.

More precisely, it wasn't Mrs Osborne's name that had caught her eye – it was seeing that Mrs Osborne lived in Belsize Park.

Belsize Park – a short distance only from Kentish Town, which was where she'd lived when she'd been Mrs Thomas Linford.

Thomas Linford – the man she loved, and through her own stupidity, had lost. The man she'd come back down to London to fight for.

A car passed noisily on the road behind her, and she felt the rush of wind in its wake.

A wave of self-pity engulfed her.

When she'd last lived in London, she'd have arrived at her destination in such a car. She wouldn't have had to make her way from Euston, carrying her bags. When she'd last lived in London, she'd been respected as part of the Linford family, owners of the successful construction company, Linford & Sons, and she'd wanted for nothing. When she'd last lived in London, staff had looked after her home.

Now she was about to become a member of someone else's staff.

And she had only herself to blame for that. She'd been so unbelievably blind!

She blinked back tears.

She must pull herself together. She needed to keep her mind on the present and why she was there. It had been *her* decision to leave her home in Lancashire for a second time, and to take up a domestic post in the south. No one had forced her to return to London, nor in such a capacity. She was there to win back Thomas, and she had to be in London to do that.

So now that she was back, it was what happened next that mattered.

Tightening her grip on her bags, she walked steadily up the drive to the dark blue front door with its stained-glass panel. Her stomach churning, she put down her bags, raised her hand to the heavy brass door knocker, rapped it hard against its backplate, stepped away from the door, and waited for her future to begin.

1

WATERFOOT, LANCASHIRE

Spring 1904

Sitting on the side of the grass-covered hill, Alice Foster hugged her knees to her chest and stared across the sprawling Rossendale Valley into the distance beyond.

Then she gazed up at the sky, took a deep breath of the fresh, clean air that enveloped her, and sighed with pleasure.

This was her favourite place. It was so much more enjoyable to be up in the hills than down among the grey brick houses, trapped beneath the layer of dense yellow smoke that blanketed the town from morning till night.

Her mam had told her that many years ago, long before she herself had been born, and her mother before her, Rossendale had been a beautiful forested valley, and the river that ran through Waterfoot had been full of fish. But the forests had long been cleared. Cotton mills now stood where once there'd been trees, and fish no longer swam in the river.

Instead of teeming with natural life, the valley was filled with factories and a hotchpotch of small houses and shops that had sprung up around the factories like weeds.

Among them, she could make out the ribbon of terraces and shops that lined Bacup Road, which bisected the centre of Waterfoot, and the lines of small grey houses that flanked the steep streets that climbed up from the road. And it was easy to see the tall narrow chimneys that grew from the medley of stone walls and slate-tiled roofs – chimneys that night and day belched forth columns of dense grey smoke.

In one of those factories her mother worked, and in all likelihood, so, too, would she when she was older. She pulled a face at the thought of it.

She turned her gaze towards the part of town in which she and her parents lived. But it wasn't so easy to pinpoint their row of back-to-back houses. She stared harder into the mass of grey, but with the light of day starting to fade, and the ever-present cloud of smoke, the houses were indistinct and she couldn't distinguish one row from another.

The hills on the other side of the valley were becoming less clear, too, and she knew it was time to leave the top of the hill, go back down into the town and make a start on the evening meal. When her mam got home, she'd be tired after twelve long hours in the hot weaving shed. And her dad, too, would be weary and ready for food when he returned from the quarry, where he'd been since early morning.

Reluctantly, she stood up, wiped the grass from the back of her skirt and started down the dry dusty path that led back into Waterfoot.

* * *

She pushed open the front door and went into the gloom of the sitting-room.

The late afternoon warmth remained outside, and she shivered.

That was one of the worst things about living in a house at the end of the block of back-to-backs – there were two outside walls. Their house was colder than those in the middle of the row, which had a house on either side. The house where her friend May lived was just as cold as hers. May's family lived at the other end of the row of six back-to-backs, very close to the stone steps leading up from the road.

It was just as well that her house was close to the steps, May always said. Her mam took in ironing every week, and by the time she'd reached the top step, carrying a large wicker basket filled with linen and clothes that weighed heavily in her arms, she'd gone about as far as she could go.

Alice liked May's mam, who was happy to talk to her and May while she was ironing, and who told them all kinds of interesting things.

Sometimes it was things she'd seen for herself when she'd gone to the rich people's houses to collect or return their ironing, and sometimes it was titbits that May's older sister, Gladys, a housemaid for the Bates's family, who owned the cotton mill with the weaving shed where her mother worked, had passed on when she'd come home on her weekly afternoon off.

She and May loved hearing how other people lived – the sort of things they did, the kind of food they ate, the clothes they wore. And about the houses they lived in, which were usually surrounded by trees and flowers and which had lots of rooms. They had far more rooms than just an attic, two upstairs bedrooms, a downstairs scullery with a stone slab for a sink and a single cold-water tap, a sitting-room, and a cellar.

The rich people's houses had a proper inside bathroom, with a privy in it. They didn't have to share outside privies with all the other families in their block. They were so lucky.

Even though each of the twelve families took turns in cleaning weekly the four privies they shared, scrubbing each of the boards with a hole in the middle that had been placed above earth-filled tubs, mopping the floors, and making sure there were sufficient newspaper squares, there was always a stench by the end of the week. It was especially bad in summer as the tubs were emptied once a week only by the council man, who made his round with the night-soil cart in the evening.

And the rich people's houses also had a bath in their bathroom.

They didn't have to use a tin tub in front of the fire, filled with water that had been fetched from the scullery and heated in the boiler that stood on one side of the large iron fireplace in the sitting-room. And they didn't have to top up the boiler as soon as any of the water had been used – a boiler that was always rusty, no matter how often her mam whitewashed the inside.

Not that such people ever went into their kitchen for water – they had servants to do that for them. They had a cook, kitchen maids, housemaids, and a housekeeper who supervised all the women servants, and also looked after the linen and china cupboards, the housekeeping money and who made arrangements for any guests. And they had people like May's mam to do the chores that the household staff didn't do.

But in her house and May's, they and their mams had to do all the work by themselves.

For as long as she could remember, she'd always had chores to do, some before she went to school, and some when she got back. And now she was ten, she'd been given even more tasks to do, such as polishing carefully the sideboard and chairs with lavender furniture wax, making sure that she didn't leave any clumps of wax in the joints or the corners.

She was now so busy that it was getting harder to find the time to play with May, who had even more daily chores. May's dad and her two brothers didn't do a thing in the house except make a mess, and as May's sister, Gladys, lived in the Bates's house, it was left to May and her mam to clean up after them and do everything else in the house.

But busy as she was, she didn't blame her mam for giving her so much to do each day.

Her mam had to be in the factory by half past six in the morning. All she had time to do before she went out was have a quick cup of tea and maybe a jam butty. If she was late, the factory gates might be closed against her, or if they allowed her in, she'd be fined. And she was seldom home before seven in the evening.

Her dad's job was even more tiring then her mam's, and his hours about as long – when there was work for him, that is. In frosty weather, they couldn't work newly quarried stone, so the men were often laid off. A couple of years ago, when there'd been a particularly long cold spell in winter, he had been laid off for several weeks, and her mam had struggled to manage as they'd been given no more than a pound each week by the quarryman's association.

Unlike her mam, her dad didn't have breakfast at home as he had to be at the quarry much too early for that. He had to be there early enough to make sure that the fires for the steam cranes were ready by the time the men arrived. After that, he and the other men would make their breakfast by putting white lard on a shovel held over an open fire, and cooking on it sausages, bacon and egg. When the food was ready, they'd sit together and eat it with thickly cut slices of toasted bread.

She asked him one day what he did in the quarry, and he told her that he worked something called a cone crusher. They tipped the bits of stone that hadn't been set aside to be used for building into a chute at the top of a steep slope, and by turning a spindle in the chute, her dad broke the leftover pieces of rock into smaller bits. The smaller bits fell further down the chute where they were broken up again into even smaller bits. This breaking up went on, he told her, until the pieces were small enough to fall through a narrow opening at the bottom of the crusher, and they'd be collected from there.

It sounded hard work, and boring, and she was sorry for her father.

If only they lived in a town with more than just mills and factories and a few small shops that were mainly family-run, she used to think. Then her mam and dad might have been able to find work that was less tiring, and more interesting.

And there *were* towns where people did all kinds of other jobs.

She knew that for sure as she and May had started to read *Tatler*. The Bates's housekeeper had got into the habit of giving the magazine to Gladys when Mrs Bates had finished with it. And Gladys, who could scarcely read, always passed it on to May.

On the pages of *Tatler*, they'd seen pictures of people whose lives were very different from those in Waterfoot. They lived in a variety of houses, and wore clothes that you'd never wear in a factory or down a quarry. And they didn't just work all day in a mill and then go home and work some more. They went out to interesting places, like parties and galleries. And when they were at home, they had time to relax and sit on sofas or chairs, drinking tea.

And there were many pictures of things that the women in such towns could put on their face to make themselves pretty. It seemed to be important to look pretty.

But her mam said that she, Alice, was a very pretty girl, and May's mam and dad said the same thing, too. With her looks, she ought to be able to work somewhere other than in a mill or a factory, her mam used to say. With a face like hers, she could make something of herself.

And by the time she reached the end of her twelfth year, she'd known for certain that that was what she was going to do.

When she grew up, she would do everything she could to avoid living in the same way as her mother and the other women of Waterfoot. She'd find the sort of job that when she got home each night, wouldn't leave her too tired to talk to her husband or sit with her children.

She didn't yet know what kind of job that might be as there was no mention of jobs on the pages of *Tatler*, where women seemed not to work at all. But she knew for certain that she wouldn't find work like that in a small town like Waterfoot. Such jobs would be found somewhere else, though, and wherever that somewhere else turned out to be, she'd go there.

That was the promise she made to herself at twelve years of age.

2

1905

In the months that followed the promise she'd made to herself, she firmed up her resolution to move to a larger town when she was older, one that wasn't dominated by mills. Gradually, too, she'd come to accept that it might even mean leaving Lancashire.

It made her extremely sad to think of moving away from her parents, but every time she felt tearful at the idea of living at a distance from them, she reminded herself that they, too, would benefit from her move. She would always send some of her wages back home, so their lives, too, would become easier. Realising that, she felt better about what she intended to do.

The thought of leaving Lancashire having taken root in her mind. Whenever she was close to people with money and education, she listened very carefully to how they spoke, and she started trying to imitate them. The other children used to laugh at her and tease her, and call her stuck-up, but she ignored them. She'd hate it if the people she met when she lived somewhere else thought 'slipper factory' every time she opened her mouth, and making sure that such a thing never happened was far more important than anything the other children could shout after her.

But she knew that it wouldn't just be her parents she missed when she moved away – it would be May, too.

May was the first person she'd told about her plan. When she'd done so, she'd secretly hoped that May would ask to go with her. It would be so much nicer to go with her best friend, rather than go on her own. But May hadn't believed she'd really carry out her plan.

'Get on with yer!' May had shrieked, and to Alice's huge disappointment, she had just laughed.

She'd been quite upset for several days after that, both that May hadn't believed her, and also that she'd showed no interest at all in going with her. But there was plenty of time for May to change her mind, she'd reassured herself, and she was going to carry on hoping that she did.

She hadn't yet told her mam and dad, though. They'd be upset, she knew, and there was no point in making them sad when she was still far too young to leave.

In the meantime, she worked hard on the way she spoke, and she heeded what her mam kept telling her, which was that if she wanted to make something of her life, she must be a good girl at all times and keep her distance from boys. She'd known from the expression on her mother's face whenever she mentioned boys, that it was particularly important to avoid them if she wanted to find true love.

And she did.

She desperately wanted to be loved in the way that her dad loved her mam, but she wanted the person who'd love her like that to live far away. She certainly didn't want to be loved by anyone who'd chain her to Waterfoot.

So she went out of her way to be a good girl.

It wasn't difficult being good. She enjoyed going to Waterfoot Junior School, and she worked hard at her lessons, and could read and write as well as anyone in her class. She did everything she was asked to do around the house. And she kept away from boys.

Keeping away from boys was the easiest part of all.

All the boys in Waterfoot seemed babyish and dull. They were very different from the smart, handsome men whom she and May used to see on the pages of *Tatler*.

It had become a particular treat for her and May at weekends, when they'd finished their chores, to climb up the hills outside Waterfoot, taking the magazine with them.

With the small stones on the hillside path crunching beneath their feet, they'd go higher and higher up the track, passing the fields on their left and the stream that ran between the trees, passing the mill owner's house on their right, and then making their way between the farmhouses on either side of the track until their reached their favourite niche, which was at the foot of a steep slope that led up to the moor. There, sheltered from the wind, they'd devour the magazine as they huddled together, their heads bent low over the pages.

'What sort of man d'you think you'd like to marry?' she asked May one day when they'd finished discussing the merits of each of the men whose picture had appeared in that issue.

'Someone who's not bad-tempered and shouty like me dad,' May told her. 'You should hear him in the morning. And in the evenings, too. I wouldn't want ter marry a man like that, not even if he had pots and pots of money. Money's not as important as being nice ter your wife. What about yer?'

Alice nodded. 'The same as you. Bad-tempered men are so bossy. Their faces get all lined and their eyes squinty. I wouldn't mind pots of money, though. But not if they had a cob on all the time. Me dad loves me mam, and I want a man who loves me like that.'

'So we want exactly the same,' May said happily. 'I knew we would cos we think alike.'

But Alice knew that she didn't want exactly the same as May.

Number one on her list was that her husband mustn't live in Waterfoot. But May wanted to stay close to her mam.

It would be nice if he had enough money so, like people in the south, she didn't have to work. But that wasn't high on her list as it was difficult to imagine what she'd do all day if she didn't have any chores. She couldn't really see herself doing nothing from morning till night. That would be boring. She just wanted the chance of a more interesting job, and to be able to visit exciting places, and to not have to live in a back-to-back or a small terraced house made of stone.

Sometimes at night, before she fell asleep, she agonised about what she'd do if someone very rich fell in love with her, who'd be able to give her the sort of life she'd seen in magazines, and who'd be willing to send money to her parents so that they, too, would have an easier life, but she didn't wildly love him. Would she marry him, she wondered.

She wasn't sure. If she didn't like him, she certainly wouldn't. Not for any amount of money. If she liked him, but didn't madly love him, it wasn't so clear.

But there was no point in worrying about what she'd do in such a situation as she was unlikely to meet a rich person like that, she'd long ago realised. By reading the society news in the magazine, she'd come to understand that it was essential to move in what was called the right social circles.

In Waterfoot, that would mean mixing with the people who owned the mills, not those who worked in them. And if she did ever happen to meet such a person, he'd never notice her. No one who owned a mill would notice someone like her.

And that would be the same wherever she lived.

However, as she wasn't looking for a rich mill owner, her background didn't really matter. What *did* matter, if she wanted the right husband in the right place, was that she never let herself be tempted by any of the Waterfoot boys she knew, or might meet. Not one of them would be suitable.

Well, just maybe, if she were truly honest with herself, there *were* two who'd made an impression upon her in the past few months – Stan Cooke, and Frederick Bates, the mill owner's oldest son.

Especially Stan Cooke.

Her stomach had recently started lurching in a most uncomfortable way whenever she saw Stan Cooke, the oldest of four boys who lived in a back-to-back a few doors down from her house. He was tall, with dark brown hair, dark brown eyes, and a ready smile, and he was so good-looking that he was sure to have been put in the pages of *Tatler* if the magazine people had ever met him.

Stan was five years older than her, and had already left school and started working in one of the mills off Bacup Road. Although all the girls where she lived liked him – including May, she was sure, although May wouldn't admit it – she could tell that she was the girl he was interested in.

But no matter how much she might wish it to be otherwise, she knew that Stan would stay in Waterfoot for the rest of his life, and that if she married him, she'd end up like her mam. And she wasn't going to let that happen, not even for Stan. So keeping her mam's dire hints about what could happen to careless girls in the fore of her mind, she'd started going out of her way to avoid seeing him.

But one Monday a few weeks ago, she'd come pretty close to forgetting to keep her distance.

Stan had returned from the factory just as she'd been starting to unpeg the sheets that had been outside on the line all day. She was later than usual in bringing them in as she'd had to stop for some mustard pickle on her way home. Because she'd forgotten to take the basin to school with her, which they'd fill with pickle from their large jar, she'd had to come back home first to collect it.

When Stan had got back, she'd been struggling to fold each sheet as she took it from the line, and he came across to help her. Together they finished folding everything, and then they'd stood talking about one of the teachers at her school.

All of a sudden, Stan's voice had sounded different. Before she could wonder why, he'd leaned down and kissed her. She'd been so surprised that she'd actually kissed him back!

It had been her first kiss, and she'd liked it very much, particularly because it was Stan who was kissing her. When he'd drawn back, and she'd felt the gap of cold air between them, she'd moved instinctively closer to him. Shutting her eyes, she'd raised her mouth towards his and puckered her lips as she and May had frequently practised, waiting for him to kiss her again.

But he didn't move.

She'd opened her blue eyes wide and stared up at him from beneath long eyelashes, a question on her lips.

'When yer a few years older, Alice,' he'd said, looking unusually serious as he gazed down at her, 'we're gonna do that again. You an' me are meant ter be, and I'm gonna be waitin' for yer ter grow a bit. So don't yer go and promise yerself ter anyone else, d'yer hear?'

She'd nodded solemnly. 'I won't, Stan.'

And in that moment she didn't intend to. She liked Stan, and she'd liked the way it had felt when his lips had been on hers, and the way it had made her feel inside. And she was sure that he'd be very nice to have as her husband.

But the effects of his kiss had worn off long before the evening was over, and by the time she went to bed, she was no longer quite so certain. Lying beneath her blanket, she'd run through in her head all the things she'd done that Monday before Stan had kissed her.

Before going to school, she'd pegged out the linen and clothes that she and her mam had been forced to wash on the Sunday, with her being in school on the Monday and her mam in the factory. On her way home, she'd bought the pickle, and then she'd gone outside to collect the washing. Doing the ironing was her chore for Tuesday, so when she'd put the folded linen and clothes in a pile on the chair, she'd prepared the evening meal. She'd cut slices of cold meat from the Sunday roast, and because her dad always said she made the best bubble and squeak, she'd mashed up the leftover potatoes and vegetables, fried them, and kept them warm on the stove, ready to be served with the meat and mustard pickle.

That's what she'd done that Monday, and it was what she'd be doing the following Monday, and on all the Mondays after that. And nothing would change if she married Stan.

But did she want that?

By the time she drifted into sleep, her only thought had been that she must never risk getting into the position her mam was in, and that meant she must never again let Stan kiss her.

Which had left the cotton mill owner's son, Frederick, who looked to be about the same age as Stan.

Frederick Bates wasn't as attractive as Stan, being a little too large in the middle and somewhat round in the face, but he wasn't unpleasant to look at, and on the few occasions she'd seen him, she'd thought what a nice smile he had. If she married Frederick, she wouldn't have to move too far from her parents and May. Admittedly, she'd still be in Waterfoot, but she was sure that people like Frederick's family managed to do more interesting things than those who worked in their mills.

Her mam would say that she was forgetting her position, letting herself think like that about Frederick, but her mam didn't know that she had good reason to do so. She seldom had cause to go to the mill, but on the few times she'd been there, she was sure she'd been noticed by Frederick, and she'd been pretty certain from his expression that he'd liked the way she looked.

In fact, on the last such occasion, he'd gone out of his way to go over to where she was standing. And there'd been something in his eyes that told her that had they been alone, he would've kissed her.

She'd started to feel quite excited about what that might mean. She was sure she could fall in love with Frederick. And with him as her husband, she'd have a better life, and she'd be able to help her parents.

But to her great misery, she'd recently had to abandon any thoughts of marrying him.

It had happened one afternoon not long after her kiss with Stan.

She and May had been sitting outside Alice's house, taking it in turns to read aloud an article in *Tatler* about society weddings, and she'd seized a chance to discover what May thought about her marrying Frederick Bates. In a jesting sort of way, she'd said that Frederick had seemed very friendly the last few times she'd seen him, and she was thinking that she might encourage him.

But May hadn't laughed. In fact, she'd suddenly got very serious.

'Is anything wrong, May?' she asked. 'You've gone red in the face.'

May visibly hesitated. 'No, nothing,' she said. 'It's just something Gladys told me mam.'

Alice's brow furrowed. 'What did she say?'

May cleared her throat. 'It's not really anything ter talk about. But it was about one of the Bates's housemaids. The housemaid told the housekeeper she was having a baby because of Frederick, and the housekeeper told Mrs Bates.' May went a deeper shade of red. 'Apparently, Mrs Bates called the housemaid a trollop, instantly dismissed her and said they'd never give her a reference.'

'She didn't,' Alice breathed, her eyes wide open in horror.

'She did,' May insisted. 'Gladys said Frederick didn't even suggest marrying her. But she said that even if he had, Mr Bates wouldn't have let him. He's got his eye on the daughter of a mill owner friend for Frederick. He knows it's Frederick's baby, though, cos everyone heard him shout that he'd stop Frederick's allowance if he didn't keep well away from the housemaids in future. Me mam said Frederick would obey his father cos he'd hate ter be cut off, and for the mill ter be given ter his younger brother.'

'I see,' Alice said quietly.

May gave her a knowing look. 'So whatever he was thinking when he was looking at yer, Alice Foster, he wouldn't have been thinking about marryin' yer.'

Alice forced a laugh. 'Just as well I was only joking, then.'

And a few minutes later, she'd found an excuse to go back into her house.

She'd learned a valuable lesson that day, she thought, as she closed the door behind her, one that would stop her from wasting any more time in thinking about the likes of Frederick and other mill owners' sons. That housemaid's situation had spelt out the danger her mother had been hinting at whenever she'd mentioned the subject of boys.

With the background she had, she'd never be acceptable to families like the Bateses, any more than that housemaid had been. Waterfoot was a small community and everyone knew where she came from. So no matter how pretty she made herself look, or how well she spoke, if she stayed where she was, she'd end up like her mother.

If she'd had any lingering doubts about leaving Waterfoot, they disappeared in that moment. When she was old enough, she'd go to a place where she'd be judged by what she was, and not by where she came from.

It meant that for the three more years before she left school, she must watch herself closely and never again allow herself to think about any Waterfoot man in such a way. And she would work even harder to improve herself, so that by the time she left Waterfoot, no one meeting her would be able to tell the life she'd known as a child.

And since there was no way she was ever going to work in a mill or a factory, she must also start to think seriously about what other kind of job she might be able to do.

And then, one year later, everything changed.

3

1906

White-faced, Alice sat downstairs with her mother on their threadbare sofa, staring at the wooden chair in which Mr Brooker, the quarry foreman, had been sitting until a moment earlier.

'Like Mr Brooker said, your dad was reet lucky that Walter Carpenter was close enough ter grab him and stop him from falling all the way into the crusher,' Ethel Foster said at last, her voice shaking. 'If Walter hadn't been there, yer dad would've lost more than just an arm.' She shook her head. 'He must have been that tired ter have leaned over so far, thinking ter unblock the chute. It's a godsend the horse ambulance got him so quickly ter the doctor's in Stacksteads and they were able to stitch him up.'

Alice felt fear rising in her throat. 'How can he work with only one arm, mam?'

'He can't, our Alice,' Ethel said flatly. 'It's as Mr Brooker said, he'll not be able ter go back ter the quarry. He'll get some money from the quarryman's association, but it won't be much.'

Feeling sick to her stomach, Alice stared at her father's empty chair. 'Shall we go to the surgery now?'

'From what Mr Brooker said, your dad'll still be reet shocked. We'd do better ter wait till tomorrow morning. If we go early, we'll see him before he's sent ter Bury Dispensary.'

Alice nodded, tears rolling down her cheeks.

Neither moved for a moment, and then Ethel stood up abruptly.

'We must have summat ter eat,' she said. 'It won't help your dad if we go hungry.' She went across to the stove, picked up a spoon and plunged it into the stew that Alice had made earlier. 'Without yer dad's wages,' Ethel said as she stirred the stew round and round, 'we could end up in the workhouse, you know.' She glanced back over her shoulder at Alice. 'I'm sorry, our Alice. But without an arm, your dad's not going ter be able ter find any work at all, and what I get won't be enough ter keep us in this house.'

Alice swallowed the lump in her throat.

'I'll leave school,' she said. 'They'll let me go when they know what's happened to Dad. I'll get a job, and with my wages as well as yours, there'll be a home for Dad when he's better – a home here, not in any workhouse. I don't need to go to school any more – I can already read and write and add up.'

Her mother stopped stirring and stared at Alice in despair. 'I had such dreams for you, our Alice. A pretty girl like you should be able ter do so much better for herself than work in a factory.' A loud sob escaped her.

'Cry for Dad, not me,' Alice said. She went across to her mother, put her arms around her and hugged her. 'That's yesterday's dream, Mam. Today, things are different. I heard they're looking for girls in Gaghills Mill. When we leave the doctor's surgery tomorrow, I'll go there and ask if they'll take me on.'

Her mother's eyes filled with tears. She wiped her face with the back of her hand.

'Yer a good girl, our Alice. But me and yer dad have always

known it. All right, then. Yer can go ter the slipper factory tomorrow, though it fair breaks my heart ter agree. But I'm going with yer. Knowing yer've a mother behind you should stop anyone gettin' ideas about you, you being the pretty girl that you are.'

* * *

Throughout a long sleepless night, Alice's body was wracked by tears – tears for her father and the difficulties he was bound to face when he came home; tears for the dreams she'd once had, but which must now be cast aside; tears for the weeks, months and years ahead of her, when she'd be living the life she'd so wanted to avoid.

'I'm scared of what me dad's going to look like,' she blurted out as she and her mother headed for the surgery the following morning.

'Me, too,' her mother said, her voice tired. 'That's normal – anyone would be.' She squeezed Alice's arm. 'We'll be all right, our Alice. You'll see.'

They didn't stay long with Alice's father.

The doctor had given him a heavy dose of laudanum to deaden the pain and he was too groggy to understand anything they said to him. Satisfied that he was being well looked after in the small side room at the surgery, and was as comfortable as they could've expected, given the seriousness of his accident, they stayed thirty minutes only, and then left him to sleep.

'Now for your job,' her mother said.

It was just as well that her mother was with her, Alice thought, her clogs reverberating loudly on the cobblestones as they headed for the large grey stone factory that they could see in the distance, its narrow square-shaped chimney towering above the surrounding houses. Had she been on her own, she'd have been greatly tempted to run in the opposite direction as fast as she could.

And if she'd done that, where would her mam and dad be?

Much as she hated the idea of working in a factory, this was the only sort of job she could go for.

There was a demand for domestics, she knew, and that would have been preferable to working in a mill. But domestics were expected to live in the houses where they worked, and living away from home would be impossible. Her mam would need her help when her dad came home.

A shop would've been better, too, but there was no point in looking for such a job. Any vacant post would almost immediately be filled by someone in the owner's family, or by a family friend, or by a girl who'd had more schooling.

How quickly her whole life had been ruined, she thought, fighting back the urge to burst into tears.

Two days earlier, she'd dreamed of the day when she'd have a better life, and her mam and dad, too.

But her dreams now lay in the dust.

And possibly, too, her friendship with May.

She'd hardly be able to meet up with May, let alone spend any time with her, the hours she'd have to work in the factory, and the help she'd have to give at home. And she'd always be tired, like her mam was. May would have no choice but become best friends with one of the other girls in their class.

And if they *did* meet, what would they talk about? May would be learning lots of new things at school, things that she didn't know so couldn't talk about.

She would become boring old Alice to May.

But thinking about it, perhaps it was just as well that she and May would hardly be able to meet in the future. Envy of May was already eating into her, and a growing resentment that May still had the freedom denied to her, and she'd hate that feeing to get any stronger. It wasn't fair on May.

'We're here,' her mother said, and stopped walking.

Alice came to a halt. She looked up at the grey building in front of her. And her heart sank even further.

The clicking room foreman was summoned. When he duly appeared, Alice explained that she'd come for a job.

He eyed her up and down with obvious appreciation, asked a few questions and, not in the least bit bothered by her lack of experience, said she could start in the clicking department the following day. They'd teach her what she needed to know, he told her.

'Clicking?' she asked.

The clickers are what they call the cutters, he explained. She'd be put on pricking and marking, and when she was familiar with the work, she'd be given the further task of guiding machinists when they were sewing together the slipper parts and putting fancy stitching on the vamps.

'Vamps?'

'The vamp's the part of the slipper or shoe that covers the front of the foot,' he said with an unmistakable trace of impatience.

All the jobs she completed would be entered on a production card he'd check at the end of the day. And she was sure from his expression that the comments he'd make if she didn't fulfil her quota wouldn't be pleasant to hear.

Then he told her mam to wait where she was while he took Alice to have a quick look at the clicking room. It would save time the following day, he'd added.

There were benches over a yard wide fixed to the walls, and also running down the length of the room. Clickers were working at clicking boards set on top of the benches, cutting around patterns for the uppers or linings of slippers. They were paid so much per pair according to the shape and number of cuts required, the foreman explained.

'The clicking boards must be regularly buffed to make sure that the surface remains level and hard,' he added. 'And they're given a weekly dressing of boiled linseed oil for protection.'

She was going to loathe every single minute in that prison, she thought, a lump in her throat as she and her mother left the factory and headed for the shortcut that would take them home.

But she wouldn't give up on the dream she'd had for so long. She couldn't. Not yet.

She'd do the job as they needed the money, but all the time she'd keep her eyes open for something else. She loved her parents very much and was glad she could help them, but that didn't mean that at twelve years of age, she had to settle for a life of drudgery. It just meant that she'd have to adapt her dream.

For a start, it could no longer be built on her leaving Waterfoot.

But even in Waterfoot, there must be something better she could do when she was older.

She'd give herself two years in the slipper factory at the most, she resolved, as she walked with her mother up the stone steps leading to their block of houses. By then, she'd be fourteen, and old enough to look for that something better. And when she found it, she'd go after it with every bit of determination she possessed.

* * *

Just two years, she promised herself again that night as she blew out her candle and slipped into her bed. Not one day longer.

4

1911

The first two years in the slipper factory came and went without Alice even noticing, and the years that followed, too.

During that time, she was promoted to upper clicking, which meant an increase in her wages, most of which she handed straight over to her mother, and she spent every minute of every day either working in the factory or working at home.

The need for her help in the early months after her father's discharge from the hospital had been great, and she and her mother had regularly toiled late into the evening. Cleaning the house, making the meals, doing the washing, looking after Alice's dad, who in his early months at home was frequently in pain, and either aggressively resentful at being unable to work, or tearfully grateful for the care that his wife and daughter were giving him – it all had to be fitted around her mother's twelve-hour day in the weavers' shed and Alice's long day in Gaghills Mill.

With all there was to do at home and in the factory, Alice had no time at all to dwell on the passing of the years.

She'd had no time, either, to think about Stan Cooke.

But not long after she turned fifteen, she noticed that he was starting to hang around while she was doing the washing, ready to lend a hand by putting pressure on the mangle if she'd let him. And several times, he'd followed her to the market at the close of day on Wednesdays, and had offered to carry her shopping.

She liked Stan better than anyone else she'd met, but being permanently exhausted, boys were the last thing on her mind. And she was also acutely aware that having a husband like Stan would condemn her forever to the kind of life she was leading, and she wasn't yet willing to abandon her dream of a better future. Not when she was still so young. Not even for Stan.

Reluctantly, he'd come to accept that she would never agree to marry him, and he'd started walking out with a black-haired girl, who worked in a local printing company.

By the time that Alice was seventeen, Stan had married the black-haired girl and had moved to a small terraced house a couple of streets away, where he'd virtually disappeared from Alice's sight.

She'd recently seen his wife several times, though, in the centre of Waterfoot, usually either going into Trickett's Arcade or coming out. And at the sight of his wife pushing a large, very old black pram, her face lined with fatigue, her belly swollen with a second child on the way, Alice had heaved a huge sigh of relief that she'd avoided such a fate.

To her delight, she hadn't lost contact with May in the five years that she'd worked in the slipper factory, much as she'd feared at first that she might. They didn't see each other as often as they used to, but this was not just because Alice was always busy – May was busy, too.

May's father worked for a local rag-and-bone man, who had a high-wheeled cart that was pulled along the narrow roads by a donkey. It was the job of May's dad to drive the cart. As he drove down each street, people brought out their rags and unwanted items, and in return, he gave them a scrubbing stone or a block of salt, depending upon the number of items they'd given him.

It was a steady business as the scrubbing stone, or donkey-stone as people used to call it, was in great demand. It was cream or white in colour and, as they didn't have floor coverings, people used to wet the stone and rub it on their floors to colour them. Also, they used to line with white the edge of their doorstep, and sometimes they even rubbed the stone on their sinks.

Unfortunately for May's family, her father seldom came straight home at the end of his day's work. Rather, he'd drop into one of the local pubs, and stay there for most of what was left of the evening, drinking up a large part of his wages.

Because of this, May's mother was always short of money for food, and was having to take in even more ironing. May had been helping with the ironing since leaving school, and was also helping her mother look after the three children of a widowed woman, who'd had to go out to work when her husband had died leaving the family destitute. And also at times, May had gone out on the cart with her dad.

So May's life wasn't easy, either, but May still couldn't see herself living anywhere other than Waterfoot, as she always told Alice on the increasingly rare occasions that the subject came up. Her dad was mean, so she'd never want to go far from her mother.

* * *

Busy though Alice and May were, they went to Bacup Fair together every Whitsun, and at seventeen, they looked forward to the Fair just as much as they'd done as little children.

It being a special day, Alice chose a cornflower blue cotton dress that skimmed her slender body, and she tied her blonde hair back from her face with a cornflower blue ribbon. May wore her Sunday-best pale grey dress, and a deep red ribbon hung in her long dark hair.

Their arms linked, they set off in great excitement.

By the time they arrived, the Fair was a hubbub of noise: stall-holders shouted out to attract the attention of the passing crowds; vendors loudly hawked their wares; innumerable clogs clattered along the lanes; horses' hooves clip-clopped on the hard ground; iron-rimmed cart wheels rattled over the uneven cobblestones; brass bands and carousel music rose in a discordant cacophony; dogs barked relentlessly and horses whinnied. Everywhere people were laughing and screaming, their voices loud and shrill.

As they neared the heart of the Fair, Alice breathed in the pungent aroma of cooked food mixed with the acrid smell thrown out by the spluttering paraffin lamps. 'I just love this,' she said happily. 'I hope I never have to work when the Fair is on. I'd hate us not to be able to come together.'

May laughed. 'Factories have ter close from Friday ter Tuesday, don't they? Whit Monday's a Bank Holiday, isn't it? So yer'll always be able to come. And me, too. Of course,' she added, a trace of awkwardness edging into her voice, 'it might not always be just the two of us coming.'

Alice dropped May's arm, and stared at her. 'May Cummings, what aren't you telling me?'

'Nothing,' May said hastily. 'It's just that with us being seventeen, we're bound ter be thinking of marryin' soon, aren't we? Things change. When we're married, our husbands might expect ter come ter the Fair with us.'

'I won't be getting married for ages,' Alice said bluntly.

May looked at her in surprise. 'But your mam and dad can manage without yer now, can't they? After all, yer dad's now working behind the till in the hardware store, and yer said he's getting on well.'

'I know he is. I have to help me mam, though, don't I? The chores still have to be done.'

'But yer know she'd manage if yer married. Every mam copes when a daughter moves out.'

'You're right, and if I'm truly honest, it's not really to do with them. It's that I'm not going to tie myself to a man from around here. I want a better life than that.'

'Where're yer going to find that better life, Alice?' May asked, a hint of ice in her voice.

'Don't be annoyed with me, May. I can't help the way I feel. To answer you, I haven't a clue! But I know I won't find it here.'

'Yer could if yer looked really hard. Yer could marry anyone yer wanted, yer so pretty. Not a mill owner's son, maybe, but perhaps a shop owner's son.'

Alice blushed. 'You've got putty brains if you think that. But what about you – d'you want to get married?' She stopped abruptly. 'Oh!' she exclaimed. She put her hands to her head and laughed. 'I'm the one with putty brains, aren't I? You've met someone, haven't you? That's why you said what you did about it not always being just us.' Ignoring the people on foot who were pushing past her, and the horses and carts that were forced to swerve to avoid her, she stood staring at May, her eyes shining.

'Not really, I haven't.' May hesitated, and then she blushed. 'It's just that the farmer's son, Ronald Morgan – yer know him cos he helps his dad with the milk round – has called for me a couple of times. That's all.'

'I've never really spoken to him. Beyond saying thank you, that is, when I've gone up to the milk float and handed him my pint measure. But I can tell you like him, so he must be nice. And you'll always have plenty of milk and butter.'

'Trust yer ter jump ahead! At most he's called for me three times.' May tucked her arm into Alice's again, and they resumed walking. 'He *is* nice, and I like him, but don't let's talk about him. After all, he might not come by again, and I don't want to build it up and then get disappointed. There'll be other girls who like him, too, and he may prefer one of them to me.'

'If he did, he'd be mad,' Alice said, beaming at May.

'You'd say that cos you're my friend. Let's change the subject, shall we? Look, there's the hoopla stall. Come on – let's have a go!'

Releasing her hold on Alice, May plunged into the sea of people and colour that was moving slowly along the road as men and boys in flat caps and shirts with starched white collars, and women and girls in their finest dresses, wandered among the medley of canvas-topped stalls, coconut shies, swings and swing-boats, wooden horses and garishly painted roundabouts that lined the lanes across which strands of colourful bunting hung.

Alice trailed slowly after May, letting what May had said sink in.

As she'd seen May's face, it had hit her with sudden certainty that this would be the last Bacup Fair that the two of them would go to together.

May was clearly ready to move on to the next stage of her life, and at seventeen, it was time that she, too, gave serious thought to her future. With her father settled in a job with hours that weren't too demanding, she could now begin her search for something else she could do.

If she didn't do so soon, it could be too late.

* * *

'That's my favourite of all the things you can do here,' Alice said as they walked away from the swingboats at the end of their allotted time, their legs wobbly, their faces flushed, their hair dishevelled. 'You feel as if you're flying, and can do anything.'

'I know what you mean. I like them best, too.' May paused and sniffed the air. 'And I also like toffee. From that lovely smell, we must be near where they're making it. Let's get something to eat – I'm so hungry I could eat a buttered frog. And we can have some toffee afterwards.'

Having found a stall selling pork carved from a spit-roasted pig, they each bought two thick slices sandwiched in crusty bread, and then, eating their sandwich, they headed towards a distant roundabout, their progress slow as every so often they stopped to stare at the show-people in multi-coloured costumes who crossed their path, and who put on a performance whenever a number of spectators grouped around them.

When they finally reached the roundabout, the wooden horses were still circling up and down, so they hovered at the side of the stand, and finished their sandwich while they waited for the music to come to a stop.

A shrill scream of fear cut the air.

It was followed immediately by a heavy thud.

Startled, Alice dropped her last piece of bread as she turned swiftly towards the cry.

The carousel ground noisily to a halt.

'Look, May!' she exclaimed, pointing to a small girl, who'd obviously fallen from the back of her wooden horse. The girl lay motionless on the ground at the side of the roundabout, an open gash on her forehead where she'd hit the metal rim that encircled the wooden base of the stand.

For a long moment, everyone stared at the injured girl. Nobody moved.

Then a woman rushed forward from the back of the crowd. 'Someone run for the hand litter,' the woman shouted as she reached the child. 'And go for her mother, if anyone knows where she is.'

Then she knelt down and opened the child's mouth very gently.

'Why, that's Nora! She's one of the clickers!' Alice exclaimed in surprise, and she inched slightly closer to have a better view. 'How does she know what to do?' she said in wonder as Nora checked first the little girl's head, and then her neck, her eyes and the rest of her body.

Then Nora pulled the light shawl from around her shoulders, folded it as narrowly as she could and tied it around the wound on the girl's head.

Alice took another step forward, but a woman in a black cotton dress covered by a dark brown pinafore apron, pushed roughly past her, and came to a stop right in front of her, blocking her view of Nora and the child. The woman looked at the injured girl, and broke out into a loud wailing.

'That must be her mother,' May said, peering around the woman. 'Poor thing. Her daughter's deathly white. She's obviously unconscious. I hope the litter gets here soon. But at least, yer Nora seems ter know what she's doing. It looks as if she's stopped the bleeding.'

Alice frowned. 'I wonder how she knew what to do. I'll ask her when I next see her.'

* * *

Determined to find the answer to her question, when the mill opened again on the Tuesday, Alice was alert for a possible moment during the day in which she could ask Nora about the accident, but the moment never presented itself. The factory having been shut for several days, the supervisor had watched them closely from the start of the day to the finish, making it clear that he expected them to work extra hard to compensate for the working hours they'd missed.

In the end, she was forced to hang around at the end of the day in order to catch Nora as she left.

As soon as Nora emerged from the factory door, Alice rushed to her side, and together they walked towards the point at which their route home took them in opposite directions. While they walked, she told Nora that she'd seen her possibly save the life of that little girl, and asked how she'd known what to do.

'I enrolled in our local branch of the British Red Cross last year, didn't I?' Nora told her. 'The Red Cross won't register you as a nurse till you're twenty-one. But the more I can learn before I'm twenty-one, the better. I really want to be a nurse. Once I've got my first aid certificate, I intend to try for a job in a hospital so that I can develop more skills. Although I'll still be too young to be registered, I'm sure I'll be of use to a hospital, having done the course.'

'What d'you learn in the classes?'

'All kinds of things. Some of the things you saw me doing at the Fair – checking the injured person's airway, seeing if they can breathe, making sure the blood's circulating, seeing if there's any bleeding, and if there is, trying to stop it. That sort of thing. And you learn skills a nurse would have to know, like how to read a thermometer and take a pulse, how to bandage the different parts of a person, and how to put splints on limbs to keep them in one position.'

'My father lost his arm in a quarry accident a few years ago, and when he came home from the hospital, I helped me mam look after him. He's got a tiny bit of a stump, and I used to wash it.'

Nora shrugged. 'So you aren't faint-hearted, then. You should come to the class with me. It's on Wednesdays – I go there straight from the factory. A good thing about being a nurse is that you'll always be able to find a job. When I'm registered, I shall look for a hospital miles away from here. I can't wait to get away from all this.' She gestured around her.

Alice beamed. 'That could've been me talking. I'll join you next Wednesday.'

5

1913

Two years later, May had married Ronald Morgan and moved to live with him on his father's farm just outside Waterfoot, and Alice, to her great joy, had received her certificate in first aid, and had taken a part-time nursing job in the new Pike Law Infirmary, which had been opened the year before in the grounds of Haslingden Workhouse.

At nineteen, she was two years too young to be registered as a nurse by the Red Cross, but she'd been determined to do as Nora had done, which was to use those two years to build upon what she'd learned in the Red Cross course, every minute of which she'd loved.

* * *

When she'd started the first aid course, going with Nora every Wednesday evening, she'd told her parents what she was doing, and why.

They were extremely surprised to learn that she wanted to become a nurse, and while they were pleased with the choice she'd made, and greatly relieved that she would be able to escape the factory, they were at first disappointed that one day she might move away from Waterfoot. But the more they thought about it, and how limited her choices were in a mill town, the more they realised she was doing the right thing. And if in order to be a nurse, she had to move away, that would be a price worth paying.

It was Alice's mother who'd first heard about the job in Pike Law.

Not long after Alice had received her certificate, her mother had been talking to a woman in the grocer's queue, who worked in a local doctor's surgery, and the woman had mentioned that the new infirmary at Haslingden was looking for a part-time nurse. The moment Alice got home, her mother had told her about the job, and she had written at once to the Haslingden Guardians, the officials responsible for overseeing the Parish.

She'd attended a short interview on the Saturday afternoon, conducted by three of the Guardians, and at the end of the interview, had been offered the post.

This had come as something of a shock, it all happened so fast, and after the initial excitement at her success, drawbacks she hadn't considered had flooded her mind. Her delight giving way to anxiety, she'd sat in the tram taking her back to Waterfoot, running through the advantages and disadvantages of working there.

When she got home, she told her parents that she wasn't going to take the job, and promptly started setting the table. After a moment's stunned silence, her mother told her to stop what she was doing and sit down. She wanted to know what it was that had caused Alice to come to such a decision.

'I can't leave you to cope with everything by yourselves,' Alice told them. 'Dad's out in the day, working, and when he's home, he's limited in the help he can give. That's true, isn't it, Dad?'

He nodded. 'Ay, it is. I do my best, but yer mam has ter do more than she should.'

'Dad's right, Mam. You work all hours as it is,' Alice went on. 'You can't pick up my chores as well your own. I'm staying put.'

Her mother silenced her with a dismissive wave. 'Yer dad and I have talked about this, and we know we'll be able ter manage perfectly well without yer, so we don't want ter hear any more about yer not taking the position. Yer've worked hard at learning first aid for the past two years, and yer deserve the chance of putting into practice what yer've learned.'

Alice looked from one to the other.

'Yer mam's right, our Alice,' her father had said gruffly. 'We want the best for yer, girl, and that means yer must be a nurse.'

Her eyes had filled with tears, and she'd jumped up and hugged them both.

Two days later, struggling to contain her happiness and her overwhelming excitement that at last she was about to become a real nurse, she'd informed the factory that she was leaving, said goodbye to her friends there, and walked out of the clicking room for the last time.

A spring in her step, she'd almost run home.

* * *

The first time she'd properly seen the workhouse was the day she started working there, the day on which she was going to be shown around and her duties explained.

When she went for the interview, she'd been too nervous to notice anything about the place. But now she was able to see that it was a large, imposing grey stone building, with a stretch of grass in front that ran for the full width of the building, with trees and a carriage drive, too.

She'd gone straight up the steps and into the entrance hall, and been instantly struck by the many pictures that hung from the painted walls, and by the friendly atmosphere.

She would be based in the infirmary, which was to the north-east of the workhouse, and she would be one of three nurses looking after approximately ninety-five patients, she was told by the Guardian who'd been sitting in one of the armchairs in the hall on her arrival, waiting to take her across to the infirmary.

'It's all so much better than I expected,' she said as they walked along. 'Both inside the building and out. You hear all sorts of things.'

'You do indeed,' he said with a smile. 'Workhouses used to have a very bad name, and many certainly deserved it. But things are very different these days. And the same can be said about infirmaries. Ours has been open for only a year.'

With her every step, she realised that she was going to be in the best possible place to learn the nursing skills she needed to know before she was twenty-one. Moreover, she was confident that she was going to enjoy working there.

She was still elated when she arrived back home at the end of her first day, and told her mother and father what she'd been doing.

'The first thing they showed me,' she said happily, 'was how to make a hospital bed. You have to fold the corners in a special way. That's something every real nurse has to know.'

Her only concern had been the money, she told them, or rather how little there'd be of it. She would be given her uniform, but with working only part-time, she'd be bringing home quite a bit less than she'd done from the factory, where although her wages hadn't been much, they'd been boosted by two promotions.

'And so,' she said, with a touch of triumph in her voice,

'before I left, I asked the Guardian, who'd come back to see if there was anything I needed to know or wanted help with, if they'd got any more paid work going, and they had! The infirmary cook needed an assistant, and that assistant is going to be me.'

* * *

The following morning, she stood in front of the entrance to the infirmary wearing a navy blue and white pin-striped dress with a detachable white collar and cuffs, and a crescent-shaped starched white cap. Over her dress, she wore a large white apron, on the bodice of which was a bright red cross. In her hand, she held a short dark blue cape with a red lining.

Filled with a massive sense of pride and relief that she was, at last, set on course to be a qualified nurse, she walked up to the door.

6

THE FOLLOWING SATURDAY

She'd go and see May that afternoon and tell her about the infirmary, she decided. Although May's mother would have told May that she was working there, she wanted to tell her all about it herself. And having finished at Pike Law after lunch, instead of leaving the tram when it reached Waterfoot, she stayed on for a further few miles.

When she got off, she walked a short distance, turned left and headed up a steep, rutted track to the farm where May now lived.

She felt really bad that it was only the third time she'd been there, and that her last visit had been over three months ago, long before she'd heard about Pike Law. But with working all day, and helping out at home in the evenings and over the weekend, she had very little free time.

And May, too, didn't have much leisure time.

She'd been worn out on the last occasion they'd met, and probably still was. Ronald's mother died a year after the wedding, and May was now looking after the farmhouse, not only for Ronald, but also for his brother and father.

She really ought to make an effort to visit more frequently, she thought, as she trudged up the last stretch of the hill to the farm, hoping very much that she hadn't come at a bad time, and that May wouldn't be too busy to stop and chat for a bit.

She'd hate May to think that she didn't care how she was getting on, because she did.

She missed her enormously, and truly wished they could meet more often, as they used to. But instead of it getting easier, in reality it was going to be even harder now that she was doing two jobs at Pike Law.

The moment May came out of the farmhouse, and exclaimed in surprise at seeing her, then rushed forward, wiping her hands on her apron and smiling broadly, she saw that, difficult though it was going to be for her to visit in the future, it was going to be even more difficult for May, who was very obviously expecting a child.

'May!' Alice screamed, and ran up to her. 'You're going to be a mam!' And she hugged her hard.

May went red. 'And don't I know it! He's been keeping me awake at night with his kicking. Or she has,' she said. 'I've about four months ter go, but I've hardly started me knitting. Ronald's really excited, too. In the evenings, he's been making a cot for the baby. I'm sure he wants a boy, but he won't say.'

'Have you thought of any names yet?'

May waved her hand in dismissal. 'There's plenty of time for that. But don't let's talk about babies now. It's reet good to see yer again, Alice. Come into the kitchen and tell me what yer've been doing. I've really missed our chats. Let's sit down and have a cup of tea. Ignore the mess. I was making a potato pie, but it can wait.'

As she sipped her tea, Alice told May about the infirmary, and that she'd also be helping the cook. 'I feel sorry for anyone who has to eat anything I cook,' she said with a laugh. 'Mind you, I'll probably be given the boring jobs to do, like peeling potatoes, and it'll be Cook who puts the lot together and makes the finished dish.'

'Won't you mind cooking? You've always said how much you dislike it.'

Alice shrugged. 'I disliked the factory, too – this won't be nearly as bad. Anyway, main job is the nursing, but I won't get paid very much, so the kitchen money will come in handy.'

'I see,' May said. 'Well, I certainly wish yer the best. I wouldn't like ter do the things yer'll find yourself having ter do.' She paused, and frowned. 'Aren't yer worried that while yer doing them, yer won't have time for courting?'

'Not at all,' Alice said airily. 'I haven't changed my mind about leaving here, you know. In two years' time, I'll be registered, and then I'm going to look for a nurse's job in a large town, probably in the South. A nurse can't be married so I won't be thinking about finding a husband for a while.'

'In the South!' May exclaimed, sitting up sharply. 'But yer'll be miles away! I know we don't meet very often these days, but Waterfoot's not that far from here and yer still feel close. If yer in the South, yer won't.'

'We'll still meet,' Alice said firmly. 'I'll come back a lot.'

'But yer won't, will yer?'

'Of course, I will. I'll want to see me mam and me dad, for a start, and we'll meet up whenever I come. We'll always be best friends, May, wherever I am.'

May gave an awkward laugh. 'Of course, we will. I'm just being selfish, I suppose. And a bit envious of all the exciting things yer'll be doing down there. Not that I'd swap with yer,' she added hastily.

'I'm sure Ronald would be delighted to hear that,' Alice said, sitting back in her chair and smiling. 'Anyway, that's enough about me. It's your turn now. Have you any news – apart from the baby, that is?'

May shook her head. 'Not really. I work hard every day, but who doesn't? And each day is pretty much like the one before. But it's the same for most people, isn't it?'

Alice nodded. 'I know what you mean. It's why I can't wait to get away from here and go somewhere that isn't so boring.'

May straightened slightly in her seat. 'Every place has got some sameness about it. But when yer married and yer love your husband, like I love Ronald, it doesn't bother yer.'

'If you say so.'

'I do,' May said with more than a touch of annoyance. 'Yer always saying that it's dull here, that the people's lives are horrible, and that yer'll get a better life somewhere else. Maybe life *is* difficult in this area, but yer can't do better than livin' among people who've known yer all your life and who care about yer. People who're good friends and who'd never let yer down. That means a lot.'

'I know it does.'

'But *do* yer, though? It doesn't sound like it from where I'm sittin'. Yer look down on the people here, just because they're poor and have ter work very hard, and don't have what yer'd call an exciting life. By that, I suppose yer mean a life where yer'd go ter parties every day, or sit and do nothing all day like the people we used to read about. But having the money ter live like that doesn't make a person nicer, or better than the people hereabouts. Be careful what yer throw away, Alice, in yer hunt for a life yer've seen in a magazine, which may not even be real, and which yer might not even like if yer got it.'

'I think I'd better go now,' Alice said stiffly, standing up. 'You seem to think I'm expecting someone to hand me the life I want on a plate. But I'm not. You've forgotten how hard I've worked for the past few years.'

'No, I haven't.'

'I think you have. Studying for my certificate on top of an exhausting day in the factory, in addition to all the household chores, wasn't easy. And being a nurse isn't easy. It's a long day, and you have to do the most embarrassing things for people, and see the nastiest of sights.'

'I know that.'

'I admit I often say how much I dislike it here, but I can't help it – that's how I feel. But when I talk having about a better life, I don't mean doing nothing all day. It's just that I want more choices about the kind of work I do, and the sort of house I live in, and what I can do when I'm not working.'

'I understand. Honestly, I do.'

'I don't think you do. You think I should be satisfied with what I've got now and be content to have the same until I die. But I don't believe it's wrong to want more from life than a monotonous daily grind in a mill, then coming back to a house where you share the privy with several other families, and where even boiling water is hard work. It's different for you out here on the farm. But I'm not the same as you – I want people around me, not fields. Anyway, I've got to go now. I look forward to meeting your baby.'

May started to stand.

'Don't get up,' Alice said quickly. 'I'll see myself out. Give my best to Ronald and the rest of his family.' And she walked out through the front door, and headed at speed down the hard mud track that led back to Bacup Road.

'Alice,' she heard May call after her.

Never once turning back, she continued walking, tears of loss streaming down her cheeks.

7

1915

War had broken out in the year before she was twenty-one, and that changed everything. The infirmary was taken over in part as a military hospital, and Alice had immediately stopped assisting the cook and started working full-time in the infirmary.

Then in 1915, she was registered as a nurse by the Red Cross.

She couldn't remember ever being as happy as she felt on the day her registration came through, the culmination of six years of hard work. And her parents were delighted for her, too, and so proud.

They'd wanted to throw her a small party and invite the people they knew, including May and her family. But with a war on, they were all working flat out on the war effort, and it was impossible to do so. And anyway, with people dying on foreign shores, no one was really in the mood for a party.

By the time that the war was in its second year, the infirmary was full of injured men, and Alice had become increasingly expert in tending horrific wounds – a kind of experience she'd never expected.

She'd learned about the different effects that war could have on men when helping daily with severely shell-shocked soldiers. At meal times, she'd put her hand behind the head of a soldier who couldn't stop shaking, to steady him while gently feeding him. Then she'd move on and do the same for the next similarly afflicted man.

And she'd write their love letters for them, too.

For those who were too shy to put their thoughts into written words, she'd begin with 'My dearest darling' and end with 'Forever yours', and in between those words she'd try to convey the thoughts they were struggling to express. For those who were completely unable to verbalise their feelings, she'd write down what she imagined they'd want to say, and read it back to them for their approval.

But despite helping to treat the casualties who were arriving regularly at the hospital, every time she heard the latest news from the Front, she felt very cut off from it all, and increasingly, she found herself wishing that she worked somewhere more central to the action.

Then her chance to do so came when she read one morning in *The Nursing Mirror* that with new patients arriving at the rate of a hundred a week, there was a desperate need for nurses at the newly opened Queen Mary's Convalescent Auxiliary Hospital, situated in Roehampton House, in south-west London.

It was a reference to amputees further in the article that particularly caught her eye.

After her father's accident, anything to do with amputees and prosthetics always stood out. As soon as she read that it was a two-hundred-bed military hospital for patients who had lost limbs, and who were to be fitted with the most scientifically advanced limbs possible, and then rehabilitated, she applied for the job.

She cited the experience she'd gained through assisting with the care of her father, as well as her subsequent Red Cross course and also her nursing experience at the infirmary, where she'd tended not only seriously injured soldiers, but also workhouse inmates who'd lost limbs through the extremes of cold or bad diets. And she enclosed references from two of the Guardians.

When she received her letter of acceptance, she jumped up and down in delight.

She would now be nursing those who'd suffered the most terrible injuries in the war, and helping them to live as full a life as possible in the future, despite their disabilities.

And she'd be doing so in London.

This was her dream come true.

She felt overwhelmed by conflicting emotions. Her joy at knowing she was about to move to a large town, something she'd wanted for years, was tempered by sadness that it had been a horrendous war that had brought this about. And by the wrench she would feel at leaving her parents, and May, with whom she'd long ago made up after their argument.

And she'd be saying goodbye to all the places, which were so familiar to her – above all, the moors – as she stepped into the unknown.

While it was an exciting thing to be doing, it was also a daunting one.

Her parents were delighted for her as they knew how much she wanted this, but at the same time, they were extremely worried about her living in London, where the Zeppelin raids, which had started in January, had already killed a number of civilians.

'No one can be certain of being safe anywhere,' she told them firmly. 'Zeppelin airships are known to have fallen wide of their mark on a number of occasions. You mustn't worry about me, and I'll try not to worry about you.'

When she told the Guardians that she'd got the job, they wished her well, and showed their gratitude for her hard work by giving her a copy of *Black's Medical Dictionary*. That was the first thing she put in her bag when she packed for Queen Mary's, which, she'd discovered, was how the hospital was known.

When it came time to leave for London, her parents went with her to Waterfoot Station, where she was to begin the first leg of her journey, and May joined them on the platform, heavily pregnant with her second child, having left her son, William, at home.

As the train approached the station in a cloud of soot and steam, Alice hugged her parents tightly, and then she and May flung their arms around each other.

'You'll always be my best friend,' she told May, her voice breaking. 'That'll be true of wherever I live, even though we won't see each other as often.'

May nodded, her face miserable at the thought of Alice going so far away – possibly even out of her life for ever. Impulsively, she leaned forward and hugged Alice again, letting the warmth of her embrace speak the words she couldn't.

* * *

Several hours later, when the last of the trains conveying her to London drew into Euston Station, she stepped on to the platform, grasped her bags firmly and headed for the exit.

Having found the way to the bus stand, she took a bus to Victoria, and then another to Roehampton, all the while staring out of the window, mesmerised by the noise, by the size of the city, and by the sight of so many people hurrying this way and that along the pavement.

It was hard to believe that she was actually in London, and

that London was where she was going to be living. In all her wildest dreams over the years, she'd never for one moment allowed herself to hope that she might find a position in London.

But she had. And she couldn't believe it.

And even when she'd unpacked her bags in the small room she'd been given in a house close to the hospital, where several other nurses lived, she still felt as if it was all a dream.

But she came down to reality fast when she started at the hospital.

With so many soldiers returning to England each day, many of whom had lost at least one limb, the demand for beds in Queen Mary's already far exceeded the number available. She found herself working harder than ever before, and moving straight from one task to the next.

As for any thoughts about finding someone with whom to share her life, nothing was further from her mind.

And then she saw Thomas Linford.

8

QUEEN MARY'S HOSPITAL

September 1918

The moment Alice first saw Thomas Linford, her breath quickened.

Owing to the severity of his injuries, Thomas had been sent back to England from France. His right leg had been almost completely blown off, and his right hand was badly damaged – he'd lost two and a half fingers, and the remaining thumb and forefinger had limited movement – while his body was extensively scarred.

As he'd lain unconscious on the battlefield, his fellow soldiers had wrapped bandages around his hand, and put a tourniquet on his leg, hoping to save it. But by the time that the field ambulance had been able to get to them, the tourniquet had been on for considerably longer than an hour, and they hadn't been able to save the leg.

When he was stable, he'd been transferred back to a coastal hospital in England, and when they'd done as much as they could for his wounds, he'd been sent to Queen Mary's to have a prosthetic leg fitted.

Alice had been in the middle of making up a Carrel-Dakin solution, a lime-smelling antiseptic mix to be fed into infected wounds, when Thomas was brought into the ward on a stretcher.

She glanced across at his face. Their eyes met, and he grinned.

Oh, my goodness, she thought, as a wave of desire shot through her, and she almost dropped the spoon of powder she was holding. Clutching it tightly, she stared at him for a moment.

Then she'd shaken herself, and continued her work, but still so acutely aware of him that she almost put the wrong amount of powder into the boiled water.

Forcing herself to concentrate on what she was doing, she finished making up a gallon of the solution, poured it into big demi-johns, and began to wheel the jars round the ward on a trolley. Wherever she came upon a gangrenous limb, she checked to see if three hours had passed since the last injection, and if it had, she injected the solution into the tubes leading into the wound.

It was something she hated doing, it was so painful for the men, and they detested it as it was so cold, but the solution frequently caused the gangrene to recede, so all the nurses scrupulously administered the three-hourly injections, day and night.

When she reached the bed next to Thomas's, which she'd made sure would be the last bed she'd come to, she deliberately placed herself so that her back was to Thomas while she studied the wound of the soldier in front of her.

To her relief, the gangrene in the soldier's stump, which had been in its early stages, was already showing signs of diminishing, and the stink of gas gangrene, which could so easily fill the ward with unpleasantness, was slight. But the wound was still suppurating, so she applied an enormous dressing of solution-soaked gauze, and wrapped it in the mackintosh-type material, which would help to keep the bed dry and the dressing moist.

Then she turned towards Thomas.

He was sleeping.

She felt a sharp pang of disappointment.

Why did he have that effect on her, she wondered as she quietly pushed the trolley away. She had looked after countless injured soldiers since the beginning of the war, some of whom had been equally as good-looking as Thomas, but she hadn't felt drawn to any of them. Yet from the moment she'd seen Thomas's face, had felt the warmth from his eyes and seen the laughter within them, butterflies had been fluttering in her stomach.

Later, as she prepared for bed, she looked back on the day, and came to the reluctant conclusion that it was just as well that he'd been asleep when he had or she might have given away her interest in him by talking in too friendly a way. That could have ended up in a most embarrassing situation.

And it would have been pointless, too.

Nurses weren't allowed to have a relationship with a patient, or to marry.

And it was out of the question in the middle of a war, when people with nursing skills were desperately needed, and when she'd come all the way down to London to tend injured soldiers, to open the door to something that could end up with her having to leave the hospital.

It was just as well, she thought with relief, that he wouldn't be in the hospital long enough for them to get to know each other.

Not that he would've been interested in her, anyway. Even without his leg, he was so attractive that he'd be bound to have his choice of women.

From her idle enquiries about him, she learned that he was expected to be in Queen Mary's for the six weeks it would take to make the prosthetic leg and to try and improve the movement in his thumb and index-finger. In addition, he would need to stay for an extra week in order to practise walking on his new leg.

But although that meant he was going to be there for longer than the average three weeks for patients in that department, there still wouldn't be sufficient time for her to get to know him, nor for him to get to know her, assuming he felt any interest in her.

But she did think, in that fleeting moment when she'd first seen him, that something had passed between them.

So, to be on the safe side, she'd have to keep her distance, she decided with real regret. She'd do her best to make sure that she was always tending another patient when it was time for Thomas's dressing to be changed.

Her plan to avoid him had worked for six weeks.

But for the whole of that time, despite knowing that she wouldn't be going anywhere near him, she woke up each morning sizzling with excitement at the thought of seeing him again that day, even if it was only from the other end of the ward.

And as she'd prepared for her shift each day, she'd paid more attention to her hair than she'd ever done before, and had carefully smoothed down her dress and made sure that her apron, cuffs and cap were spotless white and well-starched, all the while desperately hoping she'd see him, while also desperately hoping she wouldn't.

Never before had a man had such an effect on her, she thought with a sense of wonder. Not even in the days of Stan Cooke.

But with an iron will that she hadn't known she possessed, she'd kept her distance for six weeks, even though every minute that they weren't in the same room had seemed dull and empty. And even though she sensed whenever she was in his ward, that he was following her every movement with his eyes.

When the six weeks' mark passed, she felt an overwhelming relief that he'd soon be going home, and at the same time, she felt utter despair at the thought of not seeing him again.

And then she discovered that he wasn't leaving.

His stump had become infected while they'd been fitting his artificial leg. With his flesh receding and fragments of bone protruding, they couldn't attempt to fit the prosthetic leg again until the wound had healed. It meant that Thomas was going to have to stay in Queen Mary's longer than anticipated.

But Alice was determined to stick to her original plan.

He was off limits.

An extra week or two wasn't long enough to make any difference, especially when he was likely to be in a great deal of pain during that time and certainly wouldn't be interested in chatting to a nurse. She'd been strong so far, and she could certainly maintain her self-control for a little longer, she told herself with confidence.

And then she was the nurse who was tasked with syringing his stump every four hours with a solution of sterilised water and peroxide.

She couldn't pretend to herself that she wasn't delighted. She was.

The matter had been taken out of her hands. And since she was going to have to relax the strict discipline she'd imposed upon herself, she might as well make the most of every minute she spent with Thomas.

And thinking about it, that would be no bad thing as it meant she would really get to know him.

After all, she had no idea what he was truly like, having kept away from him from the moment she realised how attracted towards him she felt. But it might be as well to find out if he had any off-putting defects of character, and if he had, she'd instantly lose interest in him.

But no matter how hard she looked, day in and day out, she couldn't find any flaws.

All she saw was a fun-loving, cheerful, handsome man, who was determined not to let his injuries overwhelm him, and who seemed to enjoy talking to her as much as she enjoyed talking to him. And gradually, as the treatment started to work, and the flesh on his stump began to heal, she realised that her feelings had proved stronger than her willpower, and she'd fallen deeply in love with Thomas.

To her great joy, he seemed to feel the same about her.

This was confirmed on the day he took his first few steps on his new leg.

Despite the prosthetic leg chafing with his every movement, he managed a visit to the toilet by himself. Alice waited nearby in case he needed her help, but he didn't call for her, and came back grinning broadly.

'Those armrests on the toilet make it feel as if you're sitting on a throne!' he exclaimed.

Both laughed.

As their laughter died away, their eyes locked – his dark, exultant and alive; hers blue and sparkling with warmth and happiness; both pairs aglow with love.

She took a step back.

She knew by now that Thomas came from a wealthy background. She'd seen some of his family when they visited. They had the sort of self-confidence that came from money, and they wore the kind of clothes she'd seen in *Tatler*.

And she remembered the disgraced housemaid who'd

worked in Frederick Bates's house, and had no intention of making the same mistake. She mustn't forget what could happen to people of her simple origins when they caught the eye of a wealthy person. Not for one moment.

And it wasn't as if she wasn't fully aware of the nature of Thomas's interest in her.

Soon after she'd taken over his care, she'd accidentally brushed against his body while winding his bandage around his upper thigh. His feelings for her had been very evident.

She'd paused, and their eyes had met.

Neither had said a word, and she'd continued bandaging, acutely aware that her face was flame-red. Furiously, she told herself that she was being silly, that this was not about her – his body would have hardened in such a way no matter which young woman was doing the most intimate of tasks for him.

And yet, he did seem to enjoy being with her.

But she mustn't let that awareness get out of proportion.

He was casual and jokey with all the nurses, particularly the younger ones. She'd seen him flirting openly with them, and seen them flirting back in a light-hearted way. He obviously appreciated the care he was receiving, and equally, they appreciated the charm of a man who refused to let anything get him down.

His behaviour towards her was no more than any other casual flirtation, and she'd be a fool to make more of it.

9

QUEEN MARY'S HOSPITAL

11 November 1918

The ward telephone rang at eight in the morning. Alice rushed to answer it, but she was beaten to it by another nurse.

'It's over. Yippee!' the other nurse screamed at her. 'It'll officially be over at eleven, but really it's over now. The war's over, Alice.'

She hung up the telephone and they hugged each other. And then they both rushed in opposite directions – Alice to tell Matron the fantastic news, and the other nurse to spread the word throughout the hospital.

With excitement and jubilation exploding in the wards and along the corridors, the nurses decided to stop whatever they were doing at eleven o'clock to mark the moment with a celebration, even if it was no more than standing motionless for a minute. But when the time arrived, they were all busy, and it passed unnoticed.

Alice didn't see Thomas until early in the afternoon.

As she stood at the entrance to his ward, staring across at him, the excitement that she'd felt all day changed swiftly to misery.

The day before, she'd been standing just behind Matron, Thomas's medical notes in her hand, and she'd heard Matron tell Thomas that he was being discharged in five days, and that his family had been informed. Her heart had sunk the moment she heard the matron's words, and finding it hard not to burst into tears, she'd glanced at Thomas. He'd gone deathly pale, and looked stunned.

Matron had congratulated Thomas upon his recovery, and upon the high spirits that she'd heard so much about, and then she'd moved to the next bed.

Alice had lingered at Thomas's bedside. Wordlessly, they'd stared at each other.

Then he'd turned over, his back to her, and she'd no longer been able to see his face. She'd stood there a moment longer, and had then left, feeling utterly distraught.

The thrill of the morning's news had pushed her despair to the rear of her mind, but now, seeing Thomas at the far end of the ward, it all came rushing back.

She swallowed hard, and made her way along the ward to his bed.

'I had so wanted to enjoy the actual moment the war ended,' she told him, trying to avoid the subject of him going home. 'I knew it'd be something I'd never forget. But I missed it. And now I'm missing all the fun that's going on outside. All the visitors have been telling us what it's like in the streets, but it's not the same as being out there with everyone.'

He fixed his eyes on her face. 'People in other jobs have stopped working, or so I hear. You should, too, Alice. You never have a break. And I'd like to stop being a patient for a while and go outside. Of course, if I did, I'd need someone to push the chair.' He grinned at her. 'I bet if you worked your considerable charm on Sister, she'd let you take me out for a bit. You could say it's part of my rehabilitation. After all, if I'm going to go home, I need to get used to being among people who aren't doctors, nurses or patients.'

'That's true,' she said, in sudden elation at the thought of being outside with him. 'I'll ask Ward Sister.'

The sister had hesitated at first, and then agreed. But she stressed that Alice shouldn't keep him out too long as the day's excitement was bound to have exhausted him, although he wouldn't realise it.

With both of them wrapped up against the cold, and with a tartan rug over Thomas's legs, Alice pushed the heavy wheelchair along the pavements in the vicinity of the hospital, forging a path through the moving mass of people – soldiers on leave, women in the uniform of the Voluntary Aid Detachment, people in hospital blue, mothers with children, and elderly men and women with tears in their eyes. All were shouting themselves hoarse with joy, relief and excitement, waving flags and making a noise in any way that they could.

The roads were crowded, too. The lorries that frequently passed by were crammed with men and women, and there were cars and taxis, and buses with people on top as well as inside.

Everywhere, people were singing at the top of their voices, sometimes accompanied by makeshift bands, sometimes without. Songs such as 'Home Sweet Home', and hymns like 'All People that on Earth do Dwell', rose from the beating heart of the crowd. And 'God Save the King' was heard over and over again.

Thomas stared from one side of the chair to the other, and from what she could see, appeared overwhelmed by it all. But at the sound of 'It's a Long Way to Tipperary', he thumped the arm of his chair with his good hand, cheered, and then joined in the singing with great enthusiasm.

She glanced down at the top of his head, and wished with all her heart that the present moment would never end.

With the light fast fading, she reluctantly turned and headed back to the hospital. The lighting restrictions had already been lifted, but there'd been insufficient time to wipe the black shading from all of the street lamps, though some had been done, so their route back to the hospital was comparatively well lit. And even more so whenever they passed a hotel, since the hotels invariably had their outside lights on and their blinds up.

As they neared the hospital, Thomas started singing again. She shushed him quiet. 'Think of the patients,' she said as they reached the entrance.

He stopped singing, stretched up and caught hold of her arm.

She freed herself, put the brake on the wheelchair, and moved in front of Thomas to see what he wanted. He gazed up into her eyes.

'Your eyes have got little bits of gold in them,' he told her.

'They'll be reflections from the lights around the hospital.' She giggled. 'Is that what you wanted to tell me?'

'It's what I wanted to tell you, but it wasn't what I wanted to ask you. I love you, Nurse Alice Foster. Will you marry me?'

10

PRIMROSE HILL

Three days later

Arthur Joseph Linford, who was no longer a well man, regularly expressed amazement at the growth of Linford & Sons, the construction company he'd founded many years before. It had already been extremely successful when, before the war, he'd stepped aside to allow Joseph, the oldest of his three sons, to take over as chairman, and so, in effect, become head of the family.

And it had been even more prosperous since then.

No one had expected any rancour among the brothers at Joseph being offered the chairmanship of the company, and there hadn't been any.

The middle son, Charles, was happily ensconced in the world of banking, and the youngest of Arthur's three sons, Thomas, hadn't the slightest interest in construction. It was true that Thomas had worked for the company before the war, but he'd made no attempt to hide his boredom, nor the fact that he was there solely to make sufficient money so that he and his friend,

David, could go into the city at night and take advantage of the many pleasures on offer.

As soon as war had broken out, Thomas and David hadn't been able to enlist fast enough. No matter how hard the family had tried to persuade Thomas to claim an exemption on the grounds that he was essential to the war effort at home, as both Joseph and Charles were doing, Thomas wouldn't listen.

His refusal to stay at home would have been easier for the family to understand if the exemptions had been based on a lie, but they weren't.

When war broke out, the government knew that some highly placed bankers would be needed if money was to be kept moving, and Charles was to be one of those, and they knew that builders like Linford & Sons, with their skills and expertise, would be in great demand.

But Thomas had been deaf to their pleas, and he and David, fired up by a sense of adventure and patriotism, had gone off to fight.

David had died on the battlefield, within sight of Thomas, his body blown into myriad pieces by a buried artillery shell that he'd stepped on.

Thomas had come back to England, a severely injured man.

Linford & Sons, however, had thrived.

The wartime contracts awarded to the company had extended far beyond providing at speed much-needed shelter for people rendered homeless, and they'd found themselves moving into areas that were new to them, such as clearing airfields and building new ones in strategic locations. And now, at the end of the war, the company was stronger than ever.

And the post-war future of the company was looking good, too.

There'd already been a shortage of accommodation when the war broke out, then during the first few years of the war, relatively few houses were built, and of those, many were for wartime workers in areas that were unsuitable for peacetime needs. It meant that the demand for housing was going to be high for some years to come.

And when the government repealed the emergency act they'd passed in 1915, which had fixed rents at the pre-war level, construction would be given a further boost. And that was bound to happen – the government couldn't risk leaving a situation where it was uneconomic for construction companies to build houses for rent. The demand for housing wouldn't be met, and the government would suffer in the next general election.

But whatever happened in the future, Joseph Linford had great faith in the survival of the company, no matter the restrictions they faced. And so had his only son, Robert, who was now working with him.

Although still only seventeen, Robert, who would one day take over the running of the company, showed all the signs of being an excellent successor. He was a born businessman, with construction in his blood, and with the imagination to see ways in which the company might develop in the future. When the time came for him to hand over the reins to Robert, Joseph was confident that the company would be in good hands.

But that day was still a long way off.

And what mattered now was the present.

* * *

Joseph Linford signalled to the maid that she could leave them.

Sitting back in his mahogany carver chair, he gazed with pleasure along the length of his dining table, admiring the dark richness of the polished wood, the light on the crystal glasses, and the gleam of the silverware that was left on the table at the end of a meal that had been surprisingly good, given the voluntary rationing that was in operation, and which he obliged Mrs Morley, his housekeeper, to observe.

So far the evening had been a very pleasant one. He and Maud always enjoyed the company of his brother Charles, and Charles's wife, Sarah.

His eyes settled on the glass of port in front of him, and he smiled in satisfaction as he eyed the ruby red liquid.

'It's one of the vintage ports from my cellar,' he commented. 'There can no better port anywhere in London. The strength of my cellar is a testament to the continuing success of Linford & Sons. It's been an extremely good year for the company, and the next promises to be even better. Father was delighted when I went through the figures with him at Chorton last weekend.'

'So, Arthur is both retired, and not retired,' Sarah said with a smile.

'Exactly so, Sarah,' Joseph said, and he inclined his head towards her. 'And I'm sure the same will be said of me when I retire and hand over the reins to Robert.' He picked up his glass of port. 'Apparently, it looks as if they're going to ration meat for another year,' he remarked.

Maud glanced at her husband, and raised an eyebrow. 'And you suggested that Sarah and I join you and Charles for port this evening, in order to discuss the issue of food rationing, did you? Well, you never cease to surprise, me, Joseph.'

He smiled at her. 'A husband who still can surprise his wife after the years we've been married, my dear, must surely be congratulated. But no, in your underlying assumption, you are correct, as always. Interesting as the subject of food restrictions may be, I thought we might want to discuss Thomas's amazing news, and if I may add, very welcome news. We hadn't already broached the subject when it was time for port, so I thought we might break with tradition for once.'

'A sensible idea, Joseph,' Sarah said. 'Yes, Charles and I were absolutely thrilled when Thomas introduced us to Alice this afternoon when we visited him. We weren't in the least surprised he fell in love with her – she's a pretty little thing. Charles had actually noticed her previously on the ward when we were visiting Thomas. And we were pleased that although she comes from the North, and has presumably had little education, you wouldn't know that from the way she speaks.'

'I, too, am not surprised he fell in love with her,' Joseph said drily. 'More of a surprise is why someone as good-looking as she would choose to attach herself to a man with such a damaged body.'

Charles leaned forward. 'I can hear what you're suggesting, Joseph, and I think you're wrong. From the small amount I've seen of them together, this isn't about her marrying for money – I think she genuinely loves him. And unlike you, I'm not at all surprised. Thomas can be charming when he wants to. Losing a leg won't alter that. The hospital will ensure that he gets the best prosthetic available, and see that he can manage perfectly well. I think you'll find he's very different from the hot-headed young man who went to war. The worst of his excesses will have gone, but he'll still be amusing and good company, just as in the past.'

Sarah nodded. 'I'm sure Charles is right, Joseph. You must let us help with the arrangements for their marriage and with the decisions about where they'll live. He obviously won't want to take up residence with anyone in the family. Apart from the fact that our houses are completely unsuitable, any newly married couple would rather be on their own.'

Joseph nodded. 'I agree, Sarah, and I've been giving the matter some thought. Thank you for the offer of help, but I think the whole thing's going to be pretty straightforward. Thomas wants to marry before he leaves Roehampton so that they can live together as soon as he comes home. He wants the smallest wedding possible in a church near the hospital, and he doesn't want a reception afterwards. I can understand that. Despite our victory, there's a lot of sadness everywhere, and hardship – the war's only just ended and thousands of people died or were injured. Also, it'll be one of the first occasions he's been outside the hospital, and it's bound to be somewhat daunting.'

'What house have you got in mind?' Charles asked. 'Knowing you, I'm sure you've already got a suggestion to make.'

Joseph took a sip of his port. 'There seems to be an obvious place for them to set up home – the Kentish Town house that came with the yard. There are even vans in the yard, which could be useful if Thomas wanted to travel anywhere with the wheelchair. I know that two downstairs rooms are being used as the company offices, but that was true when Father and Mother lived there in the years before we all moved to Hampstead, and they were quite happy. Indeed, you and I were born in Kentish Town, Charles.'

'That's true.'

'It'll obviously need a small amount of work to return it to being a home again, and one that's suitable for Thomas, but as builders we're well placed to do it. I imagine we'll have to install an internal water closet and a bath in one of the downstairs rooms, and make one of the rooms into their bedroom. Thomas won't find the stairs easy.'

'I think that's an excellent idea,' Sarah said. 'It could be made into a very attractive home. That'll be something for Alice to do. The front door opens on to the pavement, which will make it easy with the wheelchair, and there's a little garden at the back. It's perfect for Thomas.'

'My thoughts entirely, Sarah,' Joseph said with a smile. 'And feeling confident that Thomas will welcome the plan, Maud and I have taken the liberty of hiring a housekeeper for him, a Mrs Carmichael. If he and Alice are unhappy with our choice, they can always change her. But domestic staff are becoming difficult to find, with alternative forms of employment for women these days, so when I heard that Mrs Carmichael was looking for a position as a housekeeper, I approached her at once.'

Charles raised his glass in a toast. 'Well done, Joseph; you seem to have thought of everything. That's the wedding and house sorted, then, and the housekeeper, too. And with Thomas very wisely marrying a nurse, we don't have to worry about hiring a woman to take care of him. As far as I can tell, it leaves one thing only to decide – a job for Thomas. But I suspect you're about to tell us that, too.'

Joseph laughed. 'How well you know me, Charles! Yes, I *do* have a job in mind. It was Maud's idea, actually, not mine.' He smiled at his wife. 'We're setting up a small division in Linford & Sons to deal with the internal decorations of the houses. We'll be going all out to meet the demand for new homes, but so will all of our competitors. It means that our houses will have to stand out if we're going to find people to rent them. Or to buy them,' he added.

Charles looked at him in surprise. 'To buy them?'

'That's right. My instinct tells me that we're heading for a time when people are going to clamour to buy their homes, rather than rent them. If so, having a designated division for interiors will be extremely useful. Thomas can be in charge of this.'

Sarah stared at Joseph in surprise. 'And you really think that Thomas is the right person to decide what will make a house attractive to people?'

'Maybe not at the moment,' Joseph said, 'but he's certainly got an eye for attractive women, and that's not a bad place to begin.'

'I take it Robert agrees with all this, and that his absence this evening isn't a sign of disapproval,' Charles said, with a wry glance at his brother. 'With him now working full-time for the company, his voice should be heard.'

'Don't worry about Robert, Charles. He's a chip off the old block, and like his father, Robert makes sure that his voice is heard when he has something to say,' Maud said smoothly, and she glanced with affection at Joseph.

Joseph laughed. 'Less of the old, if you don't mind, Maud.' He smiled reassuringly at Charles. 'Robert is right behind everything I've suggested. He isn't here because he's at Chorton House with Father.'

'Again!' Sarah put down her glass. 'He seems to be at Chorton just about every weekend.'

Joseph scowled. 'He is,' he said tersely. 'It's because of that wretched woman, Lily Brown. With Robert telling me at the end of last year that he wanted to marry her, I arranged to keep him in London for a month this spring. I regret to say it doesn't seem to have done the trick.'

'That's not really surprising. Have you seen the woman?' Charles murmured.

Joseph glared at him. 'That's neither here nor there. I've repeatedly told him that he should be looking for someone more suitable than a Land Girl without any education, background or money, which he could certainly do now that the war has ended. But does he listen? No! And Father's no help at all. He's still so deeply mourning the loss of Mother that he allows Robert to do whatever he wants when they're at Chorton.'

Charles opened his mouth to speak.

'And don't you say Alice is not that unlike Lily in terms of where she comes from, Charles,' Joseph cut through him. 'Thomas's position is very different from that of Robert.'

'Robert isn't listening to you, darling,' Maud cut in, 'any more than you're listening to all of us. We've told you on more than one occasion that your hostility towards Lily will push them closer together. You should be inviting her to join us whenever we're at Chorton. The more that Robert sees she's out of her depth on family occasions, the more he's likely to realise for himself that she wouldn't make the sort of wife he'd be happy with.'

Joseph shook his head in despair. 'You may be right. It's so hard to know. Robert used to be such an easy lad, but not these days. You've no idea how relieved I am that I don't have to worry about Dorothy or Nellie, too. Dorothy's been busy from morning till night since she was transferred to the hospital in the internment camp at Alexandra Palace.'

'I know how happy she was at Byculla, and that she'd very much wanted to stay there,' Sarah said. 'Has she settled now?'

'I think so. She knew she didn't have a choice, and she's the sort of person to make the best of what she has to do. The hospital there needed help with the huge number of German internees they're holding, and that was that. But from what we've heard, she's finding it better than she expected. I don't envy her, though, having to work among the people who cost her uncle his leg. As for Nellie, she's only fifteen and still at school, so she's too young to cause us any sleepless nights.'

'Ever the optimist,' Charles said with a smile. 'Louisa may only be seven, but even at that young age, she can be trouble.

She's far too much like her mother for there to be any harmony in the house!'

'Thank you, darling,' Sarah said lightly, and they all laughed.

'To return to where we started,' Joseph said, 'which was the subject of Thomas. Let's drink a toast to the fact that something that could have been very difficult to deal with, has unexpectedly been solved by Thomas falling in love.' He raised his glass. 'To Alice. Our family's saviour.'

11

KENTISH TOWN

September 1919

'I've never been one for the great outdoors before,' Thomas remarked as Alice pushed him into the front hall. 'I was always keener on going inside a club, than anywhere outside, despite growing up on the edge of the Heath. But now that I can't get about as much,' he indicated his missing leg, 'I'm getting more used to going out, and I actually enjoyed our walk this afternoon, even though Kentish Town isn't the most beautiful of places.'

'Me, too. We must do it again very soon.'

'In fact,' he went on, 'I rather surprised myself today. Before the war, I'd never have noticed that the horse chestnut leaves were turning a burnished gold, or that the sky had a soft autumnal pallor that would look good on interior walls if only people could see beyond dark paint and thick wallpaper. And there was a definite tang of woodsmoke in the air. But I suppose that my newly awakened senses aren't to be wondered at, being stuck as I am in the chair. There's not much else to do but look at the view.'

'And hold my shopping,' Alice said lightly. 'You're very well placed for that.' And she removed her wicker basket from his lap and put it on the small hall table that stood beneath a large gilt-framed mirror.

He grinned at her. 'There's that, too,' he said.

'And that frees my arms so I can put them around you and hug you.' She pulled off her fur-trimmed cloche, leaned down and held him tightly, her long fair hair falling over his face.

He pulled her closer. 'I love you, Alice,' he said.

'And I love you, Thomas Linford.'

'Do you?' he asked, pushing her slightly back. 'Even though it didn't work out last night? I felt such a failure. But my stump was so raw that I couldn't stand any pressure on it. And you know...' His voice trailed away, and he stared anxiously up at her.

'I *do* know,' she said gently, and she ran her fingers down the side of his face. 'If you're in pain, that's one thing. But you know, you're making it more difficult by keeping on trying to stop me from seeing your whole body. I'm a nurse, remember. There's virtually nothing I haven't seen. When you try to hide yourself, it gets in the way of what we both want to do – me, too, Thomas, and I don't care how forward that makes me sound. It's the truth. I love you as you are, every inch of you.'

'But there aren't that many inches to love, are there? I'll never get my leg back, bits of my hand will always be missing and my body will always be scarred.'

'And I'll always love you. Believe me, you'll eventually come to accept your injuries, and then you'll stop dwelling on what you can't do, and realise just how much you still *can* do. Now,' she said briskly, taking off her coat, 'why don't I ask Mrs Carmichael to bring us some tea? It's a little earlier than usual, but that doesn't matter. It'll help you to snap out of this mood.'

'Good idea.'

'Start unbuttoning your coat, and I'll help you with what you've not been able to manage when I get back. I won't be a moment.'

She went through to the kitchen, and returned a few minutes later.

'I asked Mrs Carmichael to bring the tea into the living-room as I thought we could play a game of cards while we waited,' she said, helping him out of his coat, which she hung up on the wooden stand in the front hall. 'It's only fair that you let me get my revenge for my defeat yesterday.'

'We're closer to the office. Why don't we go there?'

'Because you'll only start thinking about work. The living-room it is,' she said, and she helped him out of the wheelchair, and slid the crutch under his armpit.

'D'you want to go to the water closet first?' she asked.

'You'll be offering me a bedpan next,' he said with a trace of annoyance.

She pulled a face. 'I'm sorry. That's the nurse in me.'

He paused and twisted himself to look at her. 'I'm not your patient any longer, Alice,' he said quietly. 'I don't want to think of you as my nurse – I want to think of you as my wife, especially when we go to bed. It's hard enough to do that, knowing that you're doing things for me which most wives don't have to do for their husbands, but asking if I want to empty my bladder is quite unnecessary. If I do, I'll get up and go, unless it's something I'll need your help with.'

'I understand, Thomas, and I'm sorry.'

He nodded, and smiled wryly. 'And I'm sorry, too. I know you're just trying to help. Come on; let's play that game of cards.'

Slowly, he made his way past the staircase on the right, and went into the small living-room that led off the end of the hall to the left.

'When you think about it,' he said as Alice helped him into his armchair next to the fireplace and placed a table in front of him, 'it's not really surprising that I notice what's around me in a way I never used to. After all, it's my job to pick the right decorative details for the Linford houses – obviously within the limits of what I'm allowed to spend, which isn't a lot.'

'And you're doing a really good job. Joseph's always saying how impressed he is,' she said, and she pulled up a chair and sat down opposite him. Picking up the deck of cards from the table, she started shuffling them.

'He'd say that anyway. He wants to feel less guilty that I fought for the country, and that he and Charles didn't. So what he says isn't important. But what Lloyd George says *does* matter. He said that soldiers coming home from horrendous water-logged trenches shouldn't be expected to live in something you wouldn't put an animal in, and he was right, and that's why I do the best I can.'

'They certainly deserve a pleasant home after what they've been through.'

'Unfortunately, being realistic, not even the private builders, and all of the local authorities who've been given financial incentives by the government to start building houses, are going to be able to produce sufficient homes to meet the demand. There'll be overcrowding and sharing for a lot longer.'

Alice shrugged. 'Where I come from, that's common. There aren't enough houses to rent, and people can't always afford those there are. So, are we going to play "Old Maid", then, or wait till we've had our tea?'

'Not that new game "Strip Poker"?' he asked, raising an eyebrow. 'Is this for fear of what you might be forced to see if I lost?'

She laughed. 'On the contrary – I'd play "Strip Poker" like a shot if I thought you'd let me win. But you won't. Whatever we play, I'm always the one who loses, and I think we should spare Mrs Carmichael from a fit of vapours at the sight of me in a state of undress.'

He gave her a slow grin. 'I think we'll play "Strip Poker" when Mrs Carmichael has left. I feel a winning streak coming on.'

She blushed. 'Don't count on it.'

Mrs Carmichael came in with a tray. They waited while she put down the silver tea pot and pot of boiling water, plus two bone china cups and saucers, a jug of milk and a plate of biscuits that looked as if they'd just come from the oven. And then she left.

Thomas gave Alice a knowing glance. 'Let the game begin.'

She picked up her cup and giggled. 'We're going to play "Old Maid" till Mrs Carmichael's safely retired for the night. The joker can be the old maid.'

When they'd finished their tea, she moved the cups and plates to a different table and dealt out the cards, face down. 'Fan your cards,' she said, 'and I'll take one.'

Thomas leaned forward, lifted his right arm and went to place his hand on the cards. 'Darn!' he exclaimed, pulling his arm back. 'Wrong hand.' And resting his right hand on his lap, he reached out to the cards with his left.

There was a knock on the front door. He paused, his hand in mid-air. 'I wonder who that is.'

'Good job one of us isn't in the middle of stripping,' she said. They looked at each other and laughed.

A moment later, the door opened.

'Mr Joseph Linford,' Mrs Carmichael announced, and they saw Joseph just behind her. She stood aside, and Joseph came into the room. Alice rose to her feet.

'What d'you want?' Thomas asked brusquely, struggling to fan out his cards with his left hand.

'Do sit down, Joseph,' Alice said, and she pointed to the armchair closest to them.

'I'm sorry to interrupt,' he said, sitting down.

'Please don't apologise. It's lovely to see you,' Alice said.

'She's only being polite,' Thomas snapped.

'Mrs Carmichael will bring you some tea, if you wish,' Alice told Joseph. 'Or would you prefer a whisky?'

'It's a pleasure to see you, too, Alice, as it always is,' Joseph said. 'A whisky would be much appreciated. Thank you.'

Alice indicated that Mrs Carmichael could leave them, and she went across to the drinks' trolley and poured a glass of whisky from the decanter. 'Would you like one, too, Thomas?' she asked.

He nodded. 'I might as well. Something stronger than tea could make this unexpected, and may I say completely unwelcome, visit from my brother, more palatable.'

She filled a second glass.

'Thank you, Alice,' Joseph said, taking the glass she offered him. She gave the second glass to Thomas.

Thomas grunted.

Joseph angled his body slightly towards Thomas. 'This unwelcome visit, as you so graciously put it, Thomas, is because I've some worrying news. Father's been taken ill. He thinks he'll soon be joining Mother and the doctor's inclined to agree. He's made it clear that he wants to be buried alongside her in the churchyard near Chorton House.' He took a drink, and Alice noticed that his eyes were moist. 'That's understandable,' he added. 'Since Mother died, Chorton has been the place where he's felt closest to her.' He put his glass down on the table, took out a handkerchief and blew his nose.

Thomas stared at his untouched drink. 'That *is* bad news,' he said quietly. 'Who's with him?'

'Robert, obviously, since he and Lily are living in Hampstead with Father. We're going to try to give Robert as much time as possible away from work so that he can stay with him. They've always been very close. The rest of us will visit whenever we can. Maud and I are going at the weekend, and we can take you, if you wish.'

He nodded. 'I do wish.' He paused. 'At least he has Lily there, too.'

Joseph's eyes narrowed. 'I've suggested she move to Chorton for a while. The child's only two months old. It's highly unsuitable to have a baby there at such a time. However, Robert doesn't agree, and Lily and the nanny aren't going anywhere.'

'But Father likes her, doesn't he?' Thomas said. 'If he hadn't, he'd never have offered her a home with him, or invited them to live with him once they'd married. I imagine he'd want her there.'

'Oh, she can turn on the charm when she wants,' Joseph said acidly. 'That'll be how she trapped Robert into such an unsuitable marriage. But it doesn't mean that hers is the face he'll want to see in his dying moments.'

'Shouldn't he be left to decide? If he's got the strength to say where he wants to be buried, he's got the strength to say who he wants at his side. It's hardly up to you.'

'As chairman of the company, I'm making it my business. She'd do far better to be thinking about where they'll live when Father dies. He's always given us to understand that he'll be leaving Chorton to the three of us, you, me and Charles.'

'I'd be happy to let them stay on in Hampstead. And I'm sure Charles would, too. He doesn't need the house. And nor do you, for God's sake. Or would you rather see them and the baby on the streets?'

'Don't be ridiculous!'

'So Robert can count on you for support, can he?'

Joseph glared at him. 'I didn't come here to discuss my son's future accommodation. I wanted to bring you up to date.' He turned slightly to Alice. 'Our mother died in December a few years ago, Alice, and was buried by the church at the top of the hill near the house. You've no idea how cold it was by the graveside. It's as well that we remember to wrap up warmly again, this time to say goodbye to Father.'

He blew his nose again.

'You've no idea what real cold is!' Thomas said with a sneer. 'Muffled up as we were in the trenches with scarves and gloves, and with balaclavas under our helmets, and wearing greatcoats over our uniforms, we were still bitterly cold. That's real cold.'

Joseph finished his drink, and stood up. 'I've told you what I came to tell you. I'll now leave you to wallow in self-pity, Thomas. Thank you for your hospitality, Alice,' he said, and he smiled at her with genuine warmth. 'I appreciate it.'

'It's better than guilt,' Thomas called after Joseph as Alice walked with him to the door. A few moments later, she returned to the living-room, sat down and stared at the table. The cards had been pushed to one side, and the whisky glass in front of Thomas was empty.

'I've lost the taste for cards. I'll have another whisky, instead,' he said. 'And take that look of reproach off your face. It's not my fault they didn't do what they should've done. It makes me feel sick whenever I see them, knowing that they were safe in bed when David and I were fighting to protect them and everyone else at home.'

'You must try not to think like that, or at least, put it to the back of your mind.'

'On the contrary, I intend to rub their noses in it whenever I see them. They're cowards, and I'm not going to let them forget it.'

12

KENTISH TOWN

December 1919

Alice helped Thomas into his office, where he'd made it clear he preferred to sit during the day. While he stood leaning on his cane, she unwrapped his scarf, slid his black cashmere coat down over his arms, and threw them across the nearest chair. Then she helped him into his wheelchair, placing it so that his back was to the large sash window that looked out across the street.

'You did very well today, walking as much as you did. You must be tired. Shall I take the prosthesis off?' she asked.

He nodded. 'Please. Yes, I *am* tired. But I was determined not to use the wheelchair as I'd have looked such an obvious cripple. I must admit, though, that I was very relieved that Charles wanted to leave as soon as the will had been read. And that neither he nor Sarah felt the need for a jolly conversation on the way home. A little of my family goes a long way.'

His prosthesis removed, he angled the wheelchair so that he could look through the window at the row of plane trees lining the pavement on the opposite side of the road, stark shapes against the pale grey sky. Between the bare arms of the winter-shorn trees, the dilapidated shops that opened on to the pavement could be clearly seen.

'I prefer the view in summer when the trees prevent me from seeing those awful run-down shops,' he said, swivelling back to face her. 'Pull up your chair so that you're right next to me. You're much more attractive to look at than the view.'

She did so.

He smiled at her, leaned across and took her hand. 'You look after me so well, Alice. I'm a very lucky man. I'm sorry I get impatient at times. I get angry at what I can't do – I'm not angry with you. And I just can't get used to using the wrong hand.'

'I understand that, Thomas, really I do. I've never been happier than since we married.'

He stared at her intently for a long moment. 'Is that really true?' he finally asked. 'Even though bits of me are missing?'

She smiled at him. 'They don't matter nearly as much as the bits that are there. You're extremely handsome, and you're a really kind person, which is even more important.'

Thomas opened his mouth to speak.

'No, don't deny it.' Alice reached across and put her finger to his lips. 'I watched your family today as your father's will was read out. The minute they heard he'd left the Hampstead house to Robert, and the money to run it with, they all looked horrified, except for you. Even though Chorton House was left to you all, they seemed really angry, and were very cold afterwards to Robert and Lily. Especially to Lily. Joseph genuinely seems to hate her.'

'He has from the moment Robert introduced her to him.'

'You were the only one there who smiled at Lily after the solicitor had finished reading the will, and also the only person who said goodbye to her and Robert.'

'I always feel sorry for Lily. She seems alone in the water, encircled by sharks. And Robert's too much of a Linford to be aware of that.'

'I can't imagine why Joseph's so against her. She's beautiful, and she clearly adores Robert. You think he'd be happy that someone loved his son like that.'

'Basically, he doesn't think she's good enough for him. And he thinks she trapped Robert into marrying her by getting pregnant.'

'That's silly. Robert need not have married her. Men don't always do what they should. I know that from some of the things that went on in Waterfoot.'

'That's true. But Robert has a strong moral streak, and Lily must've known he'd marry her. It's not in his nature to do otherwise. But Joseph's also thinking about when he stands down as chairman, and Robert takes over. He believes that Robert should have the right wife at his side – someone with background and education. Like he has in Maud, who's an excellent wife to Joseph. And the others don't like Lily because she's awkward with them, and doesn't fit easily into their little world. And it'll be worse now as they'll think she put pressure on Father to leave his house to her and Robert. Joseph's always thought she was a gold-digger.'

'She'd never have done that, I'm sure. I know I've not seen her very often, but on the few occasions I have, she's seemed really pleasant, although very shy. I can't see her pushing anyone into anything.'

'Nor can I. And I can't see Father letting himself be persuaded into doing something he doesn't want. People who build up highly successful companies like Linford & Sons aren't the sort of people who let themselves be pushed around. Father did what he wanted. But clearly, the rest of the family don't agree with what that was.'

'Well, I thought you were really kind today. You didn't show any resentment that Robert had been given the house where you all grew up. And you went out of your way to be nice to Lily. Even Charles and Sarah didn't talk to her. I was a little surprised Charles didn't, as he's always done his best to make *me* feel at ease.'

'I suppose it's also a money thing. To give Joseph his due, which I do very reluctantly, with the war over and a huge demand for homes, he's understandably anxious to have sufficient in the coffers to build as many houses as possible. The thing about Linford wives is that they're expected to contribute financially to the company on their marriage, which both Maud and Sarah did. Joseph had very much hoped that Robert would marry someone who could do the same.'

'But love's more important than money!'

'Not if you're Joseph, it isn't.'

Alice sat back heavily back against her chair, and bit her lower lip.

'You look worried, Alice. What's the matter?'

'I don't have any money, or what they'd call background or education. And you can't imagine what my home was like. It was very clean – my mother and I looked after it well – but it was a tiny back-to-back in a small mill town. And nurses aren't the sort of people you see in magazines.'

He smiled at her. 'They are if the magazine is *The Nursing Mirror*.'

She smiled weakly back at him. 'You know what I mean.'

He leaned forward. 'Has anyone in the family made you feel that you don't belong? Because that's what they do to Lily.'

She shook her head. 'No, never. And as I say, some of them,

like Charles, have gone out of their way to make me feel very welcome.'

He straightened up. 'There you are, then.'

'They always look at me kindly, and with curiosity. They try not to show their curiosity, though,' she added, and she giggled.

He grinned. 'They look at me like that, too.' He put his finger under his chin and looked up at the ceiling as if deep in thought. 'Hm. I wonder why.'

She giggled again. 'I think it's quite amusing. They know you've lost your leg, but they're not sure if anything else in the area was damaged. They'd obviously love to ask, but they don't dare.'

'Thank God for that! All that matters is that you know that nothing else was damaged, and this evening, I'll prove it to you.'

She blushed.

'Seriously though, Alice, I've never seen any sign of them feeling about you as they do about Lily. Believe me, if they did, we'd both know it. Joseph never stopped telling Robert what an idiot he was being. If Robert hadn't been left Father's house, I don't know what he and Lily would've done for a home. Even though Robert's his son, Joseph would never have taken them in. And nor would he have agreed to let them stay in the Hampstead house.'

'That sounds very harsh.'

'That's Joseph for you. But I'm sure they like you, and if they've any other feelings towards you, it'll be relief that there was someone stupid enough to take me on.'

She beamed at him. 'I'm not at all stupid – I'm really lucky. I'm married to the best of husbands.'

His face suddenly anxious, he stared at her intently. 'Am I really that, Alice? At times, I worry that you might see me more as a cripple than a husband.' A trace of awkwardness crept into his voice. 'It's taking me so long to be able to do everything I want, and I still need so much help with personal things. When you look at me, do you honestly see someone you want to go to bed with? In the middle of the night, I sometimes wonder that.'

She jumped up from her chair and went and hugged him. 'Of course, I don't see you as a cripple. I love you, Thomas. I see you as my husband, as the man I want to lie next to every single night for the rest of my life, the man I hope will one day give me children. I couldn't love you any more than I do if you were absolutely whole.'

He pulled back from her. 'So that's it,' he said with sudden sharpness. 'You see me as less than whole. Like my family sees me.'

She laughed in embarrassment. 'That didn't come out right. Of course, I don't. I love you with all my heart. I have since the moment I saw you.' She went to put her arms around him again, but he pushed her away.

'But you don't think of me as whole.'

She edged back to her chair and sat down again. 'I don't know why you're talking like this,' she said, suddenly feeling very cold. 'You must know how much I love you. And that your family loves you, too.'

'My family?' He laughed dismissively. 'You don't know what you're talking about. I make them feel guilty. They'd be happy if they never saw me again.'

'You know they wouldn't. There's no reason why they *should* feel guilty,' she added. 'Charles and Joseph both told me they'd begged you not to join up. They could've really used your help during the war, with all the work they had. There's more than one way of fighting a war, you know.'

'They've got through to you, I see.'

'I'm just telling you the truth,' she said, her voice catching. 'I don't want you to make yourself unhappy by coming to believe a twisted version of what happened. That would be very bad for your recovery.'

'So I'm twisted, am I, as well as being less than whole? That's a nice way for a wife to talk about a husband.'

Clutching the handkerchief in her pocket, she stood up. 'I'd better check on lunch with Mrs Carmichael. There's no point in talking to you when you're in a mood like this. You're twisting my words, and pretending that everything I say means something different.'

And she walked out of the room.

13

KENTISH TOWN

March 1920

With a sinking feeling, Alice stood staring at Thomas's back, her umbrella hanging from her hand, water dripping on to the floor.

'You're in a mood again, I can tell,' she said flatly. 'You're in a mood more often than you're not these days.'

'If you say so.'

'Then there's probably no point in telling you what Joseph said when I bumped into him while I was out.'

'No, point at all,' he said, staring resolutely across the road.

She sighed inwardly.

She undid her raincoat, took it off and carried it with her umbrella to the coat stand in the hall, and then returned to the office. She went to a high-backed wooden chair near where Thomas was sitting, pulled it over to where Thomas could see her and she could see his face, sat down and leaned forward, her elbows on her knees.

'Joseph was going into the yard to check something,' she began, ignoring his pointed refusal to listen. 'We talked for a few minutes, mainly about the new development in North London. He said that buying up lots of land on the roads leading in and out of London has worked out even better than they'd hoped. With roads improving and the underground now extended, people can live further out, but still get into London to work.'

'Good for him.'

'He's very pleased with the progress they've made, so he's taking Charles to see it in two days' time, along with Robert and Lily. He'd like us to go, too. He said you've done a lot of work on the inside of the houses, and he thought you'd like to see how they're coming along. He'd pick us up and take us there, and then we'd go back to his house for lunch. He's going to come by tomorrow and ask if you'd like to go.' She paused. 'I'd really like to see the houses, so can we say yes?'

'You go if you want, but I'm not.' He glanced at her, and his lips curled. 'I'm sure Charles would like that. He couldn't stop staring at you at Father's funeral, nor at the will-reading. And you yourself said that he often talks to you. Good old Charles. Not that I'm surprised, mind you – his wife never stops nagging him. Being married to Sarah is enough to make a man look somewhere else.'

'I don't know what you're talking about.' She moved closer to him, and took his hand. 'Obviously, I wouldn't go without you, but I think we *should* go, Thomas. You need to get out more, and it'd be nice for you to go somewhere with your brothers.'

'You mean, so they can feel good about themselves, being seen taking an injured soldier out!'

She dropped his hand, and straightened up. 'That's not why Joseph wants you to go with them, and you know it.'

'Don't be so naïve, Alice – it's not about me, it's about them. They feel guilty about me fighting, and David being blown into little pieces, while they were safe at home.'

She groaned audibly. 'Not that again.'

'Yes, that again! I'm sorry that it's boring for you to be reminded that they shelled us in the trenches for hours on end, day and night. That I've seen people go bonkers in front of me, with a fear you could smell, certain that the next shell would be the one that got them. If they went to light a cigarette, their fingers shook uncontrollably and they couldn't. It could be their last, you see. The continual bombardment drove us mad. But why am I bothering? People who've never been afraid like that couldn't possibly understand.'

'You're wrong. Of course they know what it was like. For a start, you tell them whenever you see them. And they've seen for themselves some of the terrible injuries that soldiers have come home with. But just because a person's been injured, Thomas, he doesn't have to give up on living, and be nasty to everyone he meets. The war's been over for almost two years, but instead of getting better, you're getting worse. It's time you looked at what you've got, and not at what you've lost.' She stood up. 'That's something you could be thinking about while I check on our tea.'

'Alice!' she heard him call as she started to open the door to the hall. She paused and turned towards him. 'I'm sorry,' he said. 'You know I had those nightmares again last night, and kept on waking up, sweating. My heart was thumping like mad, and I felt terrified. It makes me so tired in the day, and then I'm really nasty to you. I hate myself for it, but I can't seem to stop.'

'I *do* understand, Thomas,' she said, and she took a few steps towards him. 'Anxiety attacks are normal after what you've been through, but they *will* pass, believe me.'

'I hope so for both our sakes.' He hesitated. 'As a peace offering, when Joseph stops by tomorrow, I'll tell him we'll go with him on Friday.'

She smiled broadly at him. 'Thank you, Thomas; I'm so

pleased. And Joseph will be, too. And now for some tea,' she said, and went out into the hall.

* * *

She closed the office door behind her, leaned back against the cold wood and took a deep breath.

Why hadn't she told Thomas that not only had she met Joseph that morning, but she'd also bumped into Charles?

She'd no idea why she'd held it back, but the moment that Thomas had made that remark about Charles staring at her at the funeral, she'd been very glad that she hadn't mentioned seeing him, too. Yet she and Charles had talked for a few minutes only, and their conversation had been completely innocent.

Thinking back, though, maybe the words 'bumped into' weren't strictly accurate. They implied that something had been accidental, and she wasn't entirely sure that their meeting *had* been a matter of chance.

She'd been on her way home, her umbrella furled as it wasn't raining, and she'd just turned the corner, gone past the Assembly House, and reached the bench at the end of her road. She'd occasionally sit there for a few minutes before going the rest of the way to the house, but it wasn't a day for sitting on the bench, given the unsettled weather, so she went to cross straight over the road, and caught sight of Charles further along on the pavement.

He'd been staring at the house from behind one of the plane trees bordering the pavement opposite, the collar of his dark grey jacket upturned. The thought had flashed through her mind that although he'd be able to see both the front door and the window of Thomas's office, it was unlikely that anyone inside the house, or in the builders' yard, would have been able to see him, and that may have been deliberate on his part.

Scolding herself for being so fanciful, she'd paused where she was, her foot in the gutter, and wondered whether to go up and speak to him. At that moment, he'd turned, looked in her direction and seen her. A hesitant smile had broken out on his face, and he'd made a movement towards her.

It *had* been deliberate, she thought.

She'd felt her heart start racing, and she'd stepped back on to the pavement instead of crossing over the road, and waited for him to reach her.

Their conversation had been very brief, and she couldn't really remember what they'd said, beyond the fact that he'd told her he'd be going to see the new development at the end of the week, and that Joseph was going to ask her to join them. And Thomas, too, of course, he'd added.

He'd laughed as he'd thrown in the mention of Thomas, but now that she was thinking about it, he'd also looked a little self-conscious.

She'd told him that she'd seen Joseph on her way out, and that he'd already invited them, and she was going to do everything she could to make Thomas agree to go. Charles had nodded his approval, and a few moments later, he'd said goodbye and left.

It was only when she was crossing the road to the house that she realised that it had started drizzling while they'd been talking, and she'd actually got quite wet.

But really, the whole thing couldn't have been more harmless.

Or could it?

She bit her lip and gazed at the olive-green wall on the other side of the narrow hall. Of course, it could, she told herself angrily. She was telling herself one thing, but in her heart, she knew it to be a lie.

There *had* been something in the air between them that

morning, just as there had been at the funeral and at the will-reading. And deep down she knew that he'd been wanting to see someone that morning, and that someone had been her.

And she also knew that every time she'd felt his eyes on her, something within her had stirred, and she'd felt a sensation that she shouldn't be feeling for any man other than her husband. She hated herself for it, but she couldn't help it – Charles was such a clever man and so good-looking, and so very kind.

And he wasn't the sort of person she'd ever have thought would take an interest in someone like her.

Whenever the other Linfords looked at her, their eyes registered mild curiosity – curiosity about whether she and Thomas lived as a normal husband and wife – and also gratitude. They clearly appreciated everything she was doing for Thomas, but they weren't viewing her as a person in her own right. She was pretty sure that although the Linfords seemed to like her, she was little more to them than Thomas's nurse, who, by being married to Thomas and living in the same house, could perform her duties more easily.

But it was different with Charles.

The expression in Charles's eyes when he looked at her showed that he saw her as a woman, and an attractive woman at that. Being appreciated by such a man made her feel warm inside. Surely, there couldn't be any harm in admitting that, but just to herself.

She took a deep breath, and straightened up. She must pull herself together and stop thinking in such a way. Of course, there could be harm in it.

And really, she was merely responding to flattery. While that wasn't surprising – she didn't get a lot of appreciation, living with Thomas – it could be dangerous to give any thought to Charles and his effect on her. Thomas should be her sole focus.

But he didn't make things easy for her.

He'd been so very different in Queen Mary's. And she understood why, although she hadn't foreseen it.

For as long as he'd been there, he'd been protected from much of the physical reality of living without a right leg and without the use of his right hand, which would be especially difficult for him, being right-handed. While in the hospital, he had yet to learn how much tougher life would be at home. Because of this, she'd had the chance to see his charm, and his sense of humour, and to see beyond the scars to the lean, muscular body she was tending.

But now that he was home, confronted daily by things he could no longer do for himself, and frequently in a significant degree of pain, everything was very different. He could see his limitations with clarity, and chafed continually against them, with the result that he was becoming moodier with each passing day, and more and more hostile and resentful towards his family.

She fully understood that.

It was just that helping him to overcome his disabilities was harder than she'd expected, and it was difficult for her to cope with his moods. Increasingly feeling tired and worn down, she was finding it harder and harder to summon the patience she needed while he came to terms with life as it was going to be for him from now on.

Nevertheless, despite everything, she had no regrets about marrying him, and even though her life as Mrs Thomas Linford wasn't at all the life she'd thought she'd find in London, she never once looked back with longing to the life she'd had in Waterfoot.

Thomas was her husband, and she loved him. And he was still very attractive to her. And when in precious moments, she glimpsed the old Thomas, charming and kind, she felt completely happy.

But such occasions were getting further and further apart, and too frequently, he seemed to treat her as another enemy, rather than as his wife.

And that was why she was susceptible to flattery.

But she shouldn't make too much of her meeting with Charles.

She'd done nothing for which to reproach herself, and she never would. Her loyalty was to Thomas, and that would not change. In the meantime, she'd try even harder to be patient and understanding, and she'd do her best to raise his spirits when he felt particularly low.

That was the reason why she'd been so keen that they join Joseph the following Friday.

It wasn't anything to do with Charles being there.

But the suspicions that Thomas had voiced, however mistaken, meant that she'd have to be extra careful how she behaved when next she saw Charles since Thomas would be watching them.

Well, let him watch, she thought, as she walked past the door that opened into the small living-room, crossed to the other side of the hall and went into the kitchen. There'd be nothing for him to see as there was nothing *to* see.

14

THE FOLLOWING FRIDAY

Friday morning arrived for Joseph after what had been a long sleepless night.

Throughout the night, a violent wind had whipped across the Heath, bending the trees in its path as it hurtled towards the empty roads of Primrose Hill. Jagged streaks of lightning sliced the black sky at irregular intervals, but no rain fell.

At last, at dawn, a vivid flash of lightning tore the sky apart, followed by a reverberant boom of thunder, and the heavens opened. Translucent sheets of rain fell heavily to the ground, and slammed with force on to glistening roofs, racing down solid brick walls and slithering thence across drenched pavements into the gutters, to be absorbed in the rivers of dark grey water speeding down the hill.

Lying awake, Joseph heard the rattle of his shutters as they battled furiously against the onslaught of the wind, and the stuttering pings of the driving rain that lashed his window panes. If it continued like this for much longer, he'd have to cancel the visit to the new development in the north of London, he thought with deep regret.

And he'd been so looking forward to showing it off.

But then, as suddenly as it had begun, the wind dropped, the shutters stilled, silence fell, and he drifted into sleep.

When he opened his eyes, his bedroom shutters had already been opened, and he was staring up at a clear blue sky. The visit could go ahead.

* * *

'What are you not telling me, Joseph?' Maud asked, sitting in one of the armchairs that flanked the open fire. 'You were distracted throughout dinner, and you hardly said a word. While on many occasions I'd be thankful for a degree of silence, this isn't one of them. I'm interested in how it went today. For a start, did Thomas go with you? You thought he might pull out at the last moment. It would have been most annoying to have gone out of your way to pick him up for nothing.'

'Both Thomas and Alice were there,' he said, settling more comfortably in the armchair on the other side of the fireplace. 'The person who didn't go was Lily,' he added, pushing his tobacco into the bowl of his pipe. 'Robert said something about her staying at home with James. It appears that James had a rotten cold. I did point out that they had a nanny, but he took Lily's side, of course. A sick child wants its mother, he said. But I could tell he was embarrassed by her absence. She's clearly no interest in the company that keeps her in a great degree of comfort.'

'But Lily *does* tend to be ridiculous about James – we all know that. She talks incessantly about the child.'

'That's because she's nothing else to talk about,' he retorted. 'She lacks any interest in anything.'

'I must agree with you there.' She picked up her glass. 'But your silence isn't about Lily, is it? We already know what she's like. I sense that you're brooding about something else that happened today.'

Joseph paused, about to put his pipe in his mouth. 'Amazing, Maud! You're almost witch-like in your sensory powers, my dear. So much so that, fearful you might cast a spell on me, I'm choosing to overlook your wish that I fall silent with greater frequency.' They smiled at each other. He put his pipe in his mouth, drew deeply on it, withdrew it again, and studied its bowl. 'But you're right, Maud – I *have* had something on my mind since I got back, and you're right again that it's nothing to do with that woman. But happen is the wrong word. It's just that something a little strange was said, and I haven't been able to stop thinking about it.'

'Strange in what way?'

Joseph laid his pipe across the ashtray, took a sip from the glass next to him, and changed his position.

'Perhaps strange is the wrong word, too.'

Maud sighed theatrically. 'Why don't you start at the beginning, Joseph?'

'All right, I will. But I'm afraid it means you'll have to wait even longer for the silence you desire.'

'My curiosity is such that I'm prepared to forgive you for that.'

Joseph cleared his throat. 'The day began well – I explained the changes in company policy, told them we'd continue to be the landlords of the houses we're building for renting, but that our emphasis would now be on building affordable houses for sale, and that we're building the houses in pairs, rather than in terraces.'

'I see.'

'They then went and had a look at a few of the houses. I'd pointed out that the internal layout had changed. With people's domestic situations being different these days, there's no longer a call for servants' quarters. The houses have three upstairs bedrooms and an internal bathroom and water closet. And a plumbed-in kitchen, too. I stressed that we'd rigidly followed the new regulations about drainage and sewage, and that there was separate clean running water for drinking.'

'So far so good, and nothing strange.'

'No, but something that was surprising was the attention that Alice paid to everything. In fact, she was quite flattering about my ability to know what people want. Of course, I credited everyone else in the team for the part they played.'

'But of course,' Maud murmured, suppressing a smile.

'The other thing I told them was that we're reducing our costs by hiring equipment when we need it instead of buying it, and we're no longer retaining lawyers. Despite business being excellent, we're cutting down on our staff. Basically, building houses for sale costs more than building houses to rent, but until the government repeals the fixed-rent act, it's uneconomic to build houses to rent. The cost of labour and supplies is spiralling, and rents are stuck at too low a level.'

'It sounds as if they had an interesting morning,' Maud said with a smile. 'Such a shame that I had to be in town all day. But still nothing strange, darling.'

'Aha, but I'm coming to that. Actually, there were two strange things,' he said, and he took another sip of his cognac. 'Firstly, Charles offered to run Alice and Thomas back home after we'd had lunch, but Thomas wouldn't have it. He insisted – quite rudely, in fact – that *I* take them home, even though it meant I'd have to go out again after lunch. I don't mind telling you, I was pretty fed up.'

'But Thomas seems to be permanently angry with everyone. I'm sure he was just being awkward for the sake of it.'

'I might have agreed with you if it hadn't been for what happened a short time afterwards. I suggested that Alice learn to drive, and said we could find a company vehicle for her. With Thomas's limited mobility, I thought it would be useful for them to have a car.'

'That's an excellent idea, darling. How considerate of you.'

'Well, Thomas obviously didn't think so! Charles immediately offered to help Alice learn to drive, but Thomas snapped at him that they didn't need his help, and that Alice didn't want to drive, anyway. The poor woman was scarlet with embarrassment, and, in fact, looked extremely disappointed at not being able to learn to drive. It would have made things so much easier for her.'

'And you don't think it was just Thomas being awkward again?'

He shook his head. 'Thinking about it, no, I don't. And what's more, I think Robert picked up on it, too. I saw the way he looked at Thomas, and then at Charles.'

'How do you account for Thomas's behaviour, then?'

He stared at her, frowning. 'I'm not sure, Maud. I just know that on the few occasions we've all been together, Charles has always been very friendly towards Alice. I assumed that like us, he's sorry for her, with Thomas being in a bad temper most of the time. But when you think about it, Thomas must feel very insecure beneath that permanent black mood of his, and he could well see Charles's kindness to Alice as an implied criticism of the way he treats Alice at times. Anyone with disabilities like his is bound to be extremely sensitive about things like that.' He drummed with his fingers on the arm of his chair. 'I'd like to think that's all it is.'

She thought for a moment. 'Charles *does* go out of his way to be nice to Alice, in a way that he doesn't with Lily. But of course, the position of the two women is very different. Robert is always considerate towards Lily, but as you say, Thomas frequently belittles Alice. Lily doesn't need Charles's kindness in the way that Alice does. I expect that Charles has picked up on Alice's need.'

Joseph nodded. 'I think that's probably right, my dear. Anyway,' he said, standing up, 'now that I've told you what I was thinking, I suggest we go to bed.'

Maud picked up her book, rose to her feet and headed across the room to the door.

Joseph trailed behind her, anxiety written across his face.

15

JACK STRAW'S CASTLE, HAMPSTEAD

April 1920

Sitting in the garden of the yellow brick three-storey building, Alice's gaze rose to the pale yellow chimney on the castellated roof. Then she looked back at the garden, at the small trees and bracken that bordered the verdant lawn, and at the flowers that wound up and around the wooden trellis that separated the tables set out for afternoon tea from the rich green lawn.

'This is lovely, Sarah,' she said happily.

Sarah smiled at her. 'I'm glad you think so. I've always thought this a rather attractive coaching inn.' She picked up the teapot and poured tea through a strainer into each of their cups.

'It's named after the rebel leader Jack Straw, who's said to have led the Peasants' Revolt with Wat Tyler,' Sarah told her. 'It all happened in the fourteenth century. Some people say that Jack Straw was actually Wat Tyler himself, but I wouldn't know about that. All I know is that he's supposed to have taken refuge here, but was caught and executed.'

'Oh, dear. Not the happiest of endings for him, then,' Alice remarked.

'Indeed, not. And Charles Dickens is meant to have eaten here. In Dickens's time, it would have been very busy as a coaching inn, but with all the cars on the roads nowadays, there's not much call for that any more.' She handed Alice her cup of tea, and moved the sugar bowl closer to her. 'I hear that Joseph offered to add you to the number of drivers on the road, but Thomas said no,' she said, sitting back and sipping her tea.

Alice went pink. 'Yes, he did, but I don't really know why. It would have been so useful if I was able to drive Thomas around. Not that everyone hasn't been really kind,' she added quickly. 'I know I can always ask for help if we need it, but it's nicer not to have to ask. There are lots of places we might've visited if I could have driven. It would have made Thomas's days more interesting.'

'Well, hopefully he'll change his mind,' Sarah said warmly. She indicated the tiered cake-stand. 'Do help yourself, won't you?'

'Thank you.' Alice took two small praline profiteroles.

'I've been meaning to invite you to the house for afternoon tea for quite some time,' Sarah went on, 'but with the weather as lovely as it is at the moment, I thought we ought to take advantage of the sun and come up here. You obviously know the area around Robert's house, but as Thomas can't walk very far, I thought you might not be familiar with this bit of Hampstead. It's the highest point in London.'

'Yes, you're right. This is the first time I've walked across the Heath, and the first time I've seen Whitestone Pond.'

'It was originally called Horse Pond – obviously because it was a drinking point for horses. There's a large white stone nearby, which is probably why the name changed over the years.'

'It's certainly beautiful up here. But I don't really know the area around Robert's house, either,' Alice said. 'Thomas turns down more of Robert's invitations than he accepts. I'm sure that's lovely, too, though.'

'Thomas really is a naughty man. We'll have to see what we can do about that.'

'If he'd let me learn to drive, I'd be able to bring him up here.'

'Are you likely to be able to persuade him, do you think?'

Alice shook her head. 'I doubt it. He's very down at the moment. Instinctively, he says no to everything I suggest, so I've stopped suggesting anything.'

'You'll have to take a leaf out of my book – keep on at him. I keep on at Charles about what he should be doing. I truly despair of him, Alice. Whenever there's an opportunity for promotion, will he apply? No. He's happy to carry on doing what he's been doing since time began, even though it's long stopped being a challenge. He should've gone for promotion years ago, but he doesn't have one ounce of ambition. It's so frustrating.' She gave Alice a guilty smile. 'I'm afraid, I must sound like a nagging shrew to you.'

'No, you don't.'

Sarah laughed. 'That's kind of you, but I'm sure I do. Sadly, my words are like water off a duck's back, and he takes no notice. The trouble with Charles is, he's no desire to further himself. When we first met, he wasn't so lacking in ambition. Or if he was, I didn't notice it. It's not that we need the money, you understand – it's just that I wish he were more dynamic, and I can't stop myself telling him that.'

'There are worse things than a lack of ambition. He could be cheating on you, for example.'

Sarah laughed. 'Not Charles. He's much too lazy to make the

effort. But if he were, I hope I'd never find out. I don't think I could deal with knowing.'

'Charles seems a very kind man, and kindness is far more important than ambition.'

'You're right, of course, Alice,' Sarah went on. 'And since I don't seem to be getting anywhere, I probably should stop. But to come back to you, you're far too young to be confined to the house month after month with a miserable husband. We must try to shake Thomas out of himself. And I've an idea. You've not really met my niece, Nellie, have you?'

Alice shook her head. 'I've maybe seen her a few times, but that's all. I've never had a conversation with her.'

'She's Joseph's youngest child. The oldest child, Dorothy, lives in Germany, but we don't talk about her. She married a German, I'm ashamed to say. Then there's Robert, and then Nellie. Nellie was still at school when you and Thomas married, but she's seventeen now, and very lively. Despite being a few years younger than you, I think you two would get on.'

'From the little I've seen of her, she seems very pleasant.'

'She is. You'll have a chance to find out for yourself when we have lunch at Robert's in a couple of weeks. I'll see that you sit together.'

Alice pulled a face. 'We aren't going. Thomas won't hear of it. He said he couldn't imagine anything worse than being in a room with Joseph and Charles. To be honest, I was surprised that he was so against the idea as he seems to like Lily. I've never heard him say anything against her, and at the will-reading, he went out of his way to be pleasant to her when… when she looked a bit lost,' she finished quickly.

Sarah gave her a wry smile. 'When we were all being fairly horrible to her, was what you were going to say, I believe. And you'd have been right. But we were all somewhat taken aback by the will. So you won't be seeing Nellie at Robert's, then, but you'll see her in June on her birthday. We're all going to Chorton House for the weekend. Maud thinks Joseph's making far too much of what's only an eighteenth, and can't imagine what he'll do for her twenty-first. But I can understand him wanting to give us all a chance to dress up, now that the gloomy war years are over.'

Alice bit her lip. 'I'm not sure that we'll be going to that, either. Joseph did mention it, and Thomas went very quiet.'

'Maybe he did, but you'll both be there for Nellie's birthday, that's for sure. It's one thing to turn down lunch at Robert's, but quite another to upset Nellie. And she'd be very upset if we weren't all there for her birthday unless there was an excellent reason why not. Joseph would be extremely angry at anyone who caused Nellie distress. Thomas will know that.'

'I do hope you're right.'

'Trust me, I am. But I warn you,' she added with a laugh, 'Nellie will drive you crazy. She's madly in love with a trainee solicitor called Walter Shawcross, who doesn't even qualify for another year. Charles introduced them – he thinks very highly of Walter. He says he'll go far. Whether or not he will, Nellie adores him, and she's keen to announce their engagement on her birthday. But I think she'll be unlucky. Joseph doesn't want her to marry Walter.'

'Do you think he'll change his mind?'

'I hope so. I had tea with Nellie a week or so ago, and I've given her some advice about how Walter might be able to win Joseph round. It's unlikely to happen by June, though.'

'I must admit, I find Joseph a little frightening, even though he's always very pleasant to me,' Alice said with an apologetic laugh.

'I suppose that's inevitable – he comes with all the trappings of success and speaks with the authority of a person who's used to being obeyed. But I feel sorry for him.'

Alice stared at her in surprise. 'Sorry for Joseph?'

'Yes, I do. He's a man with a strong sense of family. He gets on with Charles, but his youngest brother is invariably rude to him, and they were never close, anyway, not even before he went off to fight. Of his three children, the oldest, Dorothy, has been cut off and is unlikely ever to come back to England. It means that he'll never see her again, or see her children. We know she's got at least one child, or soon will have. Joseph wrote to her, telling her that her grandfather had died, and she wrote back saying that she was expecting her first child.'

'If she's in Germany, he must be quite worried about her safety. Thomas is sure there'll be another war.'

'And he could well be right. You should hear Charles on the subject. So that's Dorothy. Robert is married to a woman that Joseph can't stand. And Nellie is hoping to marry Walter, who wouldn't be his choice, either. Poor Joseph. He's learned the hard way that while he can control a business, he can't control his children's affairs of the heart.'

Alice was silent for a moment, her face anxious.

'What is it,' Sarah asked.

Her shoulders slumped. 'You know, it occurred to me the other day that if it wasn't for the fact that Thomas needs the sort of care I've been trained to give, Joseph would think I'm as unsuitable to be a Linford as Lily. He would, wouldn't he? You can be honest.'

'Oh, I'm sure, he wouldn't,' Sarah said hastily.

'Yes, he would. After all, why wouldn't he? Thomas told me that he expects a certain sort of background for anyone who marries into the family, and that they should be able to make a financial contribution to the business, and you've more or less said so yourself. I fail on both counts.'

Sarah reached across the table and took Alice's hand. 'We're all very fond of you, Alice,' she said warmly, 'and not just because of what you do for Thomas. It's because we like you. I think we all sense that you've not had the same pampered childhood as us, and as our children, but you've a strength of character that we all admire. Unlike Lily, you're interested in things, and you can talk to us. We consider you a great addition to the family.'

Alice felt warmth rush to her face. 'I don't know what to say,' she said with an awkward laugh.

'But it's true.' Sarah released Alice's hand and gestured with her palms upended. 'Look at this afternoon. Despite not having met very often, we've talked easily about a number of things, some of them quite personal. I know we're going to be good friends.'

'Oh, I do hope so!' Alice exclaimed. 'Sometimes it's like I'm dreaming, you know. When I lived in Waterfoot, which is a small mill town some way north of Manchester, my friend May and I used to look at the pictures of ladies like you in magazines. I never thought I'd meet any, or if I did, that I'd be able to talk to them. And now, look at me! At times I have to pinch myself to make sure it's true.'

'You don't sound very northern. Just the occasional vowel. And the odd expression.'

'I used to listen to how educated people spoke whenever I had the chance, and I tried to talk like them. I didn't want to open my mouth and have people instantly think, aha, she was a factory worker.'

'Is that what you did before you took up nursing?'

Alice nodded. 'Yes, and I hated every minute. But I had no

choice. My dad lost his arm in an accident in the quarry where he worked, and without his wages, we couldn't manage. I left school at eleven and got a job in a slipper factory.'

Sarah stared at her china plate for a moment, and then looked across the table at Alice. Alice saw that Sarah's eyes were glistening.

'You make me realise how lucky I am, and also Charles and my children. It's been so easy for us. And it makes me appreciate all the more how strong you are. Only an amazing person could've achieved what you have. You should be very proud of yourself, Alice, and the family should feel honoured that you've joined us.'

Alice laughed with embarrassment. 'Thomas knows about my family, but the others don't, and I'd rather it stayed that way. I've tried to leave my past behind me, and if the others knew about it, in a way it would have followed me here, and I wouldn't want that.'

'I won't say anything, I promise.' Sarah paused. 'What about your parents? They must miss you.'

'I expect they do, but I try not to think about it. I've not been able to get up there to see them, what with the war and getting married, and with Thomas needing me. I do write, though. But I'm afraid it's ages since I wrote to my friend, May. She married a farmer.'

'It must be hard to keep in touch when one person moves away, and the other doesn't. But you've made new friends now, so I hope that helps a little.'

'It does. I'd love to be able to see my parents more easily, and also May, but I'd never live up there again for anything. I love it here.'

Sarah smiled broadly. 'I'm glad you feel so settled down here.

Now, let me pour you another cup of tea, and perhaps we should each have one of those delicious-looking white chocolate and hazelnut truffles.'

16

CHORTON HOUSE, OXFORDSHIRE

Late June 1920

Early on the Sunday afternoon, Alice stood on the drive next to Thomas, who was in the wheelchair that was kept in Chorton House, while they waited for Maud to come out.

She'd enjoyed every minute of Nellie's eighteenth birthday celebration, and was really sorry that it was ending prematurely for her and Thomas, and because of Thomas's insistence that they return to London immediately after lunch, for Maud, too. She could hear Maud in the entrance hall behind them, telling Joseph that it wouldn't be worth her returning to Chorton after dropping them in Kentish Town, so she'd remain in London.

If only Thomas had agreed to stay on for the rest of the Sunday and go back on the Monday morning as the rest of the family was doing, she thought wistfully. Maud would have stayed for the rest of Sunday, too, and they would all have enjoyed an afternoon picnic by the river. A picnic like that was something she'd never done, and it would have been a real treat.

But Thomas had refused to stay longer.

Trying to quash her disappointment, she stared down the length of the gravelled drive to the wrought-iron gates that were set in the dry-stone wall surrounding the house and gardens, and to the fields beyond. Because of the house's elevated position, she could see the fields of the neighbouring farm, which lay to the right of Chorton House and also those to the south, which lay across the country lane on the other side of the stone wall.

Beyond the fields, a medley of roofs – both thatched and tiled – marked out the nearby village. Behind them rolled the undulating hills of Oxfordshire, their lush green slopes intermittently broken by clusters of dark green trees, and splinters of honey-coloured stone where houses stood alone.

She couldn't imagine anything more pleasant than a Sunday afternoon spent wandering along beside the river, and then sitting with the family, eating the food that the housekeeper, Mrs Spencer, had packed into wicker baskets that morning. It was certain to be delicious. She had made a superb dinner for them all the previous evening.

With the help of two kitchen assistants who'd come in from the local village, Mrs Spencer had set out on the large mahogany dining table a buffet of watercress salad, platters of cold fillets of bass with horseradish sauce, salmon mousse with cucumber, braised veal, a leg of lamb, homemade bread still warm from the oven, rhubarb flummery and Bakewell pudding.

It had been absolutely wonderful. The whole evening had, and she hated having to leave almost a day before the others.

Silly her for thinking that it might be different this time, and that Thomas might actually want to spend more than a minimum amount of time with his family. Admittedly, at the time of agreeing to go to Chorton for Nellie's birthday, he had told Joseph that he would want to leave immediately after lunch on the Sunday.

However, on the Saturday evening, when he'd gone downstairs to join everyone for a cocktail, he'd been in a much better mood than she'd seen him in for a long time, and she'd felt a sudden surge of hope that when it came to it, he might say they could stay on until Monday.

And he'd had every reason to be in a good mood – he'd looked tremendous on the Saturday evening.

She'd overridden his complaints that everyone was making too much fuss about the birthday, and had all but forced him to wear his smart classic black dinner jacket with black silk satin lapels. And he'd looked so handsome!

If any of them had ever wondered why she'd married him, she'd thought, as she'd moved his wheelchair to the foot of the staircase, they'd only have to take one look at him in his evening dress to have their answer.

She'd waited for him at the foot of the wide staircase, knowing that he'd prefer to walk down by himself, and she'd watched in delight as he managed to do so by resting his injured hand on the mahogany banister, and holding his cane in his good hand. When he'd reached the final step, he'd been visibly tired and had allowed her to wheel him into the main reception room, where he'd transferred to a mahogany high-back chair by the wall.

To her surprise, he'd caught her arm as she'd started to put the wheelchair back next to the wall, and had held her away from him, as if to see her better.

His eyes had slowly travelled down her white chiffon dress with its tight beaded bodice and slightly full skirt that fell to the floor. When they returned to her face, they were filled with appreciation, and with the promise of a closeness that night that had been increasingly absent in recent months.

She'd felt herself tremble in sudden anticipation.

She'd started to lean towards him, very much wanting to kiss him, regardless of what the family might think, then out of the corner of her eye, she saw Maud approaching, looking stunning in a green velvet dress that shimmered the length of her body, and which was dramatically set off by an emerald necklace and a single emerald in each ear, and she'd swiftly straightened up.

'You both look wonderful,' Maud said when she reached them.

Basking in the warmth of her approval, Alice thanked her, and sat down on the chair next to Thomas as Maud moved away to greet Nellie, who was wearing a white-beaded flapper dress with a long fringe, elbow-length white silk gloves, a long coil of pearls around her neck and a narrow white-beaded band around her head.

'It's a pleasure to see you in something more suitable for your age, darling, and not in something your Aunt Sarah would wear,' they heard Maud tell Nellie.

Bearing in mind what Sarah had told her when they'd had tea together a few weeks earlier, she wondered whether she should go and speak to Nellie. But the decision was taken out of her hands as Nellie went straight across to one of the windows that looked out over the drive, and stared out intently. A few moments later, she heard a car, and Nellie ran into the hall, where she could be heard her instructing the person who'd just arrived – presumably Walter, she assumed – to get changed as quickly as possible and come back down.

Nellie had then returned to the reception room, her eyes still fixed on the door, and Alice decided that getting to know her better could wait till later.

'You can't imagine what it was like, spending the weekends and holidays here,' Thomas said suddenly, his tone reminiscent.

Alice glanced at him in surprise, and with a rush of pleasure at hearing him talk about his life before the war, something he rarely did these days.

'It must've been,' she said, smiling at him with affection, hoping he'd continue.

He sat back in his chair. 'It was paradise. There was always something to keep us busy, inside the house and out. And it wasn't just Joseph, Charles and me. David often came, too. We'd spend the whole of the summer outside in the thickets, having one exciting adventure after another. And in winter, there were fires in every room and we'd play games such as hide-and-seek. And we were always in and out of the kitchen. Even today, I can't eat a cake without remembering how we used to beg Cook to let us have the bowl once she'd poured the cake mixture into the tin and put it in the oven.'

'How lucky to grow up in such a place, and to know that it belongs to your family. That's right, isn't it?'

'It is, indeed. Father married Bertha Chorton, who was an only child, and her father, who was a builder, too, gave them this house as a wedding present. It was relatively small then, with only a dining-room, drawing-room, four bedrooms and very basic servants' quarters. All he requested was that Father kept the name of Chorton alive by calling it Chorton House.'

'They obviously added a few more rooms.'

'They did a little more than that! Father and Grandfather built a two-storey wing on either side of the central staircase, using the same original stone. In one wing, they had a dining-room and three more reception rooms, and in the other, a large kitchen, scullery and pantry, a boiler room, a housekeeper's room and servants' quarters. And upstairs, there are now eight bedrooms, and two bathrooms with an integral water closet. It took ten years to complete all the work.'

'But what a wonderful home to have at the end of it.'

'Yes, but unfortunately for them, they could only come at weekends and holidays. They had to be in London because of Father's work. They started out in our house in Kentish Town, and then moved to Hampstead not long before I was born, into what's now Robert and Lily's house.'

'D'you like living in London, or would you rather live out here?'

'Before the war, it was the dream of every young man like me, who had a job and money in his pocket, to live in London. I worked for the company and boring though it was, they paid me well. There's less to do here, less to spend your money on, so I'd have chosen London over Chorton any day. But then I went to war.' He stopped abruptly.

'And?'

He shrugged. 'And having the wherewithal to enjoy yourself doesn't mean a thing if you aren't a hundred per cent whole. Now it doesn't matter where I live. But being in London is probably better for me, certainly if I want to work, and I do.' There was a sound by the door, and he turned towards it. 'Well, well. Here come Robert and Lily. And they look pretty good, I must say. That Lily's an attractive woman.'

Alice followed his gaze to the entrance to the reception room.

Robert was wearing a single-breasted black dinner jacket over a starched white shirt, and straight-legged trousers, and Lily carved a slender figure in a mid-calf scarlet silk dress with a dropped waist. Ignoring the fashion for cropped styles, she'd kept her blonde hair long, and had coiled it on top of her head, and threaded it with sparkling beads that matched her dress. Her long scarlet silk gloves were ringed with glittering bands of the same colour beads.

Alice had been about to remark on the loveliness of Lily's dress, when she heard a commotion on the far side of the room.

Turning, she saw that Sarah, in an ankle-length dress made up of layers of filmy black lace over cream taffeta, with clusters of heavy jet hand-sewn beads hanging from the dress, was trying to separate Louisa and Christopher, who'd clearly been arguing, without getting so close that she damaged her dress.

Louisa, in a miniature version of her mother's dress, but with pink lace over cream taffeta and without the beads, obviously had no such scruples about her outfit as she was lashing out, trying to get hold of Christopher's hair. Sarah managed to pull her away, and Christopher walked off, brushing down his dark blue velveteen jacket as he went, and looking very pleased with himself in his new long trousers.

Thomas shook his head. 'If you will dress children of ten and six in clothes that are more suitable for adults, you must expect them to behave like adults,' he murmured. 'And from my experience, that means badly.'

Alice glanced quickly at Thomas, but he still seemed to be in good spirits. She squeezed his arm and edged herself closer to him.

His good spirits had lasted throughout the buffet, at the end of which Joseph made a short speech in praise of Nellie, and they all toasted her. And they continued during the lively discussion about what games to play. But at some point before the end of the evening, something within him had changed.

She knew that he didn't like such games, so she wasn't surprised that when charades was chosen to be the first game, and Nellie announced that husbands and wives must split up into different teams, saying that she'd head one and Robert the other, Thomas had sat firm in his seat at the side of the room, refusing to join in.

He seemed happy enough for her to play, though, and she

was given a place in Nellie's team, along with Charles, Joseph and Louisa.

Lily said she didn't want to play, either, and she went and sat next to Thomas.

The others settled into the game.

Alice had heard of charades, but had never played it before. Helped by her team-mates, especially Charles, she soon picked up the rules and joined in wholeheartedly. Their team won the first game, and shrieking with laughter, they'd loudly congratulated themselves, and instantly started to play again.

'Thomas seems to be enjoying his conversation with Lily,' she told Charles at one point in the game. 'She's done the almost impossible and got Thomas laughing. Now that I know he's having a good time, I can relax.'

Charles glanced across at Lily. 'I see what you mean,' he said. 'In fact, both Thomas and Lily seem more at ease than is usual when they're with the family.'

During the next break between games, Alice noticed Lily get up and go towards the door.

She heard Sarah call 'Lily' as she hurried after her, followed by Louisa and Christopher, both of whom looked sulky.

She guessed Sarah had asked Lily to see the two children to their room, as she watched the two of them trail disconsolately after Lily as she left the room. But she was instantly caught up in the whirl of another game of charades and another after that, and then the paper games, which became wilder and wilder as the evening went on, and she forgot about everything else.

It was some time later that Sarah gently pointed out that Thomas might need some attention. He'd been watching her for a while, she told Alice, and she couldn't help noticing that he was white with fatigue. He might be ready to go upstairs, but didn't want to spoil Alice's obvious enjoyment of the evening by asking for the help he needed.

Alice put her hand to her mouth in consternation. 'I feel awful,' she said, 'getting so carried away that I forgot how tired he must be by now. I'll go to him at once.'

Absenting herself from the game, she promptly went across to Thomas. With a sinking feeling, she saw that he was nursing a whisky, and that every trace of a smile had gone.

Her instinct told her in that moment that whatever the reason, there was no longer any hope of Thomas wanting to extend the stay until Monday. They'd be leaving after lunch on Sunday.

* * *

'I'm sorry to have kept you,' Maud said as she came out on to the drive, followed by the rest of the Linfords. 'I was just thanking Mrs Spencer for serving lunch on the terrace. To enjoy such a delicious meal, surrounded by a sea of deep red geraniums, and with the scent of jasmine in the air – it was quite heavenly. And the others wanted to come out and say goodbye to you, too. I'll let them do so while I get the car.'

'After you,' Thomas told Alice when they'd finished their goodbyes, by which time Maud had driven Joseph's car to the front of the house, and was holding the door open, waiting for them to get in.

Those were the first words he'd spoken to Alice since the end of the previous evening, and they were to be the last words until they were back in Kentish Town.

During the whole of the drive back to London, Alice was in a state of bewilderment about what could have happened, and filled with great trepidation as to what he might say when they were once again alone.

17

KENTISH TOWN

Later that day

Having asked Mrs Carmichael to bring in their afternoon tea as soon as she was able, Alice went into the living-room to join Thomas, her heart beating fast. He still hadn't said more than two words to her since the night before.

He was seated in his armchair next to the fireplace. A copy of *The Daily Herald* from Friday lay unopened on the small table at the side of his chair. Beside it stood a lamp with a fringed parchment shade, but although the last light of day was fading fast, he hadn't yet switched it on.

Maud must have been very curious as to why he'd been so unusually silent throughout the journey back to London that afternoon, she thought, as she went to her chair on the opposite side of the fireplace and sat down. She and Maud had kept some sort of conversation going, but nevertheless, the atmosphere in the car had been oppressive. Maud must have been so relieved when they finally reached Kentish Town and she was rid of them.

She smoothed the skirt of her dress over her knees, switched on her lamp and picked up her sewing from the table next to her chair.

She cleared her throat. 'You haven't said a word since last night, Thomas. One minute you were fine, and the next you were in a black mood, with a face like thunder. Why? What happened to make you change like that? Were you in pain? Or was it something I did? If it was, I don't know what it could have been.'

He raised his eyebrows. 'I find that hard to believe.'

She frowned in puzzlement. 'But all I did was join in with charades and then with some other games. You said you didn't want to play, but you told me I should. In fact, you insisted I should.'

'Playing charades is one thing, dear Alice, but you and Charles were obviously playing a different game all by yourselves – a game for two only,' he said, his tone ice-cold. 'You were ogling each other all evening. I'm not blind. I'm sure the others saw you as clearly as I did. You made a fool of me last night.'

She felt blood rush to her cheeks, and she pulled her dress further over her knees. 'That's ridiculous, Thomas, and you know it.' She heard the tremor in her voice. 'And anyway,' she continued more firmly, 'I could say the same to you.'

'What on earth are you talking about? I can assure you I wasn't ogling Charles.'

'But you were ogling Lily,' she retorted. 'I'm not blind either, Thomas. You and she were as thick as thieves while I was playing charades. When you first saw her tonight, you said how attractive she looked, and the way you behaved with her throughout the evening was more than just being polite. You were openly flirting with her, so don't deny it.'

He threw back his head and laughed. 'The idea's most amusing. But the post-war Thomas doesn't flirt any more. Too scary for the ladies.'

'You flirted with the nurses in the hospital. And I know what I saw last night.'

'I was trying to help Lily, Alice. That's all. She was completely lost in a room full of people who seem to go out of their way to make her feel uncomfortable. I felt sorry for her. And I like her. But that's all it is. In case it's escaped your notice, she adores her husband. And what's more, I like Robert enormously so I'd never attempt to do the dirty on him. Despite having Joseph for a father, Robert's turned out all right.'

'And if Charles *was* being friendly, like you say he was, it will've been because he was attempting to do for me what you say you were trying to do for Lily. I've never played charades before, and I don't have much of an education. For me, it was pretty frightening to play with people who're so much cleverer and who know so much more. That's all it will have been.'

He raised his eyebrows. 'Is that so? I've lost my leg, Alice, not my eyesight. Nor the ability to sense what's going on around me. You'd do well not to forget that. Now, am I going to get my tea or not?'

She put down her sewing and stood up. 'It's not five minutes since I asked Mrs Carmichael for tea, but I'll go and see if it's nearly ready.' She hesitated. 'I'm always happy to help you with whatever you need, Thomas, and that's because I love you. But I'm your wife – not your servant, not someone you can order around, like you're doing now. At times, though, you seem to confuse the two. It can be very hurtful.'

'And you think it doesn't hurt me to see my wife and my brother making eyes at each other? You're *my* wife, not his, and I'd thank you to remember that.' He picked up the newspaper and unfolded it.

* * *

The clock struck ten.

Thomas glanced up from the paper. 'I think I'll go to bed,' he said coldly.

Her heart sank. He was still in a mood.

'That's a good idea. You look tired, Thomas,' she said, with an attempt at brightness. 'And I feel quite tired, too, which is not surprising after the weekend we've had. Mrs Carmichael has already gone to bed, and it's sensible that we do the same.'

She stood up and went to help Thomas get up, but he shrugged her off, and leaning on his crutch, made for the door and went out into the hall. She followed him out of the room.

A loud rap sounded on the front door.

Both stopped sharply.

She glanced at Thomas in alarm. 'It's late for visits. Who can that be?'

'There's only one way to find out,' he said. 'But you'll have to open the door to do so.'

With a degree of nervousness, she went to the front door and opened it slightly.

'Joseph!' she exclaimed, and pulled it wider open.

'Have you seen Lily?' he asked.

She glanced at Thomas and then back at Joseph. 'No, we haven't – not since this morning.'

'You'd better come in,' Thomas called to Joseph, 'and tell us what this is about.'

Thomas led them into the living-room, and they took the nearest chairs.

'Lily went missing this afternoon,' Joseph began. 'When they got back from the picnic, no one could find her after a thorough search. Then we noticed that Robert's car had gone. Everyone's now out looking for her. They suggested I should bring Sarah and the children back, and then come over to you on the off chance that she'd come here. You've always got on very well with her, Thomas, probably better than anyone else in the family. Apart from Robert, obviously.'

Thomas shook his head. 'No, she hasn't.'

'You were talking to her a lot last night. Did she say anything that would give you an idea of where she might've gone?'

'Not really, no. I wish I could help, but we just talked a bit, laughed at one or two things. She went upstairs to check on James and didn't come back down again.'

'I just can't think where else she could be,' Joseph said.

'I wouldn't get too worried. She probably just wants a break from the lot of you. I would if I were her. When she's ready, she'll come back.'

'Well, I certainly hope you're right, Thomas. Anyway,' he said standing up. 'I've told you now, so I'll be off. If she comes here, you'll let me know, won't you, Alice?'

'Of course, I will.' She got up and walked with him to the front door. 'Thomas is very fond of Robert, you know,' she said as she opened the door. 'You mustn't hesitate to ask us for any help you need, and that means from both of us. Thomas will want to help, too.'

Joseph inclined his head to her, turned and made his way back to his car.

18

HAMPSTEAD

The end of July 1920

Nellie settled back on to the sofa in the reception room.

Walter put his arm around her shoulders, pulled her close to him and kissed her lightly on the lips. They smiled at each other, and then Nellie rested her head against his shoulder, and they sat there, listening to the buzz of voices coming from the room next door.

'All seems well again in Hampstead,' Walter said after a while. 'I enjoyed our afternoon tea. In the absence of a family Sunday lunch, which wouldn't really be appropriate so soon after learning we're not going to be seeing Lily again, this was a good substitute. Your family's idea of a monthly lunch for you all is an admirable one.'

'Grandfather started the tradition, and Robert continued it. Robert asked Uncle Thomas to tea, too, you know,' Nellie said, 'but he refused, even though both Uncle Charles and Father offered to pick him and Alice up and take them home. It's typical of him. Not that he would have contributed anything to the day.'

Walter moved closer to Nellie. 'I wish we could take advantage of being in here on our own. There's something I'd very much like to do, but I'm daunted by the knowledge that your formidable family's in the next room.'

Nellie giggled. 'I can't imagine anything daunting you for long. Take all the advantage you want.'

'Alas, my dread of what might happen if I tried to have my wicked way with you while they're so close is insurmountable!'

'I can see that it might be,' Nellie said, snuggling up to him. 'I can't wait for us to be married. Dottie's so lucky – she's married and got her own home, so she can do what she wants with the man she loves.' She straightened up, and frowned. 'Oh, my goodness, I'd completely forgotten about Dorothy! I must bring her up to date with what's been happening. And I want to hear how her baby is. She must be about three months old by now. Her name's Elke. It's funny to think I might never see my niece.'

He looked down at her in surprise. 'I thought you didn't know where Dorothy lived.'

She pulled a face. 'That's not strictly true. Dorothy wrote to Father, and he left her letter on his desk. I copied down her address. I've a feeling he wanted me to see it. He keeps saying that Germany will never be able to pay the huge sum of money they're meant to pay by way of reparation to the Allies, and that as it's still got an air force, although it shouldn't have, and hasn't abolished conscription or handed over its weapons, he thinks we could be in for another war.'

'He could be right about that.'

'He's bound to worry that Dottie could be in danger if that happened, and he'd want her to know there was someone here she could contact if she wanted to. That someone wouldn't be him as he's told her she's no longer family.'

'You shouldn't make too much of what your father said.

Dorothy's his daughter, and I'm sure he still loves her. I've always thought your father's bark worse than his bite. I hope so, anyway, as before too long, I intend to ask for his consent to us marrying.'

'Oh, Walter.' Nellie sighed with pleasure, and reached up and kissed him on the cheek.

'I think your Aunt Sarah's plan might be working,' he said, hugging her tightly. 'I've taken her advice and kept a close eye on any possible changes in Property Law, and read up on key property cases, so these days when I see your father, I can talk to him about things of interest to him. He's no longer ignoring me in the way he used to. Perhaps ignoring is a bit strong, but you know what I mean.'

'Ignoring is fine. No need to water it down for me – I've known my father for eighteen years.'

'An unexpected outcome of this is that as my present solicitors don't specialise in Property Law, when I qualify I might actually move to a practice that does. I'm finding it all extremely interesting. Some of the cases are fascinating.'

'I think you're right about Aunt Sarah's idea working. I've noticed Father asking your advice on a number of occasions recently.' She gave a slight exclamation. 'That reminds me of something I was going to ask you a while ago, but forgot. Did you see the way Uncle Charles and Alice kept looking at each other on the Saturday evening of my birthday party?'

'You mean Uncle Thomas and Alice,' he corrected.

She shook her head. 'No, Uncle Charles and Alice. It was as if they'd forgotten everyone else was in the room, and it was like just the two of them were playing. I've a feeling that Uncle Thomas noticed that, too. He was watching them like a hawk all the time he was talking to Lily, and when Lily went upstairs, he sat and openly glared at them.'

'He glares at everyone, though, so it doesn't mean a thing.'

'Maybe. But I'm wondering if he thinks he's picked up on something, however unlikely it seems. But people have been known to think about doing what they shouldn't, haven't they?'

'Which brings us back to the thoughts I shouldn't be having,' he said, and he pulled her close to him, lowered his head and kissed her hard on the lips.

* * *

'Well, I think that went quite well,' Sarah said as Charles pulled away from the kerb and headed the car for Knightsbridge.

Charles nodded. 'Me, too. It's a shame that Thomas didn't want to join us today,' he added a few minutes later. 'Apparently, he was quite churlish in the way he turned down Robert's invitation. I'm sure Alice would have welcomed the chance to get out of Kentish Town for a while, but he never seems to consider her. He knows that Robert's cook always serves up an excellent afternoon tea, so he would have enjoyed that at least, even if he didn't relish the company.'

Sarah tossed her head. 'I've given up being surprised at anything Thomas does. He's a law unto himself.'

'Walter and Nellie seemed very close, didn't you think? I was glad to see it. He's a good lad, and it looks as if Joseph's beginning to realise that at last.'

'I hope he is. I'm very fond of Nellie and I want to see her happy. As you spotted when you met him, Walter's perfect for her, and it'd be such a shame if Joseph put any obstacles in his way. With luck, he's learned from his experience with Robert and Lily – his opposition pushed her into Robert's arms. We must remember that when Louisa and Christopher are older.'

Charles threw her a quick smile. 'It's not often we both agree. It's a pleasant feeling. We should try it more frequently.'

They both laughed.

'Since we'll be in the car for a while,' Sarah said, 'I might as well mention something that's been in the back of my mind for a while now. It's about the children.'

'Could we talk about the weather instead?'

'I'd really welcome a little support with the children in the morning.'

'Definitely switch to the weather,' he said.

'Seriously, Charles, they never eat a sensible breakfast these days, and it's important that they do. Do you realise that Christopher had two bites of toast this morning, and that's all? And I don't think Louisa ate anything. I really would like your help with this – I don't think that's asking too much.'

Charles groaned. His eyes on the road ahead, he drove the rest of the way to Knightsbridge in silence, while Sarah spelt out the type of support he could give.

19

KNIGHTSBRIDGE

September 1920

'Charles!' Sarah said sharply. 'Did you hear what I said?' She leaned across the breakfast table and pushed the newspaper away from him.

He gave an exaggerated sigh. 'How could I not have heard you when the whole of Knightsbridge must've done?' He shook the paper back into position and turned the page.

'You seem to have forgotten that a good two months ago, on the way back from Robert's, I asked for your help with making the children eat a decent breakfast. But have you helped? No. Though I don't know why I'm surprised – you so frequently ignore my wishes.' She took a slice of toast from the rack on the table and pulled the butter towards her. 'There's no reason for them not to eat properly in the morning. Rationing's ended and we can have eggs every day.'

Sighing again in irritation, he glanced at her over the top of the *Daily Express*. A stray lock of chestnut hair hung over her forehead, which was etched with furrows. Her lips were set in a thin line.

'But butter's still rationed,' he said teasingly, and he pulled the dish away from her.

She snatched it back. 'Don't worry,' she snapped. 'I won't take it all.'

'What's happened to your sense of humour, Sarah? This perpetual nagging – it's becoming a morning ritual. In a few more years, we'll be complaining that Christopher's eating us out of house and home. Let the children be.'

'That's you all over, Charles – anything for an easy life.' She spread a thick layer of butter on her toast, her movements brusque. 'Reading the *Daily Express* says it all,' she added, nodding towards his newspaper. 'Most people in your position would read *The Daily Telegraph* or *The Times*. On second thoughts, not *The Times*. I dislike the way they were all in favour of the war, and also their comment three months ago that Jewish people were the world's greatest danger. That was quite appalling. No, *The Daily Telegraph* should be the paper of choice for someone like you.'

'But it doesn't have a crossword, does it? Whoever came up with the idea of a crossword in a newspaper is a genius. By having the *Daily Express*, when I'm bored during the day, all I have to do is take out my paper and do the crossword.'

'Ah, but if you read *The Daily Telegraph*, you might see an advertisement for a job that would actually challenge you, and interest you, so there'd be no need to kill time with a crossword.'

Charles turned the page. 'For your information, Sarah, the kind of jobs that become vacant at my level seldom appear in a newspaper – not even in the saintly *Daily Telegraph*.'

'So, you've effectively admitted you're bored, but you're not prepared to do anything about it. You've no idea how exhausting it is, having to be ambitious on your behalf.'

'And you've no idea how exhausting it is, having to hear the same thing day in, day out.' He folded his paper and stood up. 'To have a bit of peace at breakfast seems a small thing to ask.' He looked at his watch. 'I'll have to go or I'll be late. Thank you for another pleasant start to the day, Sarah.'

Tucking his newspaper under his arm, he pushed his chair back and turned to leave the dining-room.

The sound of someone rushing headlong down the staircase filled the lower part of the house, and he paused in the doorway as Louisa jumped down the last two stairs into the hall. She swung round, her hand on the newel, and then charged, head down, towards him. Too late, he started to step aside, and she crashed into him.

'Ouch!' he cried, rubbing his stomach with an exaggerated expression of agony. 'Where's the fire, Lou?'

Laughing, she pushed past him into the dining-room. 'I just want a slice of toast, Mummy,' she said, throwing herself on to a chair. 'I've got to be quick – I'm meeting my friends.'

'If you'd been here two minutes earlier, you'd have seen Mrs Morris putting freshly poached eggs and tomatoes in the warming tray. You're to help yourself to those first, and then you can have toast.'

Pulling a face, Louisa got up and went across to the sideboard, throwing a look of despair towards Charles as she did so.

He gave her a sympathetic wink, turned and went towards his library.

The strains of Sarah arguing with Louisa could be heard through the walls. First it was about her breakfast, and then about her appearance. He'd heard it all before. And so had Louisa – many times. But Sarah was wasting her time. Louisa was every bit as stubborn as her mother, and the more she was pushed, the further she went in the opposite direction. Unfortunately, Sarah couldn't see that, despite the evidence on numerous occasions.

He picked up his briefcase, tucked the newspaper inside, closed it and went back into the dining-room.

'Have a good day at school, Louisa,' he said. 'And you have an enjoyable day, too, Sarah,' he said as he bent down and kissed her on the cheek.

'I may not be home when you get back,' she said, buttering a second slice of toast. 'I'm taking Louisa to get some new shoes for school. I'm hoping it won't take too long to find what we want.'

'What *I* want, you mean. They're *my* shoes so *I* get to choose,' Louisa cut in.

Sarah sighed loudly.

Charles smiled at his daughter, waved his hand in her direction and went out into the hall.

* * *

Sitting on the wooden bench close to the junction with Kentish Town Road, his hat and his briefcase on the seat beside him, Charles stared down the road towards Thomas and Alice's house.

Then he leaned back against the seat, and closed his eyes.

It was getting on for noon, and he really ought to be at the bank by now. He didn't know what on earth had possessed him to break his journey that morning, and head for Kentish Town instead. Nor why he had spent what felt like an eternity since then, sitting on a bench doing nothing.

No, that wasn't quite true.

If he was honest with himself, he *was* doing something – he was watching for Alice.

He was desperate to catch a glimpse of her. With Thomas turning down all invitations to family occasions, he hadn't seen Alice since Nellie's party, which was way back in June. And quite simply, he'd thought about her every day of those last three months.

Even though he knew he shouldn't.

He was a married man. And Alice was his brother's wife.

It was entirely wrong for him to be longing to see his sister-in-law, towards whom he didn't feel in the least bit brotherly, just to bask for a moment or two in the warmth of her obvious admiration. But he recognised that, despite knowing that he shouldn't, he *did* want to see her, and he berated himself for it.

Not that he should take on all the blame.

It was Sarah's continual criticism, her constant putting him down that was making him feel the need of approval from someone else.

Sarah had always been somewhat dictatorial, even when he'd been courting her, but in those early days, he'd found her strength of mind quite appealing. And then, during their courtship, just as he was starting to find her manner a little too much, his family, seeing that Sarah's interest in Charles was genuine, began to express in the strongest terms possible their admiration that he'd attracted a woman with both beauty and wealth, and they'd started looking at him with a respect they'd never previously accorded him.

He'd liked the way it made him feel, and he'd mentally dismissed any concern about her slightly domineering manner, and certain that he loved her dearly, had gone ahead and proposed marriage.

At first, they'd been very happy together. Sarah was excellent company and he'd felt himself falling deeply in love with her. And when she put money into the company, his status with

Linford & Sons had been high. Their early years together had been good.

With the arrival of Louisa, and then Christopher four years later, the efficient management of the nanny and household staff during wartime conditions had fully occupied Sarah for several years. But with the war over and the children slightly older, there was less for her to do in the home. As a result, she'd joined a number of committees, which was fine. And then she'd turned her attention to him, and had made his career her focus, haranguing him daily about applying for promotion. And that was not so fine.

Not being a naturally ambitious man, the relentless pressure of her ambition on his behalf, was becoming intolerable.

'Why, Charles!'

Alice's voice broke into his thoughts. He opened his eyes and promptly stood up.

She was standing next to the bench, staring at him in surprise. And with unmistakable pleasure.

'Did you want to see Thomas? I'm sure he's home. I wonder why Mrs Carmichael didn't invite you in.'

'It could be because I didn't knock on the door,' he said lightly. He gave a slight cough. 'Actually, Alice, it's *you* I was hoping to see. In fact, I sat far enough away from the house to be sure that Thomas wouldn't see me.'

Colouring slightly, she positioned herself on the other side of his briefcase. Suddenly feeling acutely self-conscious, he sat down again.

'I mustn't be long,' she said, putting her bags on the ground. 'Thomas starts fretting if I'm out for too long and it's already been a while.' She hesitated. 'What did you want to talk to me about? Was it Thomas?'

Charles coughed again. 'I feel a bit silly, to be honest. The truth is, I've no real reason to be here – no message from the family, nothing like that. I suppose I just wanted to see you.' Feeling embarrassed at how that sounded, he gave an awkward laugh.

Alice went a deeper shade of red. 'I'm glad you did. Seeing you always makes me happy.'

'You should always be happy, Alice,' he said gravely. 'Not just when you see me. You deserve to be happy all of the time.'

Their eyes met, and both looked quickly away.

She cleared her throat. 'I'd ask you to come in and have a cup of tea,' she said, 'but Thomas...' She looked down at her lap, and then back up at him. 'Thomas would make you being here into something it wasn't. Things could be very uncomfortable. You know what he's like.'

He nodded. 'Don't worry, I know what you mean. It's just as well that I'm not thirsty.'

'I suppose it is,' she said with a half-smile. 'It's just that I think he believes there's something between us,' she added, her eyes fixed downwards again. 'In fact, I know he does. He makes sarcastic comments about it all the time. And on a few occasions, he's actually accused me outright. I've sworn there's nothing going on between us. He says he doesn't believe me, but I think he does deep down. What this is really about is that he's afraid I might wish there *was* something going on. I think that's what it is.'

A moment of silence weighted the air.

'*I* wish there was,' he said quietly.

She gave a slight gasp, and sat upright, her eyes opening wide.

'I admit it.' He shrugged. 'I know it would be wrong in every way, but unfortunately, feelings don't always obey the rules and mine are certainly wayward.' He gave her a wry smile. 'I probably shouldn't have told you that, but I doubt it's any great surprise, and as I feel better for saying it, I'm not going to apologise.'

She hastily gathered her bags together. 'I must go now. Thomas will be worrying.'

He picked up his hat and briefcase, and stood up.

'Don't worry, Alice,' he said, smiling down at her. 'I'm not going to embarrass you further by saying any more, not now and not in the future. I felt a sudden urge to see you today, and now that I've seen you, my day looks brighter. We'll leave it at that. Good day to you.'

He raised his hat to her, and started walking back towards Kentish Town Road and the underground station.

He was sure she was standing there, staring after him. But keeping a tight grip on his feelings, he never once looked back.

20

OCTOBER 1920

Charles put his pencil into his shirt pocket, folded up his newspaper and put it on the occasional table next to his chair.

'That's the crossword done, then,' he said, looking around the sitting-room. His gaze settled on the cluster of silver-framed family photographs that stood on the mahogany table in the corner of the room. 'You know, I never thought I'd say this, Sarah, but I'm actually looking forward to going to Robert's for lunch today.'

She stared at him in surprise. 'And *I* never thought I'd hear you use those words. I would imagine we're all pleased that the monthly lunches are being resumed. Don't you agree?'

He raised an eyebrow. 'When are you not right, Sarah, dear?'

Sarah laughed. 'Good gracious! You don't often say that.'

'Again, you're correct, my dear.' Charles stretched out his legs, and yawned. 'Amazingly, Thomas has agreed to join us today. Joseph's collecting him.'

'I'm glad. I'm looking forward to seeing Alice again. I found her very pleasant, and good company. I must invite her out to tea again. If I take her out, I won't feel obliged to invite Thomas, too, which I'd have to do if I asked her here.'

Charles nodded. 'She's certainly a good addition to the family. You only have to think back to how enthusiastically she joined in with the games on Nellie's birthday. She manages admirably whenever Thomas lets her participate.'

'That's very true. And if she's any failings that we haven't yet discovered, she'd be completely redeemed by what she does for Thomas.'

He smiled at her. 'Yes, I would say Thomas struck gold with her. I don't know how he'd manage without her. He's very lucky to have a loving wife to look after him, rather than a hired nurse. Alice isn't quite as lucky, though. I don't know how she tolerates his terrible moods.'

'He'll adjust eventually – he hasn't really got a choice. When he does, he'll lose the aggression.'

'I certainly hope you're right, for Alice's sake as well as ours.'

Sarah glanced at her watch and stood up. 'We should get ready now. I want to be in time to make sure that nothing's been forgotten.'

'It won't have been. Mrs Bailey knows what to do.'

'Nevertheless, I'd like to be early. And it wouldn't surprise me if Nellie wasn't early, too, for exactly the same reason. In fact, I rather hope she is. I've hardly seen her since her birthday, and I'd like to have a chat with her before everyone else arrives. I'll go and hurry the children along. I do hope they behave today. I know that Maud's critical of their behaviour at times, particularly Louisa's, and I'd hate them to give her more reason to find fault.'

* * *

'I enjoyed the lunch today, didn't you?' Alice asked, kneeling down in front of Thomas, who was sitting by the fireplace. She started to remove his prosthesis.

He put his hand on hers, and stilled her movement. 'Yes, I did,' he said. 'And there was a reason for that.'

'Indeed,' she said lightly. 'And may I ask what it was?'

He grinned at her. 'As I told you before Joseph got here this morning, I like the new you that's emerging from your shell. It's so much more interesting when you answer me back, instead of bowing your head in meek submission. Although, after this morning's performance, it might be more accurate to say snapping at me, rather than answering back. You stopped me in no uncertain terms when I was in full rant, criticising various family members in my own inimitable manner.'

'That's the trouble, it wasn't very inimitable. As I told you, we've now heard it all too often. The more you go on, the less effect it has. It just becomes boring.'

'There you go again,' he said approvingly. 'You're not standing there, taking whatever I throw at you in silence – you're speaking up for yourself. Don't go back into that shell, will you, Alice?' He stared down into her face. 'In fact, it's amazing what that new you is doing to me,' he added with a wry smile. 'And what memories of our little morning spat was doing to me throughout lunch today.'

She smiled up at him. 'It's certainly doing something very strange to you if when I'm kneeling in front of you, you think I'm actually standing!'

He gave her a slow smile, and she leaned forward, slid her arms around his waist and rested her head on his stomach.

'As I told you before,' she said, her voice muffled against his waistcoat, 'if I'd known the effect that answering back would have on you, I'd have started a lot sooner. I saw the old Thomas today, something I hadn't seen for a while, and I liked what I saw very much. And you'd be amazed what it does to me – what it's doing to me.' She inched even closer to him, and pressed her body between his thighs.

She felt his response, and she tightened her hold on him.

'I don't know how you can want to do this with me, Alice,' he said quietly. 'My body's such a mess.'

'I love you, Thomas. That's why.' Gently, she pulled his head down to hers, and kissed him.

* * *

Charles crossed to the mahogany cabinet and poured himself a whisky.

'I'll have a gin while you're over there,' Sarah said, coming into the room behind him and seating herself in one of the rosewood chairs upholstered in plush red velvet. 'I'd call today a great success, wouldn't you? I must admit, James is utterly adorable. I'm glad Annie brought him downstairs for us to see him. He's so close to walking, which at fifteen months is very good.' She took the crystal glass he offered her. 'Thank you, darling.'

Charles went and sat opposite her. 'Yes, he's a pleasant child.'

'And Thomas was a revelation, too, don't you think?' she went on. 'I've never seen him as close and attentive to Alice as he was today. And she was clearly enjoying it. There was definitely something between them that I haven't seen for a long time.'

'If you say so.' He finished his whisky, got up and poured another.

'No one could've missed it. I wasn't in the least surprised that as soon as a polite amount of time after lunch had passed, they said they were ready to leave. The only surprise was that Thomas allowed *us* to drop them home. He normally spurns our offers of help and will only go with Joseph, even though it means that Joseph frequently has to go out of his way, unlike us. It's such a shame that Thomas still won't let Alice learn to drive.'

'Thomas will have known that we'd be leaving fairly early – there's a limit to the amount of time we can inflict our children on others. And Joseph was heading into the garden with Walter. Since each had a glass of whisky, it was clear that they'd be out there for some time.'

'You're right about that.' Sarah's face broke out into a broad smile. 'There's no harm in me telling you now what Nellie told me in secret before lunch – Walter intended to ask for Joseph's consent today to him marrying Nellie. He'll probably have done so in the garden. Isn't that exciting!'

'If you say so.' He took another drink of his whisky.

'Nellie thought Joseph would be in such a good mood, the family lunches having resumed, that he'd agree to just about anything,' Sarah went on cheerfully. 'I don't think there's any doubt what Joseph's answer will be – he clearly likes Walter and respects his intelligence. You can count on it, there'll be a wedding next June, which I know is what Nellie wants.'

'I can't wait,' Charles said drily.

'What with Nellie and Walter settling down, and Thomas and Alice clearly much closer than they've been for a long time, it looks as if next year is going to be a really happy one.'

Charles downed the rest of his whisky, got up and poured himself a third glass.

21

PRIMROSE HILL

June 1921

Beneath a bright yellow sun and a cloudless blue sky, Walter and Nellie became husband and wife. There had been a collective sigh of admiration as Nellie had entered the small, very beautiful church in the heart of Hampstead, on Joseph's arm, looking absolutely radiant.

And a wonderful morning rolled into a lovely afternoon.

The marquee erected in the heart of Joseph's garden gleamed white in the strong light of the day. And at the edge of the lush green lawn that surrounded the marquee, a dense array of flowers exploded with brilliant colour.

Inside the marquee, the wedding guests sat at round tables covered with crisp white linen tablecloths, and set with crystal glasses and silver tableware. A posy of white roses formed the centrepiece of each table, their fragrance filling the air.

At the head table, an ecstatic Nellie looked resplendent in a slender white gown of beaded-lace upon silk, with a round neckline and full-length beaded-lace sleeves. A tiara had been slid into her sleek dark hair, which had been cropped in the modern style. The veil of filmy white lace that had been attached to the tiara had been removed before the reception. In each ear, she wore a small diamond stud, a present given the previous evening from Joseph and Maud. As she sat at the table, her arm was tucked into Walter's, and she leaned slightly against him.

Having removed his black silk tail coat, Walter looked relaxed in a white silk shirt and an *eau de Nil* tie, which matched the bridesmaid's dress. Over it, he wore a cream silk waistcoat brocaded with a deeper cream. His dark eyes, ever on Nellie's face, shone with love.

'They make a gorgeous couple, Maud,' Sarah remarked, glancing towards Nellie and Walter. 'Today's been quite wonderful. Having only Louisa, Christopher and James as her attendants worked very well. Simple, but effective, and very beautiful. The only dampener has been Thomas's attitude.' Both glanced along the top table to where Thomas sat, angled so that his back was to Alice. 'I'm so disappointed,' she went on. 'I was convinced that things were better between them – we all were – but now look at them! I don't know what's gone wrong, but Alice looks utterly miserable.'

Maud nodded. 'I know, and I wish I could help, but I can't see how I can. I saw Charles go across and said hello, and Thomas more or less shouted at him to leave them in peace. And Joseph said it had been a struggle to get Thomas to agree that you and Charles could collect them today. If Joseph hadn't been needed at home with Nellie, I don't think Thomas would've agreed.'

Sarah shook her head. 'I don't know what's the matter with him – Alice is really pretty, and she's got some spirit, as well as a very kind nature. He should be rejoicing that she loves him, not trying to drive her away and everyone else, too.'

'I agree; it really is a mystery.'

'But something that's no longer a mystery is your wedding present to them, Maud. Nellie told me that you and Joseph had given them a small house in Camden Town. What a wonderful gift. You'll miss her, won't you, when she's gone?'

'I certainly will, and so will Joseph. The house will seem so quiet. But it'll be a while before that happens. The company's going to do some work on their house, and until it's ready, Walter's moving in, and he and Nellie will live with us.'

'I suppose all this,' Sarah gestured around her, 'must make you think about Dorothy's marriage, with no one from the family present.'

'I could say no – she brought exile on herself by marrying a German. But the honest answer is yes. Do keep that between us, please. Joseph and I don't talk about Dorothy, but I'm sure he must think of her, too.'

'He's bound to.'

'Nellie writes to Dorothy, you know. I suspect Joseph knows that, too, though neither of us has spoken about it. With the unpleasant things we've been hearing about Germany today, I think we both want Dorothy to feel she could contact at least one member of the family. We worry about her safety in the future.'

'I hate to say it, Maud, but I think you're right to be concerned. You should hear what Charles says about a man called Hitler. He's in charge of a party that's growing in strength, and Charles is quite alarmed by some of the things that Hitler's put into his party's programme. They seem to be against anyone who doesn't have German blood, especially Jewish people. Thank goodness, he's not running the country.'

The band struck up.

Sarah and Maud stopped talking and turned simultaneously towards the dance floor.

Nellie rose to her feet. Walter held out his hand to her, and she took it.

'Nellie looks really lovely, Maud,' Sarah said, moving closer to her in order to be heard above the sound of the music.

'And so does Louisa,' Maud said. 'She looks quite grown-up in her dress.'

'She does, doesn't she? When she came downstairs this morning, I had a bit of a shock, if I'm honest. I always think of her as a young child, but of course she's eleven now. Charles came down just after her. I thought he looked remarkably dashing, too. If I'm allowed to say that about my husband,' she added, and laughed with embarrassment.

'You're allowed,' Maud said with a smile.

'It was so kind of Walter to ask Charles to be his best man. He was very proud to be given such an honour.'

Maud nodded. 'He deserved it – after all, he introduced Walter to Nellie when he invited him to Chorton. But I must say, both of your children behaved admirably this morning, Christopher as well as Louisa. Alice could see them better than I could as much to Alice's disappointment, Thomas had insisted they sit near the back of the church. Joseph was furious as he'd reserved seats for them near the front with the rest of the family.'

'I was much too close to the front to see Christopher come down the aisle alongside James,' Sarah said with regret.

'I'm not sure that alongside is the right word. According to Alice, Christopher held James's hand in an iron grip. There was no way he was going to let James run free, and James seemed to sense that as he didn't even try. Given that he isn't yet two, I thought he did very well. Apparently, he had an expression of intense concentration on his face all the time he was toddling down the aisle.'

'Christopher's a good boy,' Sarah said. 'He's so much easier than Louisa, who's something of a trial, to be honest. Whatever I say she should do, she does the opposite. She's always been like it. It's why we've found it so difficult to retain nannies. If she's like that now, heaven knows how we will cope when she gets older.'

'She'll be fine,' Maud said. 'She's no different from any number of young girls today. Nellie's had her headstrong moments, too. It's a relief that she's fallen in love with a quiet man who nevertheless looks as though he will be able to control her.'

'You make her sound like a horse.'

They laughed.

'To go back to Thomas and Alice,' Maud went on. 'They seemed to be getting on much better together over the past few months, and we assumed they still were. We haven't been able to see them that much recently owing to the numerous preparations for the wedding and reception, but that little pantomime in the church today makes me wonder if we were wrong. And look at them now.'

They glanced towards Thomas and Alice. Thomas's face was sullen, and Alice's miserable. Neither was saying a word to the other.

'Occasions like this must be very difficult for Thomas,' Sarah ventured. 'Seeing so many people taking part in activities which he, too, used to enjoy, such as dancing and socialising – the kind of thing Joseph's been doing since the speeches ended – can't be easy. It must be a constant reminder of his limitations, which will be less apparent when he's at home or out with the family. I'm sure it's no more than that.'

'Well, I certainly hope you're right. Come on,' Maud said, standing up. 'Let's go and watch the children complete their first dance as husband and wife.'

* * *

'I'm afraid they want to leave now, or one of them does,' Joseph said, coming to stand next to Charles, who'd positioned himself near the entrance to the marquee, from where he'd been able to stare unobtrusively at Alice and Thomas, while wondering how on earth she could put up with Thomas's appalling behaviour.

'I don't envy you the passengers you're about to have,' Joseph commented as they watched Thomas struggle to his feet.

They saw Alice make a move to help him, but Thomas pushed her arm brusquely aside, and began to make his way slowly across to Charles, clearly out of humour. Alice trailed after him, her face pink with misery and embarrassment.

Charles groaned theatrically. 'Believe me, I don't envy myself! I won't even have Sarah's support this time. Her intimidating presence kept Thomas in check on the way to the church, and then here. But she's chatting to Maud, and it'd be more than my life's worth to interrupt her, so I'm going to have to brave this one on my own.'

'Sooner you than me, brother,' Joseph said with a wry smile.

'Since it's the only blot on what's been a lovely day, Joseph, I can't really complain. Everyone else seems to have enjoyed the occasion. Nellie looks quite beautiful, and very happy. And I must say, it was an excellent idea to hold the reception in your garden. I was surprised at first, with business as good as you say it is, but looking around, I can see why you'd choose this over a hotel.'

'It was Nellie's choice, not mine. I imagine it was out of consideration for Walter's family. She didn't want the contrast between the financial standing of their two families to be too glaringly obvious. But she could've had it anywhere. There's still a huge demand for houses, and they're selling very well.'

'But I thought you recently said that now that building costs are falling, prices are dropping.'

'The number of houses we're selling more than offsets that. People are clamouring to buy their own home, particularly those at management and administration level. In the main, manual workers still want to rent their property, but as we're building houses for rent, too, we can also meet that demand. And now that the railway and transport unions have decided not to join in with the striking miners, the potential disaster of a national strike has been avoided and we can look forward to even better prospects in the future.'

'It all sounds very good. Except for the half hour that I'm about to endure.'

Joseph clapped Charles on the shoulder, and grinned at him. 'I'll leave you to it, then, and go and dance with my daughter. There'll be a stiff drink waiting for you when you get back.' And he walked off in the direction of the dance floor.

* * *

How he'd been longing for today, Charles thought, as Thomas and Alice neared him.

Just to know he'd be seeing Alice again had filled him with giddy anticipation. It was as if a long period of drought was coming to an end, and even though it would be no more than a momentary respite in a life that was increasingly failing to excite him, it would be considerably better than nothing.

Time and again in the past few weeks, he'd made up his mind to go to Kentish Town and secrete himself where he wouldn't be seen by anyone inside Thomas's house or in the yard of Linford & Sons, just to catch a glimpse of Alice, but had decided against it at the last moment.

He wouldn't have spoken to her, of course – that would have been inappropriate. It would've been enough just to see her. But each time that he'd been on the verge of veering off to Kentish Town instead of completing his journey to the City, he'd remembered with unwelcome clarity the way in which Alice and Thomas had been with each other at Robert's lunch, and also on the few occasions he'd seen them in the first few weeks after that, and with a sharp stab of pain, he'd continued to the bank.

He knew that he should've long ago banished all thoughts of Alice from his mind, and that it was very wrong of him to feel distraught at the pleasure that she and Thomas seemed to be finding in each other at last, and he'd repeatedly scolded himself for the way he felt. He should be glad that they appeared to be rekindling their happiness together. After all, that was what he'd wanted for Alice – happiness. And now that she'd found it, he must rid himself of the sinful thoughts that had invaded his mind and taken root.

His every instinct had told him that that was what she'd want.

'I'm sorry we need to leave so soon, Charles,' Alice said as they reached him. 'But it's been a long day and we're both tired.'

'Speak for yourself!' Thomas snapped. 'My wanting to leave is nothing to do with tiredness. It's because I'm bored. I've had more than enough of the dreary company here – present company not excluded – and I'm ready to go.'

Leaning heavily on his cane, he walked past Charles and out of the marquee, and headed for the side gate that led round to the front of the house.

'I'm sorry,' Alice mouthed to Charles, as she followed Thomas.

But her eyes said more than that.

Charles's heart gave a sudden lurch as he realised that, at times, his every instinct could be wrong.

22

KENTISH TOWN

July 1921

Joseph stepped back from the cork board, unpinned the architect's plan and gave it to Thomas to roll up, covertly studying the way he managed it. When Thomas had finished, he put it on the large table next to them, and sat down near Joseph.

'I was watching you just now, Thomas, and I'm delighted to see that your movement's much improved. You deserve credit for doing so well on your new leg, and for the way you manoeuvre the crutch, despite your hand. Also for the way you're now using your left hand more successfully.' Thomas opened his mouth to protest. 'No, don't deny it. I'm obviously not saying your situation's ideal – I'm just saying that you seem to be coping a lot better.'

'If I want to be able to escape this house on my own at any point in the future, I have to work at it, don't I?'

'I'm delighted to hear you say that as I've got a proposal for you.' He paused as the door opened and Alice came in with a tray on which were several mugs of coffee. 'Ah, Alice!' he exclaimed.

'Perfect timing as always. Why don't you stay and hear what I'm about to suggest to Thomas?'

Alice glanced at Thomas, who made a point of looking away.

She put a mug in front of each of them, and sat down at the side of the room.

'About a year ago,' Joseph began, 'you came with us to look at a site on the outskirts of London, Thomas, to see some of our new houses. Houses whose interiors you're improving. You were there, too, Alice,' he said, glancing across to her. 'Plans are one thing, but actual bricks and mortar quite another, and you haven't visited any of our sites since then. I'm hoping we can soon put that right. After all, you're an invaluable part of the process.'

'There's no need to talk to me as if I'm the village idiot, who needs to be flattered,' Thomas said sullenly. 'I've lost my leg, not my wits.'

Joseph laughed. 'Point taken. The thing is, I've got to go to a building society in Birmingham on Friday. I don't particularly want to go on my own, and Charles is tied up with some charity dinner of Sarah's at the weekend. And anyway, he's a money man – construction's not his field. But watching you just now, it occurred to me that you could probably manage the trip, so why don't you come with me? We'd leave here early on Friday morning, and be back on Sunday evening. We've one or two associates in the area, and I thought we could visit them while we're there. You could take Alice, too, if you wanted.'

'And look like a cripple who needs a nurse?'

'Alice is not your nurse – she's your wife. But I was actually thinking of you coming by yourself. If you needed any help, I'd be there. I may not be as pretty as Alice, but I'm sure I can do what's necessary for a couple of days or so. You said you wanted more independence. Well, now's your chance to begin.'

Thomas looked down at his injured hand, at the bulbous

scars where once his fingers had been, and he nodded slowly. 'Okay. I'm game to give it a go if it eases your conscience. I hope you realise what you're taking on, though.'

'This is nothing to do with guilt. It's me wanting to take a trip with my brother – just him and me. Something we haven't done for far too long.'

Thomas nodded. 'I suppose you can count me in, then.'

* * *

Charles leaned back in the leather chair in the oak-panelled library of the Club, and stared at Joseph in amazement. 'Don't tell me he actually agreed to go with you!'

'Indeed, he did. There was the inevitable snide comment about Alice, of course, and a reference to his benevolence in agreeing to do something to help me reduce my sense of guilt, but aside from all that, I think he quite liked the idea. There's one person who really will be delighted, though, and that's Alice. I saw a light spring to her eyes the moment he agreed to go. She looks quite exhausted these days, and I'm sure she'll benefit from having some time to herself, however short.'

Charles nodded. 'I thought she looked a little care-worn at the wedding. She's such a pretty woman, though, that a day or two without our brother should soon restore that bloom.'

'My secretary will book us a couple of rooms in a good hotel, and follow up on our list of Birmingham contacts.'

'Well, for your sake, I hope you see the best side of Thomas up there, not the worst.'

Joseph picked up his glass. 'I'm not that ambitious. The most I'm hoping for is that he'll be civil for the short amount of time we're there.'

'Perhaps that's wise.' Charles picked up his glass, held it for a moment or two and then put it down again. 'Tell me, how's it going, having Walter in the house?'

'Fine. He's easy enough – fits in with everything. He's a good man. And he clearly adores Nellie. The more I see of him, the more I like him. Regretfully, though, they'll only be with us for another couple of weeks. I don't mind telling you, Maud and I will be sorry to see them go.'

Charles sat forward in his chair, picked up his glass again, finished his whisky and stood up. He gave an awkward laugh. 'Talking about going, I know I've only just got here, but I've suddenly remembered something I need to do. I'm going to have to head off, I'm afraid.'

Joseph raised his eyebrows, and glanced up at him. 'If you must.'

'Unfortunately, I must. Let me know how it goes with Thomas. Give my best to the family. Perhaps you'll all come to dinner before Nellie and Walter move out,' Charles said. With a hasty wave, he moved quickly towards the door.

As he hurried down the steps and away from the Club, one thought alone filled his mind – Alice.

She wasn't used to being alone and while initially she'd probably enjoy her solitude at the weekend, and relish not having to cope with Thomas's moods, she could soon begin to feel lonely, and perhaps a little afraid. Mrs Carmichael usually visited her widowed sister on Saturday afternoons, and Alice would be completely alone in the house. If that happened, she might welcome some company and be pleased to see him, should he call upon her.

But if he *did* visit, he'd stay for a short time only – just long enough to have a cup of tea and a friendly chat. Nothing more.

There couldn't be anything more than friendship between them – not ever.

They owed it to Sarah and Thomas to be true to their wedding vows, and they owed it to the whole family to respect the sanctity of the bonds between them. They must never do anything which could jeopardise Linford unity if it were found out, and hurt the people they loved.

For despite Thomas's irritability and rudeness, he loved his brother and he couldn't conceive of making his life more difficult than it already was. However badly Thomas treated Alice, deep down he acknowledged that it was born out of Thomas's insecurity, and that he loved his wife and must live in fear of losing her.

He must never let himself forget that.

And Alice would know full well that Thomas truly loved her. That awareness would explain why she put up with his unpleasantness towards her. She, too, would feel that whatever the attraction between them – and there definitely *was* an attraction – it must never be acted upon. It would be very wrong of them to do so.

But offering to pay her a friendly visit in Thomas's absence, and keeping her company for a while, couldn't hurt.

As he got into his car, he decided that he'd detour to Kentish Town on the way to the bank the following morning. If he timed it right, he'd catch Alice on her way back from doing the shopping, and he could then suggest stopping by the house on the Saturday afternoon.

Although he'd told Joseph that he had to be around that afternoon to help Sarah prepare for the charity event to which he'd accompany her in the evening, that hadn't been strictly true.

Sarah had made it clear that she had everything under control and didn't need – or particularly want – him at her side during the day. The evening was a different matter. Being on hand for the evening, a smile on his face and a readiness to put his hand in his pocket, was what was required of him.

So he, too, looked like being at a loose end during the day, and that was another reason to pay Alice a visit.

* * *

Sitting on the bench next to Charles, Alice stared at the ground. Wisps of fair hair fell around her face.

'You're so lovely, Alice,' Charles said quietly. 'So very lovely.'

She went pink, and glanced at him. 'You don't have to say that.'

'I know I don't. But it's what I feel. Every time I look at you, something in me fills with joy. And with longing.' He leaned forward, rested his forearms on his knees and looked sideways at her. 'I'm not trying to push you into anything, dearest Alice,' he said gently. 'If you don't want me to stop by on Saturday, then I won't. I realise you might not think it appropriate for me to visit you while Thomas is away, and I respect that, but I also know that there won't be many opportunities like this. That's why I'm hoping we might take advantage of this one.' He gave her a half-smile. 'Did you hear me say we? I'm making the assumption that you, too, want us to spend time together.'

Alice bit her lip.

'Do you, Alice?' he prompted when she didn't reply. 'Or is it just wishful thinking on my part?' He waited. 'Please say something, dear Alice; I beg of you.'

She turned again to look at him. 'When you talk about spending time with me, you really mean more than that, don't you?'

He stared at her for a few minutes, and then looked down at the ground in front of him. 'If you'd asked me that an hour ago,' he said at last, 'I'd have denied it. I'd have assured you that I meant nothing more than a friendly visit. I'd convinced myself of that. But now, sitting next to you—' He turned and looked into her face. 'Being so close to you, feeling as I do about you, I can't give you that assurance.'

'I understand.' Her voice was a whisper.

'As I said, I just want to see you. I've no intention of coercing you into something you don't want to do. I care about you far too much for that. I'd settle for just a cup of tea and a friendly conversation, if that was all you wanted.'

'You say you feel strongly about me, but you haven't been here for so long,' she said, her voice taking on an accusing tone. 'I thought you were busy with other things and had lost interest in seeing me.'

He straightened up and looked at her in surprise. 'Oh, no, you've completely misunderstood! When Sarah and I saw you at Robert's that time, you and Thomas seemed to be getting on so much better. And also on the few occasions we've seen you since then. There'd definitely been a spark between the two of you that we hadn't seen before. And it wasn't just my imagination because the others said the same. We were pleased because we want you to be happy. That's the most important thing.'

'Oh, I see.' Her voice was so soft that he had to strain to hear her.

'I'm ashamed to say, I wasn't quite as pleased as the others,' he continued. 'But I knew I was being selfish, and that I had to stand back. There hasn't been a day when I haven't thought about you, though. But when I saw you at Nellie's wedding, I realised at once that things were no longer as we'd thought.' He frowned. 'What happened?'

'You're right, things *were* better for a short time. But it's so difficult for Thomas with his disabilities. He's convinced that I must be repelled by his injuries, and he won't believe me when I tell him he's wrong. And because he can't relax about his body, he can't do what he wants to do.' She went bright red. 'You know what I mean. So he finally gave up even trying, and became angry and resentful again.'

'I'm so sorry, Alice. I wish I'd known.' He leaned forward and brushed her hair from her face.

She moved swiftly back. 'Don't do that! If Thomas saw us, he'd get the wrong idea.'

'The wrong idea?'

She raised her head to look into his face, her blue eyes steady. 'You know what I'm saying.'

'You're right, I do.' He hesitated. 'And I also know how much I'd like to come over on Saturday afternoon. But it's your decision.'

She swallowed hard and looked back at her feet.

'I'm not saying that I don't feel the same way as you, because I do,' she said, her voice shaking. 'But we shouldn't be thinking like that, and even if we are, we mustn't do anything about it. Thomas is your brother. And he's my husband. And what about Sarah and your children?'

'I know all that, and it's been weighing heavily on me. The trouble is, it doesn't alter how I feel about you.'

She sat without moving.

'I know it's wrong, Alice, and there's no moral justification for my feelings. Quite the contrary. But life is short, so I still can't help hoping – praying even – that at some point before too long, we're going to ignore the right-thinking voices that are screaming loudly within us, and do exactly what those voices are telling us not to do. Are we?'

She gathered her bags and stood up. 'I must go now. Thomas will start to worry.'

He got to his feet and faced her. 'Are we, Alice?' he repeated.

For a long moment, she stared up into his face.

'As I said, I must go now,' she repeated, her voice cracking.

'I have to be back in Knightsbridge on Saturday evening. I'll be across the road from your house from one o'clock on Saturday. I'll stay there all afternoon, if necessary. If you don't open the door to me, I'll not go home until the latest possible moment, and we'll never refer to it again.'

'You might have a wasted visit.'

'I'll take my chances.'

She gave him a nervous smile, and then stepped on to the kerb, swiftly checked that nothing was coming in either direction, and walked quickly to the other side of the road.

He stared after her. If she turns to look back at me before she enters the house, she'll get into bed with me on Saturday afternoon, he told himself.

He watched her hurry along the pavement to her house. When she reached the front door, she put her key in the lock, and paused. Then she turned round and looked at him. Neither moved. Turning back to the door, she pushed it open, went inside and closed it.

Smiling broadly, he headed for the underground station.

23

THE FOLLOWING SATURDAY AFTERNOON

From his seat on the bench, Charles stared down the road towards Thomas's house. The grey front door was closed.

He looked at his watch. It was exactly one o'clock at last.

His heart beating fast, he smoothed down his hair, took a deep breath, stood up and walked swiftly towards the trees that lined the pavement opposite the sash window where Thomas usually sat.

Taking up a position behind the plane tree with the thickest trunk, he glanced nervously up and down the pavement. But there was no one coming from either direction, and to his relief, the dilapidated shops behind him seemed to be deserted, too.

Not that anybody he knew would shop there, he thought, turning to face the house. Even Thomas didn't expect Alice to use those shops. And anyway, as he didn't know anyone who lived in the area, apart from Thomas and Alice, it was highly unlikely that anyone would recognise him, or wonder why he was standing half-hidden behind a tree, opposite the house where his brother lived.

He stared at the front door. It remained closed.

His gaze slid to the open window upstairs. That had been Joseph's bedroom as a child. Charles couldn't see into it, covered as it was by a flimsy curtain, but he knew – he just knew – that Alice was standing behind the window, staring down at him.

Feeling her eyes on him, he started to walk quickly across the road – the sooner he was inside the house and out of sight the better. The sooner he was with Alice...

A wave of panic hit him, and he stopped abruptly in the middle of the road.

Alice. His brother's wife. He shouldn't be going to see her alone like this, desperately hoping she'd let him take her to bed. He shouldn't want that with Alice. Not with his sister-in-law.

He just couldn't do it.

The horn of a car sounded. He jumped, and quickly finished crossing the road.

The front door faced him.

He raised his hand to the brass door knocker, but paused in mid-air. Standing there, his fingers inches from the knocker, he was paralysed by guilt.

This was all wrong.

It was insane to take such a risk.

Suppose they were found out! It would be the end of his marriage for sure – Sarah wasn't the sort of woman to forgive and forget. And as for Thomas. What would it do to Thomas, damaged as he was and already so fragile? It would destroy him completely.

What had he been thinking of?

He was a man, not an animal. He didn't have to give in to this yearning for Alice. He was stronger than that.

And he was going to prove it.

He spun round and started back across the road. By the time he reached the trees on the opposite side, he was almost running.

Slowing down, he made his way steadily along the pavement towards the bench where he and Alice had sat several times. Never once did he look back.

When he reached the bench, he stood still.

His feet wouldn't carry him past it.

But they had to.

It was the right thing to do to leave now, before it was too late, before he gave into a desire that he shouldn't be feeling. He was strong enough to turn his back on temptation, and that's what he was going to do.

And if he hurried, he could surprise Sarah in the hall where her charity event was taking place that evening, and he could offer to help with the preparations. Whatever she'd said about not wanting him there, he was pretty sure that if he turned up in support, it would really please her.

A satisfied smile hovered on his lips.

He'd be doing the right thing, which was helping his wife with her charitable work.

It was about time he put his family first, after all. Too often recently he'd been preoccupied, his mind on Alice. But Sarah, Louisa and Christopher – the family he dearly loved – should have his full attention. They deserved better than to be putting their trust in someone who'd come close to doing something so very wrong that afternoon.

Alice, too, who looked after his injured brother so well, deserved his help and support. But instead of offering that, if he had entered her house that afternoon, he would have been taking advantage of her, exploiting the problems in her marriage to a man she had loved and looked after – and probably still did love in a way – but whose insecurities made him difficult to live with at times.

He must get as far away as he could from her house while he was thinking clearly.

And yet he couldn't move.

One more quick glance at her house couldn't hurt, for memory's sake, he told himself. Just one last time and then he'd head straight for the underground station, and wouldn't look back.

Turning, he re-traced his steps until once again, he stood opposite the house. He gazed up at the bedroom window. He was sure that she was up there, watching him, wondering what he was going to do. Helpless with longing, his eyes on her window, he could almost feel her in his arms.

The palms of his hands felt sweaty.

And then he saw her. She'd pulled the curtain aside and was staring down at him.

He caught his breath and lowered his eyes to the front door.

It was slightly ajar.

As if bewitched, he found himself walking across the road, his eyes focused on the grey door ahead of him, open to him. Reaching the door, he raised his hand to tap lightly on the wood, but the door opened wider.

Alice stood there.

For a moment, neither moved, and then she stepped aside, and he entered the house.

24

LATER THAT NIGHT

A hollow feeling within her, Alice lay on her side and stared at the wall ahead of her. She'd done something terrible that day, something that would destroy Thomas if he ever found out. And she should feel wracked with guilt. But did she?

Yes, but not as much as she should.

Thomas was her husband, and she loved him, despite what had happened with Charles. And she understood where Thomas's appalling moods sprang from. They were born out of misery and frustration.

For an active man, as he had been before the war, it must have been quite devastating to find himself suddenly and permanently restricted in the life he could live and the activities he could pursue. And she couldn't comfort him and reassure him that he would get better, that he'd grow a new leg. She could tell him, though, that it would get easier for him as the months went by, and she did so virtually every day, but it was hard for him to accept this, gripped as he was by acute despair.

She understood that, of course. And she greatly sympathised

with him, and was doing all she could to make him comfortable and more content.

But at the same time, *her* happiness mattered, too. As Charles had said.

Yet she was increasingly miserable.

And despite understanding the reasons for his moodiness, she was finding it harder and harder not to resent the impact his behaviour was having on her life. When she looked back at the past few months, she was amazed at just how long it was since she'd felt happy in herself.

She was being made to suffer because *he* was suffering.

And that was hardly fair.

It was no wonder that she'd been drawn to Charles. He was charming and very attractive. He'd been unfailingly kind to her whenever they'd met, and he always seemed appreciative of the way she looked and what she said. He made her feel like a woman, a desirable woman, not an object of no account.

So while she felt guilty for betraying Thomas, he was partly responsible for what she'd done, and that lessened her remorse.

And what's more, if Thomas didn't improve his manner towards her, she would agree to another meeting with Charles. She knew he wanted to see her again, just the two of them together – that had been clear from his every word and loving glance. And she knew within herself how much she was looking forward to feeling Charles's arms protectively around her again.

She was only human, after all.

It wasn't wrong to want to feel loved.

The memory of the reverence with which Charles had kissed the length of her naked body flashed into her mind, and she shivered with pleasure. Yes, he'd definitely made her feel loved.

Pulling the sheet up to her throat, she curled up her legs, and took a deep breath.

Unless Thomas came back from Birmingham a very different man from the man who'd gone there, she was at risk of falling as much in love with Charles as he was with her.

* * *

Charles looked up at the ceiling, and then across at the twin bed in which Sarah lay. She was fast asleep. He stared back at the ceiling and smiled. He'd been hugely relieved that she'd been so tired after the charity event that evening that she'd fallen into bed and gone straight to sleep.

She didn't normally initiate sexual activity between them, being much too well bred for that, but it could have been one of the rare occasions when she'd felt so in the mood that she'd cast aside her inhibitions.

Had she done so, he'd have found it difficult to work up the necessary enthusiasm, having quite exhausted himself earlier, first with Alice, and then having to be social to Sarah and her committee, which had been doubly demanding as all he'd really wanted to do was relive every moment of his afternoon with Alice.

But happily, sleep had been foremost in Sarah's mind when they'd got home, and she'd been fast asleep before he'd even emerged from his dressing room.

And that freed him to think about Alice.

And he didn't feel in the least bit guilty for wanting to do so.

He was a good husband to Sarah, but did she appreciate him? No.

She never stopped nagging him about one thing or another. Especially about seeking a promotion. But he had a good position at the bank, one that wasn't overly demanding, and he couldn't see why he should strive for something he might not enjoy as much, and which would give him less time to himself during the day.

So if he wanted to think about Alice, he would.

Feeling at liberty to do so, his mind took him back to the hours they'd spent together that afternoon, hours they'd filled with ease, that had been so pleasant that they'd both been left wanting more. She'd like to meet him again, of that he was sure. And as for him, since the very thought of her was enough to make his exhausted body spring into action, he, too, very much wanted that.

But where to meet, he wondered, turning on to his stomach in the hope of finding an area of cold sheet that might cool him down.

He could hardly ask Thomas if he could pop upstairs for the occasional hour or two with his lovely wife!

And while the bench along the road was satisfactory for short conversations, talking was not what he had in mind, so that would hardly do. He smiled into the pillow at the thought of the expression on the faces of passers-by if he and Alice, overcome by desire, unleashed their passion in so public a place.

The answer, of course, was easy when he thought about it – he would buy a small house not too far from Thomas's house, and then they'd have somewhere comfortable and private to meet. It would be well worth the expense as every bone in his body told him that this was the beginning of something that was going to last a long time, and greatly enhance the years ahead for both of them.

And as there was no time like the present, he'd start looking for a house the following day.

He raised his head and glanced at Sarah's bed. Wouldn't she be amazed to know just how decisive her husband could be, and how rapidly he could get moving, when the prize was something as luscious as Alice?

25

PRIMROSE HILL

December 1921

Leaving Charles to finish off in the dining-room, Joseph headed for his favourite armchair by the marble fireplace in the dark oak-panelled library at his Club. He sat down, waived away the waiter's offer of an after-dinner drink, and waited for Charles to join him.

For the past couple of weeks, he'd been anxiously looking for a time when he could speak privately to Charles about a highly sensitive matter, so it had been a relief that his suggestion to Maud and Sarah that they might like to take Louisa and Christopher to Chorton to decorate the house for Christmas had been enthusiastically adopted, with the result that he and Charles had found themselves with a family-free weekend.

Not surprisingly, given the subject, he'd been somewhat nervous as he made his way to the Club, and very anxious for the evening to go well.

And so far it had.

Over dinner, he'd discussed with Charles a few general

matters relating to Robert and how he was getting on, and the family.

Charles asked what had happened about the Birmingham associates that Thomas had offended on their short trip there in July.

He'd groaned in horror. He said that he never again wanted to be reminded of that ghastly weekend, and how Thomas had gone out of his way to make everything more difficult than necessary. Fortunately, Joseph concluded, Thomas hadn't managed to drive away any of the associates, and they were still working together. He could only assume that they'd recognised that Thomas's disability had badly affected him, and had not allowed themselves to take offence at his rudeness.

Charles had remarked that Thomas wasn't the only awkward character in the family – Louisa came a close second. And he'd gone on to say how very badly she and Sarah were getting on, and then they'd moved to the family business, and a welcome new investment.

The investment had come from a builders' merchant Joseph knew.

A while before, he'd mentioned to Charles that a Henry Ames was thinking about investing in the company, but Charles had never met him. Of that Joseph was certain. So when Sarah had mentioned two or three weeks earlier that Charles was frequently out of the office as he'd been regularly meeting up with Henry Ames, a potential investor, Joseph had known that to be untrue.

He'd assumed at the time, therefore, that Charles was having an affair, and had cautioned him against such irresponsible behaviour.

But now he knew for certain that he was.

'Ah, here you are,' he said as Charles approached the fireplace, and went and sat in the armchair opposite. 'Why don't you sit here?' Joseph told him, and indicated the chair next to him.

Glancing at Joseph in mild surprise, Charles went and sat where Joseph had suggested.

'This is a break from tradition,' Charles said with a smile. 'We normally face each other. As you're a man who places a high value on tradition, that does surprise me. And you don't yet have a brandy, which is another break from tradition.'

'I'm not sure that taking armchairs opposite each other constitutes a tradition,' Joseph remarked, 'but if it does, so be it. I doubt there's a tradition in the world that hasn't been broken at some point or other. I can't stay much longer, which accounts for the lack of a brandy, but before I go, I wanted to talk to you without us being overheard. It's as simple as that.'

Charles changed his position in the chair. 'To me that sounds ominous rather than simple.'

'I know for certain that you're cheating on Sarah, Charles.'

Charles went pale. 'I don't know what you're talking about.'

'Oh, I think you do. And I know who you're cheating with.'

Charles didn't move.

'You're cheating on Thomas with Alice.'

'That's rubbish,' Charles said, his voice a croak.

'I wish it was, but it isn't. I clearly remember how Thomas was before he went to fight,' Joseph said, his eyes on his brother. 'He was full of spirit and energy and with a sense of adventure. We knew he'd leave the family business as soon as he could – that was clear from the outset. It was a miracle he stuck at it until he was twenty-eight. He needed excitement, did Thomas, and Linford & Sons just couldn't provide the sort of excitement he wanted. But the war could, and he couldn't get there fast enough. It killed David, and although Thomas came home, a part of him died, too. We lost the old Thomas the day his leg was blown off. And now you risk destroying the little that's left of our brother.'

Charles gave an awkward shrug. 'You're talking rot.'

'No, I'm not. You're sleeping with his wife,' Joseph said bluntly. 'You're not stupid, Charles, and nor am I, so don't act as if we are.'

Charles opened his mouth. 'I'm not—'

'Yes, you are,' Joseph cut in. 'Kentish Town Road was blocked the other day. I had to find another way back to the yard, so I took a road I'd never normally use. I saw the two of you draped over each other, going into a small house. It would've been obvious to a blind man why you were going there.'

Charles slumped back in his seat.

'Alice is your sister-in-law, for God's sake! You're taking advantage of the misery she must feel when Thomas's temper is at its worst. I'm ashamed of you.'

Charles raised a finger to summon the waiter. 'Cognac, please,' he said. 'Do you want to change your mind, Joseph?'

Joseph shook his head, and the waiter went off towards the bar.

'As you know, I've been pretty certain for a while that you were up to something like that, but I never dreamed it would be with Alice. How could it be, I would've said. She rarely leaves Thomas's side. But clearly I must be wrong. Whose house is it, by the way?'

Charles gave him a wry smile. 'You're not the only one with an interest in property – I bought the house some months ago. It's small, but it's close to the shops she uses. That's the one thing she does by herself – go to the shops. From the start, she's insisted that *she* does the shopping, not the housekeeper. I know what she buys on the different days, and I get the provisions in for her. It gives us that little longer together. She's told Thomas that she always takes a roundabout route home in order to get some fresh air.'

'So that's how you've arranged it.' Joseph paused. 'Well, it has to end now, before Thomas gets wind of it. You owe it to him as his brother, and you owe it to him as someone who went to war so that you could sleep safely at night. Not to mention what you owe Sarah. I can't believe you're betraying a woman like Sarah. It's incredible. What you're doing is completely wrong, Charles. It's immoral.'

'I hardly think *you're* the one to talk about morality!'

Joseph shrugged. 'Anything I've done in the past was done out of necessity. But there's no necessity for you to sleep with Alice, and it's got to stop.'

They paused as the waiter put a cognac on the table next to Charles's armchair, and then left.

'That's down to Alice and me, don't you think?' Charles retorted. 'As you just said, Thomas doesn't go out on his own, so he's unlikely to find out. And if you hadn't seen us together, you'd never have known.'

'That might be what you want to think, but you could be wrong. It's obvious that poor Thomas has long sensed that there's a mutual attraction between you and Alice – I'm sure it accounts for a lot of his brusqueness and his tetchiness. One slip by either of you is all it would take in his heightened state of suspicion for him to rumble it.'

'It's all very well to focus on *poor* Thomas, but what about poor Alice? She's done so much for Thomas, and by extension for the family, yet he's continually rude to her. At times he treats her worse than you'd treat a servant. Surely she's got every right to receive affection from someone else.'

'That's a moot point. Didn't she make a vow at her marriage that it was for better for worse? And as I said, much of his bad temper may be caused by his suspicions. And what about *your* marriage? Whatever the rights and wrongs of Alice and her situation, *you've* no excuse for being unfaithful. You couldn't have a better wife than Sarah.'

'You mean because she's brought money to the business? Well, that's not the only measure of a good wife, you know. *You* try being nagged at day after day, and constantly belittled, and made to feel that you're failing someone's expectations of you. Try that, and then try to imagine how hard it would be to turn away from someone who clearly respects you and loves you for who you are and as you are.'

Joseph made an impatient, dismissive gesture. 'Now you're just making excuses. Nothing justifies what you're doing to our brother. Nothing. And it's got to stop.'

Charles's lips set in a firm line.

'D'you hear me?' Joseph thundered.

'I do, and I'm sure that everyone else does, too. I'm wondering if I'm going to be hearing an "or else",' Charles said quietly. 'And if I do, what the threat will be.'

Joseph sat back and shook his head. 'There isn't one. I'd do anything to stop Sarah and Thomas from discovering what you two have been doing, so I'd never threaten you with exposure, if that's what you think. And I'm well aware that I owe you a debt of gratitude for the help you've given me in the past, which went against the grain with you.'

'As I recall, I don't think you gave me a lot of choice,' Charles said caustically.

'Be that as it may. No, I'm going to have to trust that you'll think about the hurt you could cause, and do the right thing. You might find it helpful if you try to imagine the consequences when your affair is eventually exposed.'

'It might not be.'

'Oh, yes, it will. These things are always discovered in due course. You're fooling yourself if you believe otherwise. You cited Alice's present situation with Thomas. Do you really believe she'd be better off thrown out on to the street, which would surely happen? You know Thomas as well as I do. And do you honestly think that a woman like Sarah would carry on as if nothing had happened? Of course she wouldn't, and you know it.'

Joseph stood up.

'You've more to lose than I ever realised, Charles, till I saw the two of you together. And when you lose it – not if, but when, which will happen if you continue in the same way – you'll bring tremendous grief to our family whom I hold very dear. Is such a dalliance really worth the risk? Think about it.'

And he walked out.

26

CHORTON HOUSE

Sunday, mid-June 1922

The loud wails of Walter and Nellie's daughter, Emily, sounded throughout her christening in the church that stood atop a hill not far from Chorton House. Her vehement protests travelled from the baptismal font along the aisle, up the grey stone walls on either side of the small church, and spread out across the vaulted ceiling that arched above the congregation.

'I'd cry, too,' Charles told Nellie and Walter later on as together they went to join Thomas and Alice who were already in the sitting-room, 'if someone was throwing cold water over me on a chilly day. Despite the sun, it's surprisingly cool for June.'

'That's a little disrespectful, Charles, don't you think?' Sarah said, following him into the room, with Christopher and Louisa just behind her. 'Christening's an important ritual.'

'That you don't believe a word of,' he said, sitting down. 'The only times you go to church are for births, deaths and marriages.'

'Were *we* christened?' Christopher asked, flinging himself on to the floor next to his father's chair and leaning back against the leg.

'Of course, you were, darling,' Sarah said. 'And here at Chorton, too.' She turned back to her husband. 'I may not be a religious person, Charles, but I assure you I'm still able to appreciate the gravity of such a rite. And to have such a discussion today of all days is hardly appropriate.' She sat down on the empty seat on the sofa next to Nellie, who was looking tired and miserable, and put her arm around Nellie's shoulders. 'She'll settle soon, Nellie, darling. You'll see.'

'I thought girls were supposed to be meek and quiet,' Nellie said, close to tears, 'but Emily isn't. Everything seems to make her cry, and at full volume, too. I feel guilty at my relief when Nanny Jane takes her away from me. I must be an awful mother.'

Sarah hugged her. 'You mustn't expect too much too quickly. You're still getting over the birth, and you're bound to be exhausted. Things will feel better when you're not so tired. Trust me.'

'I do hope so. Was I as noisy as Emily when I was that age, Mother?' she asked as Maud came into the room with Joseph and Robert, and took a seat on the sofa opposite hers.

'You most definitely were,' Joseph cut in cheerfully, going to sit next to Maud. 'And Robert was just as bad. Being noisy seems to be an inherited characteristic.'

Nellie glanced at her father. 'And what about Dottie?' she asked sharply. 'Was *she* noisy, too?'

'Your father wouldn't know, darling,' Maud cut in smoothly. 'Parents didn't see much of their children when you were young, not like nowadays. We would spend about an hour each afternoon with you, that was all. And as for Dorothy, she was a quiet child, the quietest of the three of you.'

'Since we're not eating for a good hour and a half,' Charles said, stretching out his legs and yawning, 'and I, for one, could do with some exercise, why don't we go for a walk? If we put a jacket on, it should be quite pleasant.'

'D'you think you can manage a walk, Thomas, if we stick to level ground?' Joseph asked.

'If I wanted to, I could. But the crucial question is – do I want to? And the answer is, no, I don't.'

Alice's face visibly fell. 'I'll stay with Thomas,' she said with forced cheerfulness.

Robert glanced at Alice's expression. 'There's no need to, Alice. I'll skip the walk. There are some work details I want to discuss with Uncle Thomas, and it'll be nice to have the chance for a chat with him, too.'

Thomas gave him a wry grin.

'If you'll excuse me, I, too, will absent myself from the walk,' Maud said. 'I've yet to succumb to the joy of clambering over muddy stiles and disentangling my person from weeds and nettles. And as for risking an encounter with a bucolic horror such as a cow...' She shuddered. 'I, too, haven't said more than a word or two to Thomas for simply ages, so I'd enjoy the chance to do so now.'

'I *am* in sudden demand,' Thomas said drily. 'That lets you off the hook, then, Robert. Your mother has lifted the burden of my entertainment from your shoulders. You can go off with the others.' Robert opened his mouth. 'No, don't protest. You know you want to.'

Robert gave a slight shrug. 'Well, if you're sure you don't want me to stay.'

Thomas grinned at him. 'I'm fine, really. You go for your walk.'

Walter turned to Nellie. 'What about you, Nellie? Would you prefer a lie-down before lunch?'

'Tempting though that sounds, I know that some fresh air would do me good, so I'll join you.'

Charles stood up. 'Let's be off, then. On with those walking shoes, everyone. Back here in ten minutes.'

* * *

Christopher jumped down from the top of the first in the series of stiles and walked straight ahead, flapping his arms at his sides. Charles followed him over the stile, and walked quickly to catch up with him.

'Whoa, Christopher. You're not taking the slightest notice of anything around you. The countryside's beautiful. Why don't you slow down and let yourself enjoy it?'

Christopher stopped in his tracks. 'D'you mean, I should've noticed that the japonica flowers have fallen, and that everywhere, the cornflowers are in bloom, not to mention the meadow buttercups and poppies? Should I have noticed that the sycamore trees are now almost completely covered in yellowy leaves and greenish-yellow flowers? Is that what you mean?'

Christopher started walking again.

Laughing, Charles followed him. 'Wow, I'm impressed by your powers of observation, Chris. That's not bad for an eight-year-old. In fact, I'm not even sure that *I* took all that in.' He glanced at Christopher. 'I feel I've just learned something about you, son,' he added with a sudden awkwardness. 'I'd no idea you were so interested in nature.'

Christopher shrugged.

'Is Louisa as keen on the countryside as you? When I last saw her, she was dawdling along with Sarah, Nellie and Alice, so it was hard to tell.'

Christopher pulled a face. 'Not really. She prefers shopping and giggling with her stupid friends.'

Charles laughed again. 'That's girls for you. And talking of girls, perhaps we ought to let them catch us up, and also Uncle Joseph and Walter. We don't want to come over as anti-social as Robert, who disappeared almost at once. I suggest we pause at the next stile.'

'If you want.'

There was a slight thud behind them, and they felt a sudden rush of air. Turning, they saw that Sarah was fast approaching, panting slightly.

'My, you must really have got a move on!' Charles said. 'The four of you were miles behind us when we last looked. Or maybe we slowed down without realising. Christopher's been impressing me with his powers of observation – you'd be amazed at what he notices. We were going to go as far as the next stile and then wait for the others.'

'So I heard. We'll have to go back after that, though. Mrs Spencer won't be best pleased if we're late for lunch. I suggest we go as far as the stile after the next one, and then start back.'

Charles nodded. 'That sounds good to me.'

With a smile at both, Sarah continued briskly along the foot-path, gradually leaving them behind.

'We were saying that we'd worked up quite an appetite,' Joseph said as he and Walter caught up with Charles and Christopher. 'We heard the tail end of Sarah's suggestion, and we agree.'

Squinting, Charles glanced beyond them to the track along which they'd walked. 'We seem to have lost Louisa, Nellie and Alice,' he remarked.

Walter glanced briefly over his shoulder. 'I expect they'll soon speed up, if they haven't already. I doubt we're the only ones thinking about food. But as for walking fast, Sarah's in a league of her own.'

'Mummy always leaves everyone a long way behind,' Christopher said.

'She does, indeed, Chris,' Charles said, ruffling his hair. 'I think this is the one thing in which your sister doesn't take after her.'

Christopher laughed. 'She certainly doesn't. Louisa's a slow-coach. Mummy's always telling her so.'

By the time they reached the next stile, Sarah had cleared it and was standing, waiting for them. 'It's quite high,' she said. 'I wanted to warn you to be extra careful. The girls will probably need help getting over it.'

Charles glanced up at it. 'I can see what you mean. Why don't I wait here, then, and see them safely over? You're right, it does look a bit of a bugger. Sorry, Chris – bad choice of language.'

'Fine. I'll leave you to it,' Sarah said, and she headed for the point where they had agreed to stop. A few minutes later, Christopher, Walter and Joseph had also cleared the tall stile and were heading after Sarah.

* * *

'Well done, Nellie,' Charles called, as Nellie successfully climbed the stile and dropped to the other side where Louisa was waiting for her. 'Time's moving on so why don't the two of you go after the others? I'll see that Alice gets over without a hitch, and we'll catch you up.'

'See you in a minute, then,' Nellie said, and she and Louisa followed the path towards the others.

He watched them go, and then turned to Alice. 'Right,' he

said, 'let's see what you can do.' He slid his hand around her waist, and stopped.

She looked up at him, and their eyes lingered on each other.

'It feels an eternity since I've held you like this,' Charles murmured.

'A week is hardly an eternity,' she said in amusement.

'Is that all it is? Well, it feels so much longer.'

'And for me, too.'

As she raised her arm to push back the strands of fair hair that had come adrift from the loose chignon at the nape of her neck, her eyes all the time on his face, the sleeve of her jacket rolled down her arm.

His gaze slid along the silky smoothness of the pale skin on the lower side of her upturned arm, and he felt his body harden.

'I love you, Alice,' he said quietly. 'It's been unbearable this weekend, being so close to you, but unable to touch you. There hasn't been one single minute when I haven't desperately wished that it was just the two of us here. I can't have enough of you.'

She took his hand, lifted it to her lips, kissed it and let it fall. 'It's been the same for me, Charles. But I can feel Thomas watching me all the time, and I don't dare look at you, much as I long to. And I do so long to. It's only because of Robert and Maud that he let me come out on the walk without him.'

'Then we should make the most of it, don't you think?'

His words hung in the air between them.

With the hint of a smile, she undid the top few buttons of her light jacket, reached out for his hand, placed it between her jacket and her blouse, and let it rest just above her hardening nipple. Then her hand lightly pressured his, shaping it around her.

'I do think,' she said. 'As you can tell.'

The knot in his groin tightened, and heat pulsed through his body.

'The others are a long way ahead,' he said, his voice breaking, 'and we're hidden by the stile, so I'm going to kiss you. But we can't risk anything more than that, not here.'

She released his hand, and let her arm fall to her side.

He took her upturned face with both his hands and gazed into her eyes. 'Dear Alice,' he said. 'I love you. I wish I could always be with you.' And he lowered his mouth to hers.

'What the hell d'you think you're doing?'

Their hearts juddered in panic. They jumped apart and stared in horror at the top of the stile.

From her position astride the uppermost beam, Sarah stared down at them, green eyes blazing in a face that was white with rage.

27

KNIGHTSBRIDGE

The following morning

The cold light of dawn slid through the shuttered windows of the guest room, slicing Charles into narrow strips of pale grey as he lay motionless on his back at the end of a sleepless night.

Neither he nor Sarah had spoken to each other since the moment she'd come upon him and Alice the previous day. He'd stood with Alice, petrified, shaking with fear as Sarah had jumped down, brushed past them and headed for the house without uttering a word.

Leaving Alice standing there, he'd hurried frantically after Sarah as she'd raced ahead, her stance grim. In the distance behind him, he could faintly hear the sound of Alice following him. He hadn't dared look back at her, but he'd easily been able to imagine the panic which would be written across her face.

It would be the same panic that had convulsed his stomach and dried his mouth all night long as he'd lain in fear, uncertain what the morning would bring.

Well, he'd soon know. The dreaded conversation was bound to take place that day.

What would Sarah say?

And what did he want the outcome to be?

Over and over again, when he and Alice had been together, he'd told her how much he wished it could be just him and her, that they could be together forever. But in the chill light of the burgeoning day – the day upon which his future hung in the balance – he wasn't sure if that *was* what he really wanted.

Numb with fright by the time they'd got back to Chorton the day before, he'd been physically trembling. And when he saw Thomas up ahead, leaning heavily on his stick as he watched them approach, and Sarah going straight towards him, he thought his knees would give way.

'I was just getting some exercise. I didn't expect you back quite so soon,' he'd heard Thomas tell Sarah. And then, as if he'd picked up on the tension between them, Thomas's eyes had gone from Sarah's face to his, and thence over his shoulder to Alice, and he'd seen Thomas's expression harden.

'I felt sick,' Sarah had told Thomas, 'and I still do. When the children have had their lunch, we're going home. Now if you'll excuse me.' And she'd gone into the house.

A wave of intense relief had rocked through him, leaving him weak in its aftermath. He'd glanced quickly behind him, and seen Alice's shoulders relax a little.

'I came back with Sarah as she didn't feel well,' he'd said, turning again to Thomas. 'And Alice came, too, in case Sarah needed a nurse's help.'

There'd been a movement of air as Alice walked past him. Without a backward glance, she went up to Thomas. 'Can I get you anything, Thomas?' she'd asked, and she'd rested her hand on Thomas's arm.

There'd been an unmistakable tremor in her voice, and he'd held his breath.

Thomas had stared at Alice intently. Then he'd pushed her hand away, turned from her without a word, and followed Sarah into the house. Alice had trailed behind him.

He'd released his breath, and gone quickly after them.

Fear had sat at his side throughout the lunch, during which Sarah had stayed in her room feigning sickness, and also throughout the journey home, which had been completed in deafening silence.

They'd left Chorton immediately after lunch, pleading Sarah's ill health as the reason for their rapid departure, with Louisa and Christopher in the back of the silent car, their faces sullen with resentment at having to leave Chorton earlier than they'd expected.

But the silence had been a relief to him as it had given him time to think, to work out a story before they reached home.

But in the end, he hadn't had to say anything.

Sarah went straight to her room as soon as they reached the house. She didn't come down for supper, and she hadn't emerged at all during the evening. When he'd finally climbed the stairs to go to bed, he'd found, as he'd expected, that the bedroom door was closed against him, and he'd gone straight to the guest room as was his habit when he returned late from the Club.

All through the night, wakeful and restless, he'd alternated in his mind's eye between an image of Alice's frightened face, and a montage of everything that Sarah had brought into his life since they'd married.

And as the thin watery light of morning slithered between the shutters, one thing had begun to stand out very clearly.

Much as he hated to admit it to himself, his state of panic was induced in part by the prospect of his pleasant life coming to an end, and he absolutely did not want that. Not even if losing his present comforts meant that he could live openly with Alice. And he knew that in spite of his affection for Alice, and strong attraction to her, he intended to fight as hard as he could to save his marriage.

What he dearly wanted, he'd finally seen with the utmost of clarity, was to carry on living with Sarah, and being a father to his children.

But it wasn't that he'd deliberately lied to Alice.

In the heat of their passion, he'd meant it when he'd said that he wished they could always be together. And if things had been very different, that might have been what he would've chosen.

But things *weren't* different.

Not in the real world.

In the real world, choosing Alice would mean the end of a marriage that had given him a comfortable life, a splendid house, two lovely children, and the support of Linford & Sons. The company was sufficiently respected that his position at the bank was guaranteed for as long as he wanted without him ever having to prove his worth. And it would mean the end of his standing among the people he knew and valued.

It would also mean leaving a beautiful woman who, despite a tendency to nag, was a wife of whom any man could be proud.

And it wasn't just that walking away from his marriage would terminate all its benefits, and heap shame upon him, it would also involve revealing the truth about his affair with Alice.

With luck, he'd been wrong in thinking that Thomas suspected the truth.

Almost blind with fear by the time he'd got back from the walk, he could have easily been mistaken when he thought he saw hurt as well as anger on Thomas's face. Hopefully, Thomas remained in ignorance of what his wife had been doing with his own brother, and thought that the obvious estrangement between him and Sarah yesterday was the result of a totally different issue.

There'd been no reason for Thomas to suspect that Alice had been involved.

His heart beat faster. Did he truly believe that Thomas was unaware of the truth, or was that just what he fervently hoped?

If Thomas really did know about the affair – and he could hardly bring himself to think that could be the case – it would have a devastating effect on Thomas's life. And he would have incurred Joseph's everlasting wrath.

He'd seen first-hand what Joseph could do when angered. He'd shunned his own daughter for marrying a German, and he'd come down unbelievably hard on Lily because he didn't think her good enough for his son, Robert! If Thomas's suffering was increased because of him, Joseph would punish him, and that was for sure.

But to his surprise, it wasn't primarily his fear of Joseph that had determined him to fight to save his marriage. Nor was it that he didn't want to lose all the things that made his life so enjoyable, although that thought was powerful in his mind. It was that in the past twenty-four hours, he'd discovered that his home, his children, his relationship with his wider family and, most of all, with Sarah, were genuinely the most important things in his life.

In truth, they were far more important to him than Alice.

If discarding Alice, and putting up with Sarah's bossiness and complaints about his lack of ambition, were the sacrifices he had to make to keep what he had, then so be it – it was a small price to pay. The alternative of stepping hand in hand with Alice into an unknown abyss suddenly held absolutely no appeal.

Now that he knew without any doubt what he wanted, his priority was to secure it, and he might as well begin at once – hiding in bed, scared to emerge, wasn't going to get him anywhere. He took a deep breath, threw back the bedclothes, got up and walked across to the dressing room in the corner.

* * *

Lying in bed, Sarah heard the guest room door close behind Charles, and the sound of his footsteps going down the stairs. She didn't move. The bedside clock was loud in the heavy silence, ticking off the minutes since she'd seen Charles together with Alice.

It was just a kiss, he'd said, and he'd tried to brush if off. It didn't mean anything.

But she'd known he was lying – it had been so much more than that.

In the split second before she'd screamed at them from the top of the stile, she'd seen how they'd looked at each other – the expression in their eyes, the way they were drinking each other in. And in that instant, she'd known the truth.

And now, in a few moments, she'd have to get up, get dressed, go downstairs and eat the breakfast that Mrs Garner had set out. And anguished though she was, she'd have to act in front of the servants as if nothing had happened. And when the children came down, she'd have to keep up the pretence that all was normal until they'd left for school.

Most importantly, she mustn't break down. And she mustn't lose face.

No one must know that Charles had just had – maybe was still having – a sordid affair with his brother's wife. At least, not until she'd made up her mind what to do with her discovery.

She, who'd always known her mind in the past, on this occasion had no idea how to proceed. The discovery had stultified her ability to think. She, who'd always seen herself as a strong person, ever in control, and with a clarity of vision, now felt so distraught, so confused, so betrayed, that she could no longer see the way forward.

She turned on to her side.

But thinking about it, the issue was not what she should do, but how she now felt about Charles.

Was she grieving at his betrayal – for grief it was – because she loved him, or was her anguish merely born out of hurt pride? She'd always assumed that she loved him – after all, they were married – but she'd never actually questioned it. Not until now.

But while she was suffering so, she couldn't see clearly how to answer her question.

And there was another question, too. Whatever she felt about Charles, could she put this behind her? In other words, could she ever trust him again?

And also, did she want him to stay or move out?

She didn't know the answers. She hadn't yet thought it through – it was all too raw.

All she knew was that she didn't want to speak to him. Not yet. They'd obviously have to talk at some point, but before they did, she must work out exactly what she wanted. And before she could know that, she'd need to clarify her thoughts.

But whatever her decision, if he was downstairs waiting for her, and the servants were there, too, she'd have to speak to him. She dreaded the thought, but she wouldn't be able to avoid it.

She strained to hear if he'd already sat down to breakfast.

And then she heard the front door slam. He'd clearly left without breakfast, she realised with relief, so, he, too, wasn't ready to talk.

She felt herself relax a little.

Now that he was out of the house, it gave her time to prepare herself for when they broke the silence between them. Above all, she mustn't appear weak. Tears rushed to her eyes. Oh, how could Charles do that to her? How could he destroy their marriage in this way?

It showed how little she'd really known the man she'd married.

If she'd been asked two days ago if he'd do such a thing, she'd have laughed at the very thought of it. Not Charles, she'd have said. He'd never have the guts to cheat on her. Not the rather lazy man she'd married, who lacked impetus and ambition, who always took the path of least resistance, who had to be pushed into taking the smallest initiative. Not Charles, who lacked the energy to betray her, she would have said with complete confidence.

But he *had* betrayed her.

And what's more, with Alice.

A pretty girl, yes, but from a very humble background, and one who'd had little education. Not Alice's fault, she realised, and she'd done a great deal with the little she had, but nevertheless, Alice had married into a family that automatically bestowed on her both status and financial security for life. It was bewildering that she would risk all that for a fling with someone like Charles.

And furthermore, to sleep with the husband of the woman who'd taken Alice under her wing, invited her out to tea, helped to put her at her ease with the family. How could Alice have repaid her in such a cruel way?

She mentally shook herself – this brooding was getting her nowhere. Now that Charles was out of the house, she must get up. She'd think more clearly downstairs. And apart from that, she mustn't arouse the suspicions of the staff or the children.

The children! She put her hand to her head in abject despair. Heaven knows what any hint of their father's betrayal would do to the children. They must be shielded from the consequences as much as humanly possible.

She jumped out of bed, washed quickly, dressed in the first outfit that came to hand, and went downstairs.

As she opened the door to the breakfast room, she made a huge effort to compose her face for the moment she saw Louisa and Christopher, but neither was there.

'They've already gone,' Mrs Garner told her, coming into the room behind her with a rack of hot toast. 'They left early for school.' She put the rack on the table and left the room.

Sarah sat down, took a piece of the toast and spread it with a thick layer of marmalade.

What should she do after breakfast, she mused as she bit into the toast. She'd been planning to attend one of her charity committee meetings that morning, but certainly didn't have the strength to face it – they'd just have to manage without her.

She probably ought to begin with a bath, she decided. She'd had only the swiftest of washes that morning and had dragged a brush through her hair. She was usually so well-groomed that anyone who saw her looking like that, so tired and so unkempt, would know that something serious was amiss. And experience had taught her that if she was well turned out, she felt more confident and more in control. So that's what she would do – she'd have a bath, don a smart outfit and put on a little rouge.

When she was more formally dressed, it would help her clarify her thoughts about the future. And when she'd done that, she'd know what to say to Charles when he came home.

If he came home.

Maybe he wouldn't.

She bit into her toast again, and wondered how she'd feel if he didn't come back. But the truth was, she felt so overwhelmed with anguish about what had happened that she didn't really know.

28

TWO HOURS LATER

Sarah heard the maid open the front door, and a moment later, close it again.

Charles must be home.

A glance at the gilt clock on the mantelpiece showed her that it was two hours since she'd had her bath. She realised in surprise that she'd been sitting there all that time, her book unopened on her lap, the cup of coffee given her by Mrs Garner, untouched.

She placed her book on the table, got up from her chair, smoothed down her skirt, and turned to face the door as Charles opened it. He stood a moment in the doorway, staring at her, hesitation mixed with anxiety. Then he came into the room, closed the door behind him and walked slowly towards her.

Standing beside the fireplace, he faced her, visibly fearful.

'I didn't know if I'd be welcome,' he said, putting his hand on the mantelpiece as if to steady himself.

'You're not.' She glanced at the grandfather clock in the corner of the room. 'Shouldn't you be at the bank?'

'I made an excuse. I couldn't face it. Not when I didn't know what you were thinking. Nor how I could make this right.' He slid his hand along the mantelpiece and stepped closer to her. 'We need to talk, Sarah. We could get out of the house – go for a walk and have lunch somewhere. Or the other way round.'

'What's wrong with talking here and now?' She heard herself sounding shrill, and coughed. 'After all, the children are at school and the servants are busy,' she said, steadying her tone of voice.

He nodded. 'If that's what's you want, then that's what we'll do.' He went and sat in the armchair opposite. He nodded towards her chair. 'Why don't you sit down?'

She lowered herself on to the chair, her back ramrod-straight.

He leaned forward, his elbows resting on his knees. 'I'm so very sorry, Sarah.'

'Sorry for what? For wrecking yesterday for me? For lying to me on countless occasions for I don't know how long? For making a fool of me? For betraying me in the first place, and then continuing to do so? For behaving worse than despicably with your brother's wife – your sister-in-law, of all people?'

'Sarah—'

'Don't Sarah me!' she said, her voice cold. 'How long has this been going on? And I want the truth. And don't say that yesterday was the first time, as I'd know you were lying.'

'Three, maybe four times over the past few weeks. But it was more or less over before this weekend. It's just that when we found ourselves alone yesterday, one thing rather led to another.'

'Oh, for Christ sake, Charles – credit me with some intelligence! It just so happened that when I came upon you yesterday, about to rut like animals, your sordid affair was actually over. Is that what you truly expect me to believe?' Her voice rose.

'I suppose not,' he said quietly.

'So how did you get your act together, so to speak? And there'll have been a lot of acting involved, won't there? You must have lied to me and lied to the bank about where you were going when you went off for this… this liaison. And she must have lied to Thomas, your brother! Lying's a form of acting, isn't it? And trying not to let me see that you were almost certainly thinking of her when you were with me. That's acting, too, isn't it?'

'I'm truly sorry, Sarah.'

'Sorry's no more than a word.' She stood up, knocking against the table as she did so. Her coffee spilled over the side of the cup. 'I can't bear to look at you – you make me sick. I want you to go.'

Charles rose quickly to his feet.

'We've not started talking yet, and we must. Let's take a walk. Please, Sarah.' He leaned towards her, the palms of his hands upturned in a gesture of pleading. 'I'm sure we can overcome this if we talk it through. Alice is in the past. I'm desperately ashamed of what happened, and I bitterly regret it. But it didn't mean a thing, and it's over. All that matters now is the future – our future together, just you, me and the children.'

'I'm not sure we've got a future, Charles.'

'Let's walk across Green Park and try to clear our heads in the fresh air. We've built so much together. Don't throw it all away for a moment of madness on my part. I've been such a fool, and I know that. It will never, ever happen again, I promise you. I love you, Sarah. I can't bear the thought of losing you.'

She met eyes that were red-rimmed, and pleading.

'Don't imagine that being surrounded by trees and birds will make any difference, Charles. The facts will still remain the same. We'll talk here,' she said icily. She sat back down again, and Charles did, too.

Silence fell heavily between them.

'You're very quiet,' he said after a few minutes, his tone both anxious and questioning.

'That's because I'm thinking.'

'About what?'

She stared at him in scorn and disbelief. 'What do you think? I've been trying to make sense of what you told me, trying to understand why it happened. Trying to work out what to do next.'

He reddened. 'What are your thoughts so far?'

'Why did you need to go to bed with someone else? I think that's what I want to understand. Why, Charles?'

He shrugged. 'Lots of men of my age have a moment of madness.'

She shook her head. 'That's feeble, as well as unconvincing. I thought you were better than that. You're barely forty so you can hardly blame your weakness on age. And you can hardly claim to be recapturing your lost youth when you haven't yet lost it.'

'I've no other explanation.'

'Don't be so stupid! Of course, you have. You know your own mind.'

'Stupid. That's what you think of me, Sarah, isn't it?' he said, bitterness edging into his voice. 'Well, perhaps that's the reason you're looking for. According to you, I'm stupid, lack ambition, and found wanting in other ways. You're always doing me down. How d'you think that makes me feel?'

'I obviously didn't mean that you were literally stupid.'

'I don't think it's obvious at all,' he retorted. 'I know exactly what you think of me – you tell me often enough. You tell me when we're alone, when we're with the children, when we're with the family. You're always belittling me. Don't you realise that if you continually proclaim loud and clear that someone is a failure, it will eventually corrode that person's self-confidence? Is it any wonder that I turned to someone who appeared to think very highly of me?'

'So, it's my fault, is it?' Tears of anger filled her eyes. 'You go to bed with your sister-in-law and it's all *my* fault! Do you intend to accept any responsibility at all for your actions?'

He put his hands to his head. 'Of course, I do. I'm not saying that it's entirely your fault that I had an affair – of course, it isn't. It's *my* fault, and I fully accept that. But some of it is down to you, too. D'you think I'd have so much as looked at anyone else if you hadn't regularly scorned me as you did? You're beautiful, you're clever, you're capable of turning your hand to anything, and you're the mother of my children. We have a lovely house and a good life. Why would I have looked at Alice, or at anyone else for that matter, if I hadn't felt driven to it?'

She heard a tinge of uncertainty in her dismissive laugh. 'I didn't drive you to anything.'

He moved slightly forward on his chair. 'Oh, but you did, Sarah. Maybe not consciously, but on some level. The way that Thomas treated Alice gave me the opportunity to see myself in a better light. I took advantage of it and offered her friendship, and I tried to comfort and reassure her when he'd been harsh. After all, we didn't want her to leave Thomas – he needs her. To my surprise, she started looking up to me with a sort of respect and admiration. I hadn't intended this, but I suppose I was flattered. Yes, it's as simple as that, I was flattered. And I felt that I was helping her, and that made me important to her. I can't remember when I last felt important to you, it's so long ago.'

She felt her cheeks pale beneath the rouge.

'Be fair, Sarah,' he said quietly. 'Can you say, in complete honesty, that you don't frequently nag and criticise me?'

She hesitated. 'Well, I did mention to Nellie a while ago that I was afraid I lectured you rather too much, and I told Alice, too, I think. When we had tea together.' She pulled a handkerchief from her sleeve, and clutched it tightly.

He gestured with his hands. 'There you are, then. And

because of the way that made me feel, I was in a vulnerable state of mind and responsive to Alice's open admiration. It was nothing more than that, and it's over now.'

He leaned still further forward.

'Please, don't jettison our whole marriage because of my moment of weakness,' he said, his voice taking on an urgency. 'We've built so much between us. Look at Louisa and Christopher – they're lovely children. We must never do anything to hurt them. Were we to separate, or divorce – God forbid – the public disgrace would stick to them, as well as to us.' He paused, and straightened up. 'I desperately want to put this behind us, Sarah. Do you think that's possible? I suppose what I'm really asking is if you think you'll be able to forgive me.'

She looked him in the face. 'The worst thing is, and this has been going through my mind since you left this morning, I'm not sure that I'll ever be able to trust you again,' she said, her voice shaking.

'I promise, you will! I'd never do such a thing again. Please, please, forgive me. I promise you on the lives of just about everyone I hold most dear, I'll never betray you again. You *can* trust me.'

She twisted her handkerchief in her fingers. 'But that's it – I'm not sure that I can. And you have to be able to trust your husband. Unless, of course, you're willing to turn a blind eye to his philandering, which I'm not. It's nothing to do with forgiveness. I don't even know what forgiveness means. Do I say I forgive you and it doesn't matter that you slept with Alice? Well, that wouldn't be true – of course, it matters. Or do we pretend it never happened? Which is impossible – such knowledge can't be mentally deleted.'

He ran his hand across his forehead. 'So, what are you saying?'

'That talking about forgiveness is meaningless and irrelevant. The question is, can I live with what happened and bring myself to trust you again? If I can't, I'd never have any peace of mind, and even divorce would be preferable to that, shameful though it would be.'

'You *will* be able to trust me again. I swear to you. Don't let this one foolish aberration destroy our marriage. I love you, Sarah,' he said, his voice rising in desperation. Then he paused, and his shoulders sagged. 'Forget trust and all that, I suppose it comes down to whether or not you still love me, fool that I am,' he said quietly. 'Do you?'

She shook her head in despair. 'I don't know, Charles – I wish I *did*. It's all so painful that I don't know what I feel about anything at the moment.'

'Then I beg you, don't do anything rash. At least, give me a chance to prove my love for you, and to show you how much I regret my actions. Please, Sarah.'

She stared at the floor in front of her. 'The only way I'm going to be able to come to a decision is if we spend some time apart,' she said at last. 'I accept that my attitude towards you may have contributed to what you did, but that's in the past. I need time on my own to consider the future. I think it's best for now if you move out—'

They heard a short, indrawn gasp from the doorway.

Louisa stood there holding the door handle, her face ashen. Behind her, halfway up the stairs, Christopher was clutching the banister, staring towards them, a look of confusion on his face.

'Why aren't you in school?' Sarah asked sharply.

'Christopher was sick. I said I'd walk him home.'

Sarah glanced up towards Christopher. 'I'm sorry you're not feeling well, darling,' she called to him. 'Go upstairs and let Nanny take care of you,' He hesitated a moment, and then ran up the rest of the stairs. She watched until he was out of sight, and then looked back at Louisa. 'It was kind of you to come back with Christopher, but you must return to school now. You can get a glass of milk from Mrs Garner first, though, and a biscuit.'

Louisa didn't move.

'Did you hear what I said, Louisa?'

'I'm not going anywhere till you and Daddy stop arguing.' Louisa thrust out her lower lip.

Sarah stood up and took a step towards her daughter. 'It's not your place to issue ultimatums, young lady!'

Charles moved forward, and put a restraining hand on Sarah's arm. 'All parents argue at times, Lou. It's nothing to worry about. Now do as Mummy said. Get yourself something to drink and then go back to school.'

Louisa looked directly at Charles. 'You'll be here when I get home, won't you, Daddy? You've got to promise you will be. I don't want you to leave.' She glanced at Sarah. 'You're not to make him leave. I'll never forgive you if you do. Promise that Daddy will be here when I get home.'

'This is none of your business, Louisa,' Sarah said sharply.

'Yes, it is. I'm not a baby any longer – I'm twelve now. Everything is *your* fault. You're always moaning at Daddy, and you're always moaning at me.'

Sarah took a step forward. 'Be quiet! I can't imagine what the servants are thinking! Your father and I were in the middle of a private conversation, and we've no intention of resuming it while you're in the house. Kindly have some milk, and then go. And I don't want to hear another word from you.'

Louisa glared at her. 'Promise me that Daddy will be here tonight,' she repeated.

Sarah hesitated.

'Promise.'

'I promise. Now I insist you get off to school.'

Louisa pointedly turned her back on Sarah. 'I'll see you tonight, Daddy,' she said, and she left the room and went towards the kitchen.

Charles went across and closed the door, and then returned to his armchair. Both sat in silence until they heard the front door close behind Louisa.

Charles waited, scarcely able to breathe.

'I've changed my mind,' she said at last, her face stony. 'You have Louisa to thank for that. I'm prepared to try to live with this.'

He felt a huge sense of relief surge through him. He covered his mouth with his hand, and drew in a few deep breaths.

'I'm allowing you to stay partly to avoid the shame of a broken marriage, but mostly for the children's sake. Louisa's made her position very clear, and I imagine that Christopher would feel the same. And I'm doing so also for Joseph and the family. I have a lot of respect for your family, and I've no wish to cause them embarrassment.'

'Thank you, Sarah,' he said, feeling weak and shaky.

'Furthermore, I care about Thomas. Under that rude exterior is a desperately vulnerable, insecure man. He's been through enough already, and I wouldn't want to see him hurt any more. I think we can assume that he's completely unaware of your deception, and that's how it must stay. But if I ever, for so much as one minute, have reason to think you're involved with Alice again, or with anyone else, that will be the end of us, disgrace or not. I hope that's clear.'

'It is. Never again.'

'And one last thing. We both agree that you've behaved abominably, and until I've fully come to terms with this, you'll sleep in the spare room. Is that understood?'

'Of course, it is. I'll do anything you say, no matter what it is. I know how wrong I've been, and I regret what I've done from the bottom of my heart. I'm so very sorry, Sarah.'

'And I'm sorry, too,' she said. 'I'm not absolving you from blame,' she added, her voice slightly softening. '*You're* responsible for your actions, not me. But I'm sorry that I undermined you in the way I did, and I promise that will change.'

'You've the right to do whatever you want – I deserve it. Thank you. You can be sure that I'll never betray you again, and that I'll do everything possible to earn back your trust.'

29

THAT SAME MORNING

His good hand gripping the top of his chair, Thomas was standing in his office, facing the door when it creaked open and Alice entered.

At the icy contempt in his eyes, her steps faltered. She clutched her bag closer to her chest, her knuckles white.

'Poor Alice, I feel for you,' he said, his voice solicitous. 'This must all be such a worry for you. You'll be frantic to learn what's been happening in Knightsbridge, but you won't know how to find out.'

'What are you talking about?' she asked, her heart racing.

She pressed her feet harder to the ground, trying to stop her legs from shaking.

'Why, about Sarah discovering you with my brother yesterday, of course!' he exclaimed in feigned amazement. 'It's only natural that you'll want to know whether he's leaving Sarah to set up home with you.' Shaking her head, she opened her mouth to speak. With his injured hand, he gestured her to remain silent. 'No, silly me – my mistake. You won't have been wondering if he's going to leave Sarah – you'll have been assuming he is.'

'I don't know what you're talking about, Thomas,' she cried out, fear making her voice break.

He grabbed his stick from beside the chair and took a few awkward steps towards her.

'Don't lie to me, Alice. You demean yourself. I haven't the slightest doubt that you've been congratulating yourself since the day you first opened your legs to my brother that I'd never realise what was going on. Poor unsuspecting Thomas, you'll have said to each other, as you curled up in your love-nest. And I'm sure there's a love-nest somewhere – our Charles doesn't like discomfort and I can't see him fumbling behind a tree like a dog.'

'You're wrong. I—'

'Poor Thomas hasn't got a leg, you thought,' he continued, cutting through her words, 'and there are bits missing from his hand, which means he hasn't got a brain, or eyes, either. Lucky us. We can do anything we want. His wife can even fornicate with his brother and get away with it.'

Her mouth fell open. She stared at him.

He took another step towards her, and his voice took on a smooth, soothing tone. 'Oh, I'm sorry. I shouldn't use such a word in front of my lady wife, should I? Not even if she *is* fucking my brother. Yes, my own brother!' he screamed into her face, and he straightened up.

She let her bag fall to the floor, and put her hands to her ears.

'Did you actually think I hadn't noticed anything amiss yesterday? That I hadn't seen the hurt and anger in Sarah's face as she came towards me, or the panic in Charles's eyes, or the way you looked at them both in a mixture of fear and uncertainty? Did you really think I wouldn't guess why Sarah chose to stay in her room throughout lunch, and why they all left immediately afterwards? Come on, Alice.'

Alice felt cold. 'I don't know what you're talking about,' she said, struggling to hold her voice steady. 'Sarah wasn't well and that's why she didn't have lunch, and it's the reason why they went home early. That's what they said.'

He leaned towards her. 'Well, they lied, then, didn't they?' he mouthed slowly, as if talking to someone with limited understanding. 'And you're lying now,' he said sharply. 'Pretending you believe that pathetic excuse. Surely you can't think I'm that blind and stupid.'

'I don't think you're blind and stupid at all.'

'That's good. Because it's not poor blind Thomas you should be sorry for – it's poor blind Alice.' He gave a mirthless laugh. 'That's right. You're the one who's blind, not me.'

She looked up at him, her heart hammering in her chest. 'What d'you mean?'

'You couldn't see what was in front of you. You heard his words, and because they were what you wanted to hear, you believed them. Poor gullible you. You don't really know the first thing about my brother, do you? Well, let me enlighten you – Charles is a bloody coward.'

'Is this about the war again? If it isn't, I don't really know what you're talking about.'

'You'll find out soon enough. Poor innocent Alice, blind to the fact that Charles doesn't have one iota of guts in his body. The idea that he would leave a woman like Sarah to set up house with you is laughable. He'd never voluntarily give up his safe, comfortable life. Not our Charles. He'll have been fighting all day to stop Sarah from kicking him out. He'll have been down on his knees, begging forgiveness from her, willing to pay any price to keep her.' Pausing, he raised his eyebrows knowingly. 'And what do you think that price might be?'

'I don't know,' she whispered.

He took a step closer to her. 'It'll be ditching *you*, Alice. And don't think he'd attempt to carry on with you in secret, because he wouldn't. Being caught by Sarah will have frightened him to his craven core. Everything will have shrivelled, and he won't be able to play, or even want to play, with fire again. Not even if you offered yourself to him stark naked.'

Alice gestured her helplessness. 'You're wrong, Thomas. Truly you are. Clearly you think there's something between Charles and me, but there isn't, and never has been. We're just good friends.'

For a long moment, he stared at her, unspeaking, his expression hard. 'That you're still lying somehow makes it even worse,' he said finally. 'It's an insult to my intelligence, Alice, a real insult. To expect me to believe your pathetic words rather than the evidence of my own eyes, just shows the contempt in which you hold me.'

'I don't hold you in contempt, I—'

'I've long sensed that Charles felt attracted to you, as you well know, and noticed the way you sucked up to him. And I saw yesterday where that attraction has led you both. If you own up, you'll at least accord me a degree of respect. And if you harbour any hope at all of this marriage surviving, you must be honest with me. It's the very least I deserve, don't you think?'

She bit her lip in indecision, wavering between admitting the truth or continuing to plead ignorance.

He could be bluffing. How could he know for sure?

But then she saw the ice in the depth of his eyes, and she knew that it wouldn't matter what she said by way of denial – nothing would make him believe she was innocent. Perhaps she ought to admit to the truth.

But the trouble was, the things he'd said about Charles had shaken her, and although she didn't believe a word of it, she wouldn't want to leave Thomas before she'd spoken to Charles.

Her stomach gave a violent lurch.

All along, she'd taken it for granted that she'd be leaving Thomas for Charles. But faced with the possibility that it was actually going to happen, is that what she really wanted – to end her marriage and begin a new life with Charles?

The reality of leaving Thomas – of walking away from him, perhaps never to see him again – overwhelmed her with sudden force.

A sharp pain cut through her.

In a moment of blinding self-realisation, she knew it was Thomas she loved, not Charles.

She'd loved him since the day she'd first set eyes on him.

During the four years of their marriage, there'd been times when he'd been so difficult to live with that she'd lost sight of the depth of her feelings for him. But the Thomas she'd fallen in love with in the hospital was still there, and would eventually emerge. He just had to work through the stages of anger, grief, self-blame and the blaming of others. And when he'd done that, they'd be happy again, as in the early days of their life together.

Oh, how could she have been so stupid as to let herself lose sight of that?

If she went off to live with Charles, she wouldn't be there when the old Thomas returned.

And she desperately wanted to be.

If she was going to have any chance of saving her marriage, she'd have to do as he'd said and confirm what he knew to be the truth. And that would prove to him that she was determined henceforth to be honest at all times with him.

'All right, then. You're correct, Thomas,' she said quietly, her eyes on the floor. 'I slept with Charles, and I'm truly sorry. I was flattered by the attention he paid me, and I finally gave in to his wishes.' She looked up at him, her blue eyes pleading with him.

'You've no idea how deeply I regret what I did. I'm going to do my very best to make it up to you. I love you with all my heart, and I promise I'll never again give you cause to doubt me.'

'Well, that's a start, I suppose.'

'It's just that you were so unkind at times, and Charles seemed to be there whenever I felt really low, saying all the right things. I appreciated the sympathy he showed, and one thing led to another.'

He shook his head. 'Oh, dear. That's not a good continuation, I'm afraid. I won't have you blaming *me* for your sins. And they *are* sins – two sins at the very least. The sin of adultery, and the sin of committing that act with your husband's brother. Your behaviour is *your* responsibility, and no one else's. But of course, Charles, too, will have spent the day blaming someone else, and that someone will have been you, so maybe you've caught the tendency from him.'

'I'm sorry,' she repeated. 'I genuinely regret what I did, and that I've hurt you as I've done. I truly love you, Thomas. I don't know what else I can say.'

He stepped back. 'That's because there's nothing to be said. I don't want a wife who's willing to lie on her back for someone other than her own husband, just because a few kind words have been whispered to her. What happens if Joseph remarks that you look pretty in a dress, for example? I can't imagine what Maud would say if you promptly got down in the gutter, pulled up your skirt and spread your legs for her husband!'

Her eyes filled with tears. 'Please forgive me, Thomas, I beg you. The fling with Charles is finished – nothing will ever happen again, I promise you.'

'At least, you're right about that. Because you won't be here. You'll be back up north in Lancashire with your mother, or anywhere else that you choose.'

She gave a slight start.

'To be very clear, dear Alice, I want you out of my house before the end of the day. The very sight of you revolts me.'

She felt the last drop of blood drain from her face.

She took a step forward, and stared at him in panic. 'But I love you, Thomas. You have to believe that. I really do. I was weak. I gave in to Charles, mistaking my gratitude for his kindness for feelings of love. But I didn't love him. It's you I love, and I always have from the moment I first saw you in the hospital.'

He looked at her in exaggerated reproof. 'Oh, dear, that's not a good line, either, Alice, asking me to forgive you for sleeping with my brother on the grounds that you didn't love him. It rather makes you sound like a filthy slut, don't you agree?'

She gasped. 'Don't say that.'

He moved closer to her. 'Why not? It's true. You're soiled goods for the worst of reasons, and you admit it. Well, I don't want soiled goods in my house. One ravaged body in this place is more than enough. You'll leave this afternoon.'

'No!' she cried out. 'Please, no!'

'I'll give you the money to get to your mother's or wherever you want to go, and a bit extra to live on till you find a job,' he went on. 'But I never want to see you after today, or hear from you again. If you find someone else stupid enough to marry you, I'll do whatever's needed to free you. But your solicitor must contact Walter, not me. Our marriage is over. When you're ready to leave, you can see yourself out.'

He turned away from her, went back to the chair facing the sash window and sat down. He propped his stick against the side of the chair, folded his arms and stared in front of him.

'But who will look after you?'

'I'll hire someone,' he said, his gaze on the street outside. 'It's what I would've done if I hadn't met you. Now, unless the door's moved in the last few minutes, it's behind you and it's open. Go through it and get out of my life.'

She hesitated. 'I'm so sorry, Thomas.'

He didn't move.

Trying to hold herself with dignity, she turned slowly, went out of the room and closed the door behind her.

Sitting alone in his office, he stared with unseeing eyes at the line of run-down shops beyond the plane trees, silent tears falling unchecked down his cheeks.

30

KNIGHTSBRIDGE

That same day

Daylight was starting to fade, but still Alice stood at the end of the road, her two suitcases at her feet, in a dark blue coat that was too warm for the weather, but which it was easier to wear than carry. Her gaze never wavering, she stared at the house halfway down the road where Charles and Sarah lived, waiting for him to appear.

There was a very slight risk, she realised, that Sarah and the children might leave the house before he did and come in her direction, either by car or on foot. And if they did that, they might see her backed into the doorway of the dress shop. But it was a chance she had to take. She couldn't think where else to go.

And after all, if they *did* see her, what would it matter? Sarah must know by now that she was the woman Charles loved, not Sarah. It would soon be Alice and Charles, not Sarah and Charles.

It was no longer Alice and Thomas.

Her stomach did a violent somersault.

Yes, she had pleaded with Thomas to let her stay and told him repeatedly how much she loved him. But was that true?

She wouldn't really have risked losing Thomas if she hadn't genuinely loved Charles. Surely she wouldn't. Not really.

Her heart beat fast.

Her pleas to Thomas must have been the anguished cries of someone consumed by fear – the fear of being cast adrift into an unknown future, and of losing the security she'd become used to. She'd panicked in the face of Thomas's anger, and unable to think clearly, she'd done the only thing she could – desperately assured Thomas that she loved him.

But now that she was away from his scornful contempt, she could see that it was Charles she truly loved.

It had to be.

She couldn't have been so blind to her true feelings that she'd betrayed the man she deeply loved, and lost him. A wave of anguish shot through her.

She brushed it aside. Of course, she hadn't.

It was true that she'd fallen in love with Thomas the moment she'd seen him, but since then, he'd altered beyond all recognition. Instead of improving in spirits, he'd allowed his disabilities, and the resentment he felt towards his brothers, to infect his mind, and that had changed him.

The man she'd originally loved no longer existed.

And she'd come to love Charles – Charles, who'd unfailingly shown her kindness and consideration.

Whatever Thomas had said about Charles never willingly leaving Sarah and his comfortable life for her, she knew otherwise. Charles was a good and upright man, and not the sort of person to lie. He'd told her many times that he adored her, and that he wished they could be together forever, and that will have been the truth. And his words were backed up by the fact that he'd bought a house just so they could meet.

Thomas would know how honest his brother was, and he'd just been taunting her with words that sprang from anger and a desire to hurt her. He'd wanted to punish her for the pain she'd inflicted upon him. That pain would have made him lie about Charles. It meant she could safely dismiss from her mind any seeds of doubt he'd planted. She and Charles were going to be together at last, and it was just a matter of time before he came out to her.

And she couldn't be happier.

She swallowed the lump that had come to her throat, and focused again on Charles's house.

Poor Charles, with everything now out in the open, he must be as frantic to be with her as she was to be with him. His delay in joining her must be because he needed to pack his bags and deal with any domestic matters that had to be settled before he left.

That was all it would be.

She glanced anxiously at the house. He must be there. He hadn't been in the Kentish Town house that he'd bought, so where else would he be?

She knew he wasn't at the Kentish Town house because as soon as she'd found herself out on the street, dazed and in shock, with everything she possessed in two suitcases, she'd unthinkingly gone there expecting to find Charles.

After all, Sarah now knew what had been going on behind her back – her awareness had been written across her face on her return from the walk at Chorton, and Thomas had seen it. And Sarah wasn't the sort of person to ignore her husband's betrayal, so Charles would have had to leave Sarah. It had seemed obvious that he'd go to his little house in Kentish Town.

And he'd assume that with Thomas now aware of her betrayal, she'd leave Thomas, and go there, too.

But she'd been wrong about finding Charles at the house.

And for a minute or two, she'd stood in the empty hall, at first feeling lost and disorientated, and then increasingly alarmed as Thomas's words about Charles and cowardice stormed into her mind.

Momentarily engulfed by a wave of fear and panic, she'd managed to calm herself by the realisation that he was surely more likely to be at the Knightsbridge house, where all his clothes and possessions were. And she'd gone quickly there to wait for him.

But she hadn't expected to have to wait for so long.

The front door opened. Relief coursed through her, and she straightened up.

He came out on to the front step, gazed up at the sky, and then glanced down the road in the opposite direction from where she was standing. He was looking for her, she thought, her spirits leaping.

She couldn't see his suitcases, so they must still be inside the house. He was probably just making sure she was there before he picked them up and came out to join her. Excitement started to bubble within her.

And relief.

She pulled her dark blue cloche more firmly on to her head, tucked a fair curl behind her ear, and stepped out from the shop doorway.

He turned and looked in her direction.

Their eyes met across the void, and held. She felt the heat of his gaze on her face. A tremulous smile hovered on her lips.

Then he stepped back into the house, and closed the door firmly behind him.

She didn't move, couldn't move.

Despite the distance between them, she'd seen the shadow of fear in his eyes, followed by deep regret, and then resolve. The door that was shut against her told of his decision.

Thomas had been right! Charles *was* a coward! It had been lies, all lies!

She gave a loud sob.

All the words she'd used to convince herself that it was Charles she loved fell away.

The truth stared her in the face.

Clutching her stomach, she bent over, wracked by an agonising grief. She'd cheated on the man she truly loved with someone who'd merely played with her heart. Oh, what a fool she'd been, what a blind, stupid fool! Thomas had been absolutely right about her.

Charles had taken advantage of the situation she was in.

He'd wanted her body, and he'd known exactly what to say to break down any resistance she might have to the idea of sleeping with him. He would have obviously realised that she'd never give herself to him if she didn't believe he genuinely loved her, so he'd repeatedly told her he did.

She'd never forgive him for that lie.

Or for causing the end of her marriage to Thomas.

She stood there, trembling with anger and misery, desperation and fear building within her. She was completely alone, with no idea what to do or where to go.

Her eyes filling with tears, she thrust her hand into her pocket to find her handkerchief. As she did so, her fingers touched the money that Thomas had given her so that she could return to her family in the North.

'Oh, no,' she cried aloud. 'Not that.'

But she had no choice – she'd have to go back to Lancashire. It was getting dark, and she'd nowhere else to go.

With tears streaming down her cheeks, she took a suitcase in each hand, turned and slowly made her way towards the underground station, her steps heavy. She was about to begin a journey back to her past, back to a life that for many years now, she'd been overjoyed to believe she'd escaped forever.

Lowering her face to her coat sleeve, she wiped her cheeks as she walked forward, a yawning emptiness within.

* * *

Charles sat back in his armchair, listening as Sarah prepared for bed upstairs, padding back and forth between her dressing room and the bedroom. A little later, he heard her check that the bedroom door was firmly closed, and then cross the room to her bed. He imagined her slipping out of her silk peignoir, kicking off her slippers, and sliding between the sheets.

The dark oak frame of the bed creaked, and for the first time since his affair was discovered, he felt himself relax.

Unsurprisingly, she was going to make him wait before she allowed him to climb into her bed, but that day would come, he was sure. Until then, he was just grateful to be in their spare room and not consigned to a hotel, which for a short time he'd feared might be his fate. Or even worse, that he might have been forced to stay in that wretched house in Kentish Town.

At one point, Sarah had seemed frighteningly close to telling him to leave, and to being prepared to endure the stigma of divorce, rather than try to save their marriage. And to his huge surprise, faced with the sudden awareness that he really could be losing her, he'd been overwhelmed by anguish.

In that moment, he'd known for the first time the truth of

what he felt about Sarah, and that he didn't want to live with anyone else but her. Quite simply, over the years of their marriage, he had grown to love his wife, but he hadn't realised, until that instant, quite how much.

He'd been flattered by Alice's admiration, and in his weakness, sensing where the physical pleasure that her respect for him could lead, and enjoying the scene of the chase, he'd got carried away and rather exaggerated to her what he felt for her, while deluding himself somewhat, too. He did genuinely like Alice, and in all honesty, he'd enjoyed sleeping with her, but he'd never loved her.

In the last twenty-four hours, it had suddenly become very clear to him that it was Sarah he truly loved, and always had.

And he couldn't lose her.

Panicking when it looked as if Sarah was about to throw him out, he'd attributed some of the blame for his affair to her constant hectoring.

That accusation must have been put into his mouth by the gods. He'd seen her expression change, and had known at once that this was the line to pursue. But while it had slightly softened her, it hadn't sufficiently swayed her into agreeing that he could stay. He owed her change of heart to his stubborn, outspoken daughter, who had dedicated her life to opposing everything Sarah wanted.

But the fact that Sarah was allowing him to stay was proof that she did still love him.

Had she not, nothing that Louisa had said would've persuaded her to let him remain in the house. And equally, he knew that it was only a matter of time before she would allow him back into her bed.

But never again would he be able to use Sarah's criticisms of him as an excuse for anything. Not that he'd ever want to, of course, he hastily told himself.

Sarah had independent means, and for all that she liked being a Linford, he realised with absolute certainty that she'd never give him a second chance if he strayed again. He knew, too, that although he could rely on Sarah's discretion about his infidelity on this occasion, if he ever did such a thing again, his whole family, and not just Joseph and those immediately concerned, would learn that he had betrayed his own brother – a pretty treacherous way to act by any standards. And if that became known, their allegiance would be to Sarah.

But that wasn't going to happen. Not now that he realised how strongly he still felt for his wife, and how much he desired to be with her.

It was sad about Alice, he thought, as his mind went back to the moment he'd seen her earlier that evening.

He knew his brother very well, and much as he'd tried to kid himself that Thomas hadn't suspected the truth when he'd seen them come back from the walk, he'd never really believed that he hadn't. From the moment he'd caught sight of Thomas's face, and seen the hurt in his eyes, he'd realised that Thomas had guessed about the affair.

And knowing Thomas as he did, he'd been certain that Thomas would throw Alice out of the house. And he'd been equally certain that Alice would come looking for him. Why wouldn't she, after all, given everything he'd said to her over the past year?

But for all that he'd been expecting her to be waiting for him somewhere nearby, the moment he'd actually seen her, he'd felt sheer terror. What if Sarah, or one of the children, had spotted her lurking in the entrance to a shop at the end of the road? It didn't bear thinking about. He certainly couldn't risk going up to her and trying to explain.

Decisively closing the door on the past had been the only way to handle it.

He deeply regretted ever embarking upon the affair, and bringing such grief upon Alice. And he hated himself that he'd had to cause her additional pain by his behaviour towards her that evening. But he'd had no choice. The whole sorry mess had happened, and Alice must be left in no doubt that their liaison was over.

Keeping Sarah was his sole priority.

As he sat in his armchair, thinking how close he'd come to losing everything that truly mattered to him, the palms of his hands felt moist, and he rubbed them against his trousers.

For the rest of his life, he was going to strive hard to prove himself worthy of Sarah's love.

The many accusations she'd hurled at him over the years had been accurate. He *was* lazy, spineless and unambitious. All she'd done was try to encourage him to exploit to the full his opportunities and talents. Without her at his side, he would have been even less of a person than he was.

But from that day on, he resolved, his idle, self-centred days were over. He would do everything he could to make Sarah happy, and to show her in every way possible, how much he appreciated and loved her.

In short, there'd be no more playing around – he was finally going to become the man and husband she deserved.

That was a promise he made to himself.

31

CAMDEN TOWN

The next day

'A whole day's passed and you haven't yet asked for my view of what happened at the weekend,' Walter remarked as they waited for their pudding. 'May I congratulate you, Nellie, on your praiseworthy reticence.'

'You mean about Emily's christening? I thought it went well. Apart from the fact that she screamed throughout, both in the church and in the house, and they all had to sit on their hands to avoid rudely covering their ears,' Nellie said with a rueful laugh.

He smiled. 'No, not that. The trouble between Sarah and Charles.'

She stopped laughing and stared at him. 'What d'you mean? Did I miss something by having lunch alone upstairs? It's just that I was really tired after such a long walk, on top of the christening.'

'I could tell you were – you slept in the car all the way home. Not that I'm complaining about the lack of conversation – just about the snoring.'

They exchanged affectionate smiles.

He straightened his pudding spoon and fork.

'I'm waiting, Walter,' she said, tapping the table with the handle of her cheese knife. 'I'm not letting you change the subject. I want to know what I missed?'

'I shouldn't have said anything.'

'You certainly should.'

He shrugged. 'Sarah and Charles would appear to have quarrelled. Not that they spoke to each other – they didn't. Sarah went straight upstairs after the walk, and didn't come down for lunch. And the four of them left for London immediately after the meal. But something was definitely wrong.'

She bit her lip. 'I wonder what it was. Uncle Charles never argues with Aunt Sarah. He's far too wise for that – he'd certainly lose and he knows it. How strange.'

Walter opened his mouth, and then closed it.

'What were you going to say?'

'Nothing.'

'Yes, you were. I know you, Walter – you never miss a thing. What are you thinking?'

He sat back. 'There must have been something in the air – things didn't seem right between Thomas and Alice, either. Alice is normally so relaxed, and is always comfortable about joining in, but she didn't say a word during lunch. I thought she looked quite nervous, in fact. And Thomas was clearly in a mood. And upset, too, I'd say. Mind you, it's harder to tell with Thomas as he's so often sullen.'

'So you think they, too, quarrelled, and that it could've involved all four of them? Uncle Thomas could have insulted Aunt Sarah, for example. It's the sort of thing he'd do. And Uncle Charles would've been furious if he had.'

'Possibly so. I wouldn't like to put it more strongly than that.'

She put her elbows on the table, and rested her chin on her hands. 'Stop sitting on the fence like a lawyer, Walter, and put it as strongly as you can.'

He smiled at her. 'That's how rumours get started. People say something that's based on assumption, and pass it off as a fact. And that false fact is passed on to someone else, who accepts it as the truth. And so on and so on. We don't know that they quarrelled. It's a supposition. I could be completely mistaken, and they might have just been tired. After all, it'd had been a busy weekend. I should've kept my thoughts to myself.'

She exaggerated a pout. 'I don't like this lawyerly way of speaking. Have you ever thought about becoming a builder?'

He laughed.

'I'm not people, Walter – I'm your wife. You can safely say more. Aunt Sarah's the only one of the family I'd ever confide in, and since you think she might be involved, I'm hardly likely to say anything to her. You can rest assured that your words will go no further than my ears.'

The door opened. Nellie's expression cautioned Walter to wait. The maid came in, placed a bowl of rice pudding in front of each of them, and left.

'You were saying,' she said, picking up her spoon.

'Just that it seemed to me that Charles, Sarah and the children left rather abruptly. And Thomas and Alice also made a hasty departure immediately after lunch. Unusually for them, they'd intended to stay on for tea. I think one might safely deduce that something serious had occurred between them, such as a harsh verbal attack on Sarah or Charles, as you suggested. It's the sort of thing Thomas would do. Alternatively, it could be something to do with Linford & Sons.'

He sank his spoon into his rice pudding.

Nellie sat with her spoon poised above the surface of the pudding, frowning. 'If it's serious, it's most likely to do with money, don't you think?'

'I really don't know, Nellie. The argument, if there were such an argument, could have been about any number of things.' Walter continued eating. Then he suddenly raised his head and listened. 'Did I hear someone at the door just now?'

Nellie quickly finished her pudding.

A moment later, Joseph was shown into the dining-room.

The maid swiftly removed the dishes and left the room as they rose from the table to greet Joseph.

Nellie went forward and kissed her father on the cheek.

'Sit down, both of you,' Joseph said. 'You mustn't let me interrupt your dinner. But it occurred to me that Walter might be thinking of having a brandy at around this time. And if so,' he said, sitting down and angling his chair towards Walter, 'I'll join you, if I may.'

'And so will I,' Nellie said brightly. 'But not for brandy. I'll have a Bucks Fizz without the champagne, please.'

'Are you sure that Emily doesn't need you, Nellie?' Joseph asked with a smile, and indicated the door.

Nellie didn't move. 'Quite sure, thank you. It's why we support that great institution called the nanny.'

Joseph glanced at Walter and raised his eyebrows.

Walter put his elbows on the arms of his chair and brought his fingertips together.

'Nellie will leave us if this is about work or something genuinely private. If it's to do with the family, though, and is something she'll have to know at some point, she might as well stay. If for no reason other than that it'll prevent her from developing a painful ailment in her knees, caused by her getting down on the tiled hall floor and positioning herself at the keyhole in order to listen in.'

Nellie laughed.

Joseph grinned at her. 'I think we've both met our match in your Walter, Nellie. Right, you can stay – it *is* a family matter.'

'We've just been talking about it, in fact,' Nellie said.

Joseph glanced from Nellie to Walter. 'Is that so? And what, exactly, is *it*?'

Nellie opened her mouth to speak.

Walter silenced her with a look. 'I think it better to let your father speak, don't you, Nellie? But first things first.'

He got up, went across the room to the cocktail cabinet, took out two brandy snifters, and poured some brandy into each. When he'd placed them on the table, he poured a glass of orange juice for Nellie, and put it next to her.

'Your health, Joseph,' he said, sitting down and picking up his snifter.

Joseph raised his glass, and took a sip. 'I'm afraid I've got some upsetting news,' he began. 'Thomas has separated from Alice. Apparently, he asked her to leave the house immediately, and for good. I popped over to Kentish Town late this afternoon as I'd been concerned about one or two things over the weekend, and I found Thomas completely alone. Apart from a bottle, I'm sorry to say. And before you ask, he didn't volunteer any further information. He's a proud man and I wasn't going to push him.'

'Of course not,' Walter said.

'He's clearly desperately unhappy at the moment – Alice obviously meant far more to him than he showed – and it's hard to know how best to help him. But the first thing must be to get him some extra help in the house. With personal things. You know what I mean, I'm sure.'

'Poor Uncle Thomas,' Nellie said. 'How awful for him. I'm sure he'd never have sent Alice away without good reason. What a shock. Shall I go and see him this week? It'd be some company for him. What d'you think, Father? I know he's not keen on visitors.'

'It's a kind thought, and you should go. But don't be surprised if he turns you away with a growl. You know what he's like.' Joseph turned slightly towards Walter. 'I'd originally intended to drop in on Sarah and Charles after seeing Thomas, but instead I went home to talk things over with Maud, and we decided I should have a word with you. And here I am.'

'We're always pleased to see you.'

'I know you are, my boy, and I'm grateful.' He coughed. 'Assuming that at some stage, Thomas will want to divorce Alice, I'm keen to know his position. Or the position if she wanted to divorce him. It's as well to be prepared, even if it proves unnecessary.'

'While I've obviously covered the requirements and procedure for divorce during my legal training, this isn't my area of expertise—' Walter began.

'And you don't have to make it so,' Joseph said with a half-smile. 'I'm hoping this is a one-off situation for the family. You don't need to take the approach you did with Property Law in order to get through to me. I'm already on your side.'

Nellie giggled.

Walter smiled. 'I'll bear that in mind, sir. Well, my advice would be that Thomas refrains from doing anything for a year or so. It looks as if the law governing divorce will change before too long. Word is that women will be the main beneficiaries of the changes, but there'll be advantages for men, too. Divorce will become much easier and cheaper, for a start.'

'I hope you're right about that.'

'I think you'll find I am. Sadly, the war gave rise to so many divorces that there's now a huge pressure for change, especially from groups representing women. But that's hardly surprising. Now that female householders over thirty have the vote, they're bound to want to see women put on the same footing as men. And after all, why *should* a woman have to prove cruelty, rape or incest, as well as the adultery? A man doesn't.'

'So, you think he should wait. That's very helpful, son.'

'If he's set on divorce, yes. But whatever the changes that come about in the divorce law, adultery is certain to remain the sole ground for divorce for many more years. And the adultery will still have to be proved, no matter who brings the petition, and that could be problematic. There are alternatives, though.'

'Which are?'

Walter cleared his throat. 'This is a bit delicate, but given Thomas's physical condition when he returned from the war, and the fact that there aren't any children, it might be easier to request a declaration of nullity. It means that the marriage would be considered invalid.'

'Annulment, you say? I hadn't thought of that.'

'Not annulment – a declaration of nullity. They're not quite the same. An annulment is one stage earlier, if you like. Annulment is a form of legal separation that protects the wife's rights. Any children are considered legitimate, but neither party can remarry unless the other dies. I'd advise Thomas to go for nullity from the outset. It means that if he had children, they'd become illegitimate – but he doesn't. Most importantly, with nullity Alice would lose her right to inherit from Thomas. And Thomas would be free to marry again, should he so wish.'

'You *are* clever, Walter, even if it does sound as if you've swallowed a law book,' Nellie said, beaming at him. 'Isn't he, Father?'

Joseph nodded. 'Yes, he is, Nellie. That's extremely helpful, Walter, and it puts my mind at rest. I'm most grateful to you.' He finished his drink. 'And if it isn't too presumptuous of me, I'll have another brandy. Now that we've a strategy in place for Thomas, should it come to it, I'll enjoy this one even more.'

32

WATERFOOT

July 1922

From their vantage point on top of a pile of large boulders, Alice and May stared across the wild, windswept Lancashire moors to the far-distant hills that shimmered purple and blue where they met the horizon. All around them, the air danced with myriad insect wings.

'After being home for a full four weeks, today's the first day I haven't woken up crying. That's a step forward at least, I suppose,' Alice said, and she gave May a weak smile. 'It's thanks to our walks on the moors. There's nothing better for clearing your head.'

'Are there any moors where yer used ter live?'

'Hampstead Heath is probably the closest thing. It's a massive open area that's completely unspoiled. Thomas's nephew, Robert, lives in Hampstead, and the family used to go there for lunch roughly once a month, and then go for a walk over the Heath. But Thomas didn't really enjoy family occasions, and couldn't cope with the walking, so we didn't go very often.'

May looked at her curiously. 'Yer've hardly mentioned Thomas since yer got back.'

'That's because you never stop talking about William, Martin and Susan,' Alice retorted with a laugh. 'But I'm not complaining. I love hearing about them.'

'Yer should try doing for them all day long!'

'I know it must be hard work,' Alice said, 'but you look as if you're thriving on it. A good thing about being back is that I'll be able to watch them grow up. And it's wonderful to see kestrels again,' she added, nodding towards one as it dropped vertically towards a dense thicket of bracken growing near the base of the cluster of boulders. In a single swoop, it grabbed its prey in its talons, and with one swift bite, killed it.

'Ugh! I know they've got ter eat ter live,' May said, shuddering, 'but I hate ter see one animal kill another. And me a farmer's wife, too!'

'People are killing each other all the time,' Alice said quietly. 'And not because they need to live.'

May glanced quickly at her. 'That seems ter be bringing us back ter Thomas, doesn't it? When yer talk about watching the children grow, it sounds as if yer not planning on going back ter him.'

'I'm not. It's over. At least, I think it is. I haven't heard from him so it probably is.'

'You don't look or sound too happy about it.'

Alice sighed. 'To be honest, I haven't a clue what I feel. All the way here on the train, I kept thinking how much I loved Thomas, and that I was going to return to London as soon as possible to try to sort everything out. It's such a mess, you see, and it's all my fault. But now that I've had more time to think about it, I'm not so sure whether to do that. I know that I still love Thomas, but I don't know if he still loves me.'

'But if there's a chance that he does, and if yer want ter be with him, shouldn't yer go and find out?'

'But there're other things to consider, too. Mam and Dad are getting older, for a start. It really hit me when I saw them again after so long, how much they'd aged. They may be fine now, but that won't always be the case. Writing to them as I used to isn't the same as being here with them.'

'They've got good friends and neighbours. Yer don't have ter worry about them.'

'I know that. And also, you're here, too,' Alice went on. 'I hated that time we fell out and didn't see each other for ages, and I'm so glad we made up before I went to London. I really missed you when I was down there. I know Mam always passed on my messages when she saw your mam, but if I go back, it could be another few years before we met again, and I'd hate that. All in all, I'm beginning to wonder if I mightn't be happier forgetting about Thomas, and staying here.'

'And yer might not. D'yer honestly think yer could be happy living up here again, married ter someone local, who'd never in his life been outside the area? Try ter imagine spending the rest of yer life in a small stone house after what yer had in London. Believe me, the novelty would soon wear off.'

'You don't know that.'

'Yes, I do. All yer talked about when yer were little was getting away from here and having a different sort of life. Yer worked hard ter get it, and now that yer know what it's like ter live in a large town and be part of a wealthy family, I can't see how yer could ever come ter terms with living here again. Or why yer'd want to.'

'To be nearer you and my parents, of course.'

May looked at her doubtfully. 'I'd say it's just as well yer don't have ter decide anything for the moment. Not unless you're thinking Thomas might come after yer.'

Alice shook her head. 'He won't.'

'Then there's no rush, is there? When next week comes, and yer start in the draper's in Trickett's Arcade, yer'll get the feel of working up here again, and that might decide yer what ter do. You're reet lucky ter have got that job.'

'I know, and it was a really easy interview, too. All they wanted to know was if I was good with figures. But you have to be, if you're a nurse. I'm hoping to be put in the haberdashery section. I don't much like sewing, and I'd hate to be stuck on fabrics.' She grimaced.

'Just think, yer might meet someone really special while yer working there.'

Alice laughed. 'You don't give up, do you? But you keep forgetting, I'm already married.'

'But maybe not for much longer. If yer no longer together, he'll surely end the marriage. He's got money, hasn't he, so he can get a divorce. All he has ter say is that yer guilty of adultery. Even if it's not true,' she added quickly.

Alice bit her lip. 'I wonder.'

May stretched out her legs and examined her short black leather boots. 'I still think yer should've gone back ter Pike Law Hospital, rather than got a job in a shop. It's a reet shame ter give up on nursing. They've got a maternity unit there now, and there's talk that they're going ter be building a nurses' home, so yer wouldn't have ter do all that travelling.'

Alice shrugged. 'If I got a job in Pike Law again, it'd almost certainly keep me in Waterfoot, but I don't yet know for sure if that's what I want. I think it is, though. And if I decide for certain that I do, I can always ask if there's a vacancy. But for the moment, the shop will suit me fine. I like that it's close to the house, as it means I'll be able to help at home with the chores. Since I can't send money like I did when I was in London, I want to help in other ways.'

'Yer were never one ter sit still.'

'Nor is Mam. It's such a relief that she's no longer at the factory.'

'It must be. When our Gladys told me mam there was a job at the Bates's house, and Mam said she'd rather stay at home and carry on doing the ironing and child-minding, we instantly thought of your mam.'

'And we're really grateful you did. Mam's hours are so much better now. She could still use some help in the house, though. Dad does his best, but there's a limit to what he can do.'

'Well, I hope it turns out ter be what yer want. And by that, I mean everything, and not just the shop. I like having yer back.' May stood up and brushed down her skirt. 'I hate ter say it, but I think we'd better be getting back. I can't expect Ellen ter look after the children for too long.'

Alice rose to her feet. 'D'you like Ellen?'

'She's quite nice. Ronald's brother could've done a lot worse fer himself. And it certainly helps ter have another woman around the place – both fer company, and ter help with the work. It'll be a while before Susan's old enough ter help with the chores. At present, her main goal in life seems ter be ter add ter my work.'

'And I should go, too. I'd like to get the ironing done before Mam gets back. Before we met up, I pegged yesterday's washing on the line, and it'll be ready for ironing.'

With a last gaze across the heather and windberry-covered moorland, they turned and headed back to the path.

* * *

Having dipped the collars of her father's white shirt into the solution of starch she'd prepared, knowing how much her father liked to have a stiff white collar on the shirt that he wore every Sunday, she covered the worn oak table in the centre of the room with a blanket, and began to iron the clothes and bedlinen on top of it.

As she was coming towards the end of the first of the bed sheets, she glanced across at her father, wondering if he might be able to help her fold the sheet when she'd finished it. But he was fast asleep in his chair, his head lolling against his chest, the arm of his jacket hanging empty, and she knew she'd have to manage by herself.

As she started on the next sheet, she realised to her annoyance that the iron had lost the heat from its base, and she'd have to replace the cold cast-iron slab with a hot one.

Sliding open the door in the back of the iron, she removed the cold slab, and replaced it with another one, which she'd earlier put into the fire. She then put the cold slab into the fire to heat up again, picked up the hot iron, and resumed the ironing.

Sadly, she still had the patching and darning to do, she thought, as she finished the ironing, and removed the garments that needed repair from the pile of ironed clothes. Taking the wooden mushroom from the wicker sewing basket and some wool, she picked up the first of her mother's stockings which had a hole in it, sat down in the armchair in the corner of the room, placed the mushroom behind the hole, and started stitching across the hole from one side to the other.

She was good at darning she knew, but the thought of having to repair something or other every week was utterly boring.

And it *would* be every week.

The knees and heels in her mother's all-wool stockings were forever wearing out, and with wool easy to get, and money tight, the stockings were repaired as often as possible. And only when it was truly impossible to darn the feet any more would they join the other stockings that they'd rolled up the wooden table legs to protect the table legs from knocks and damage.

And it wasn't just stockings that needed regular repair. Her dad's jerseys invariably wore through in the elbow of his good arm, and every so often the backsides of his trousers, because of the amount of time that he'd sit in his chair in the one position, would have to be patched.

Later that evening, when her mother and father had gone to bed, she finished the darning by gaslight, relieved that the gas mantle gave them a better light than the naked flame used to do, and then she leaned back, closed her eyes and thought about the past week.

On the Monday, she'd helped with the washing, and on the Tuesday, it had been ironing day. Wednesday was market day. The market was open till eight in the evening, it being summer, and she'd gone there half an hour before closing as her mother always said that the stallholders, reluctant to take their produce home, would usually be selling at a knock-down price by that time.

Nothing much had happened on Thursday, but on Friday it started again. That was cleaning-up night. She and her mother had mopped the floor, and black-leaded the oven, stove and fire grate. They'd swilled the flagstones in front of their house with water, and donkey-stoned the doorstep and window sill until they shone.

On Saturdays, people worked until noon, and her mother did, too, as would she when she started at the draper's.

On Saturday afternoons, her father and Stan Cooke's father used to go and watch the cricket, and when winter came around, they'd go to the football. Her mother would potter around the house for a bit, and then, more often than not, drop in on a neighbour.

She'd got quite friendly with Stan Cooke's mother, and the two of them had got into the habit of sitting in front of one or other of their houses, chatting, and sometimes May's mother would join them. And on occasions, if the Stacksteads Brass Band was playing nearby, they'd all go together and listen.

Although her mother's place of work had changed, that had basically always been her mother's week. And if she were to stay in that area, and possibly marry again, it would almost certainly be *her* week, too, for the rest of her life.

But could she be happy with that, she wondered.

She didn't know that she could.

It wasn't the smallness of the house and its lack of modern conveniences – she was used to that. And it wasn't that she'd have to work hard – she'd worked really hard as a nurse, and had thrived on it. It was that there'd been a challenge to her work as a nurse in a large hospital that was totally missing from her life at home. Every nursing day had brought something new, and the work was really interesting and varied.

And just living in London had been so exciting.

There'd always been things to see and learn about, and different people to meet, even with the restrictions placed on their movement by Thomas. It was hard to imagine living anywhere else after seven years in such a city.

Up on the moor that afternoon, May had made her begin to think seriously as to whether she'd ever be able to reconcile herself to living the kind of life she'd struggled so hard to escape, a life that would almost certainly be devoid of the interest and stimulation she'd become used to, in order to stay with her family.

May had obviously thought she wouldn't. And as she looked round her, she feared that May might well have been right.

But to go back to London now and try to persuade Thomas to take her back, could she do that, given the bitterness of his rejection of her? And given her fault in the whole matter?

She couldn't. Not yet. It was much too soon. He would need more time to discover how he truly felt about her, and whether he could forgive her.

And she needed time, too.

She'd been convinced of her love for Thomas when she'd begged him to let her stay, and again later, when she'd come to see her feelings for Charles as something so much less. But with the passage of time, she'd started wondering if she *did* still love Thomas as much as she'd done on the day they met.

Was it possible that he'd changed so much in the four years they'd been together that even if he ultimately reverted to being his old self, his behaviour towards her had irreversibly destroyed some of her love for him?

Before she went back to London, she needed to know the answer to this.

Nothing that she might say to Thomas in the future should be based, without her realising, upon a mistaken belief about her feelings for him. To fight tooth and nail to live with him again, pleading true love for him, when in no time at all she might realise that she no longer loved him, would be another form of betrayal.

She'd betrayed him once, and she must never do so again.

So, for the foreseeable future, while she took stock of how she felt, her mother's week was going to have to become her week, too.

33

WATERFOOT

End of June 1923

As she stepped out from the canopied walkway made of decorative iron and glass which formed the frontage of Trickett's Arcade, Alice glanced up at the clock above the canopy. It was eight hours since she'd started work, but it felt more than twice as long.

It wasn't that the job was difficult, because it wasn't, she thought, smoothing down her hair that had been cut in a short bob and shingled at the back, and pulling on her green felt cloche. And the people she worked with were pleasant enough. It was just that each day was undemanding and monotonous.

When she'd been a nurse, time had flown by, and although she'd been tired at the end of each shift, she hadn't been nearly as tired as when she left the draper's each evening, even though she'd worked fewer hours and it was physically easier.

Her boredom had grown throughout the year, and she knew she would have to do something about it. Either she must go back to Pike Law and ask for a job, or she must return to London. She couldn't continue as she was for much longer.

She could certainly afford to go back to London as she still had the bulk of the money that Thomas had given her, having so far spent only a small amount on clothes and a little more than that on items to make her parents' lives more comfortable.

There were clear advantages in going back to London, apart from the fact that she'd loved living in the city.

For a start, Thomas was still in the forefront of her mind, and she wasn't going to know what she truly felt about him until she saw him again. He'd obviously no intention of approaching her, so she would have to go to him.

And increasingly Charles had crept into her thoughts.

But those thoughts were filled with anger, not longing.

He'd been cruelly careless of her happiness.

If it hadn't been for him, she'd still be with Thomas. By now, Thomas might have resolved his issues, and they might have been as happy together as they'd been in the beginning. It was grossly unfair that Charles had never been made to pay for taking advantage of her situation. If she were back to London, there might be something she could do to remedy this injustice.

But she was trying hard not to let herself dwell on the anger she felt towards Charles. She'd seen only too clearly what bitterness could do to a person, and she wouldn't want to become such a person herself.

Maybe the solution *was* to go back to Pike Law, she thought, as she crossed the road. If she went back to nursing, she'd certainly find more stimulation than in the draper's, and that might help her to feel more settled in Waterfoot. If that happened, she might lose any desire to return to London.

Of course, there might not be a vacancy at Pike Law, and then she'd be no further forward.

Thanks to the demand for nurses during the war, there were now considerably more nurses. It had become a much more attractive career, and nurses were more respected than they used to be. With so many more nurses around, it was quite likely that any vacancies at Pike Law would have been filled immediately.

'Ah, here you are!' At the sound of her mother's voice, she stopped in surprise and turned round.

'What're you doing here, Mam? I thought you'd be at home.'

'I've been ter the market, haven't I? I paid nine pence for a piece of meat that would normally cost two shillings. And instead of getting thirteen bananas ter the shilling, I got twenty-four. I'm reet pleased with myself,' she added with a laugh.

'So you should be,' Alice said with a smile. She took her mother's shopping from her, and together they continued in the direction of home.

'I went ter get something else, too,' her mother said, throwing Alice a sly glance as they walked along. 'I bought yer a magazine. I'll give it ter yer at home.'

Alice laughed. 'I rather think that the days of May and me drooling over the pages of *Tatler* are over, don't you?'

'It's not that magazine, our Alice – it's *The Lady*.'

'*The Lady*!' Alice looked curiously at her mother. 'Thank you. But why?'

'Because yer unhappy,' her mother said bluntly. 'I've seen the magazine at the Bates's house. They've got lists of jobs for people to fill – jobs for the sort of people who read *The Lady*.'

Alice started to protest that she was fine as she was.

'No, yer not,' her mother said. 'Yer doing a job that yer finding reet dull, and yer missing yer Thomas. Don't think I don't know me own daughter. Yer a good daughter, our Alice, and yer've done your best ter settle down, not wanting ter hurt yer father and me, which you think yer'd do if yer left again. Don't think we don't know that, and we're reet grateful. But me and yer dad are all right. Or we would be if we felt yer were content. There are some fine jobs advertised in *The Lady*, and we thought there might be something in there that'd suit yer. If yer found such a job, yer'd go with our blessing.'

Alice stopped walking and stared at her mother. Tears filled her eyes.

Her mother reached out to her and hugged her.

'We've never asked what happened in London, love,' her mother said as they resumed walking, 'as it's none of our business. But whatever it was, my instinct's telling me that it's business that isn't yet finished. But as long as yer Thomas is down in London, and yer up here, yer'll not be able ter finish that business. Yer need to go back ter London ter sort this out.'

A sob escaped Alice.

'And I think deep down yer know that,' her mother said as they went into their house. 'Now sit down and look at yer magazine,' she ordered, taking the shopping from Alice. She removed the magazine from one of her bags and handed it to her. 'I'll finish tonight's Stir About. All it needs is boiling. There's nowt for yer to do, so yer can sit there and find a job. And when yer get down south, yer can see yer Thomas again, and if yer find it's not what yer want, yer know yer'll always have a home up here.'

34

BELSIZE PARK

End of July 1923

A brown leather bag in each hand, Alice stood on the pavement and stared up the drive at the large Victorian house in front of her. The house stared back at her.

The advertisement in *The Lady* had been for a companion, available to start at once, for a Mrs Violet Osborne, a widow who lived in Belsize Park. Mrs Osborne, she'd read, who was generally of sound health, had just returned from hospital following a recent fall, and was seeking a trusted companion upon whom she could rely in the period before she returned to full strength. While the post was expected to be for six months only, there might be the possibility of an extension.

It was not anticipated that Mrs Osborne would need much in the way of personal care, the advertisement had informed readers, and the companion would not be expected to cook, clean or shop. Other staff were employed for those purposes. She would be required to live in the house, in which she would have a comfortable room in her own quarters. The house had indoor plumbing. All meals would be provided. She would have a break every afternoon, and would be entitled to a day off every two weeks, the details of which would be arrived at by agreement.

Alice's initial thought when she'd first seen the advertisement had been that it wasn't a nursing post, which she'd originally wanted, although it might come to that if Mrs Osborne proved to be elderly, and became unwell or infirm. While she was described as being in sound health, the fact that she'd just had a fall suggested that she could be on the frail side. And if that were so, any applicant with nursing experience was sure to have an advantage.

But was living as someone's companion really what she wanted to do, even if it were for only six months?

It would mean giving up the freedom she'd fought to have for so many years. She'd be as much a prisoner of her environment as if she stayed in Waterfoot. Even more so as she'd be at the beck and call of someone else. While it was for six months only, those six months could easily come to feel like an eternity.

And at the end of her contract, she might not have had the opportunity to achieve either of the things she'd come to London to do. She might be no clearer in knowing what she felt about Thomas, or he about her, and she might not have been able to put right the wrong done to her by Charles.

And while, in the absence of a car, the underground network would allow her to travel between Belsize Park and Sloane Square, the station closest to Charles's Knightsbridge house, and to go to Kentish Town, it was more than just getting to the houses – it was what she might find when she got there. She'd been in the North for a year, and Thomas might well have found someone else by now. And if the front door in Charles's house was slammed in her face, there wouldn't be much she could do about it.

Also, living and working in someone else's home, with limited free time, meant that for the length of her contract, she was unlikely to be able to enjoy to the full the many advantages of living in London.

In a sudden wave of uncertainty about the choice of job she'd made, she was hesitant about walking up the drive and knocking on the front door.

The moment she'd seen the advertisement in *The Lady*, offering the chance of a temporary home in Belsize Park, she'd been convinced that she'd only ever been biding her time before she returned to London – she just hadn't been aware of it – and she'd promptly applied for the position. But in doing that, she'd brushed aside the cautions of her mother and May.

Perhaps she shouldn't have done.

Both had urged her to consider whether she wouldn't rather return to hospital nursing than be a companion. Mrs Osborne might be bad-tempered or petulant, and she would have the right to tell Alice what she could and couldn't do, and she might expect to be to waited on hand and foot.

But she'd ignored them.

They couldn't know that the location of the job was its real attraction. And anyway, a Ward Sister had the right to tell her nurses what to do, so being given instructions would hardly be a novelty.

But perhaps she *should* have given more thought to what they'd said.

She must pull herself together, she scolded herself, and she gripped her bags more tightly.

Even if Thomas rejected her a second time, or she realised that she no longer loved him, she would be in London, and although it might be six months before she could profit from that, at least she was back where she wanted to be. Her year in

Waterfoot had shown her that she wouldn't want to live there again.

No, she'd made the right decision, and she must stop agonising about something it was too late to change, and get on with this next stage of her life.

Her eyes fixed on the front door, she started walking up the drive.

Halfway along the drive, her steps slowed.

Should she knock on the front door, she wondered, or see if there was a side door or back entrance for the staff, for that's what she was? At the Kentish Town house, the staff went round to the back. Of course, that might have been because of the yard, but she knew that her mother had to use a side door when she went to the Bates's house – she wasn't allowed to go in through the front entrance.

But where did she stand as a companion?

Biting her lower lip, she stared at the house for a moment or two, and then made up her mind. She'd go to the main entrance.

Taking a deep breath, she walked up to the dark blue door, put her hand on the brass doorknocker that hung between two narrow stained-glass panels, rapped it hard against its backplate, stood back, and waited.

35

MINUTES LATER

Having left her bags in the entrance hall as instructed, Alice followed the housekeeper, who'd introduced herself as Mrs Waters, past an elegant staircase, across a spacious hall tiled in cream, salmon and brown terracotta, and beneath an archway which led into a large reception room.

It was a high-ceiled room, was her first impression, with walls which had been painted cream, and the ceiling white. In the centre of a polished parquet floor, lay a delicately toned cream, salmon and dark blue rug.

As she entered, the housekeeper announced her name, and she saw looking towards her, a slender woman, some thirty years or so older than her, sitting in a mahogany-framed armchair that had been upholstered in dark blue velvet. With a smile, the woman extended a pale, fragile-looking hand.

She went forward, took the offered hand and shook it. Then she stepped back, her arms hanging in front of her, her hands clasped together.

'I'm Violet Osborne,' the woman said.

Her thin, delicately boned face was framed by silver-grey hair neatly arranged in a chignon at the base of her neck. The pale blue eyes that gazed at Alice were kind.

'Sit down, won't you, Mrs Linford?' Violet pointed to the armchair beside hers, of a similar colour and style. 'I asked Mrs Waters this morning if she and Daisy would move the chair closer to mine. I imagine we'll want to be able to talk to each other without shouting,' she added as Alice sat down. 'At least, I hope so.'

'Thank you,' Alice said. 'Yes, that was a good idea.'

'Mrs Waters will be getting us some tea as we speak,' Violet went on. 'I assumed you'd be quite tired after your journey from Lancashire, and I asked her to prepare it as soon as you arrived. I've never been to Lancashire myself, but my nephew, John, has, and he tells me that it's quite a distance away.'

Alice nodded. 'It is. The train journey seemed never-ending, and then the underground from Euston. Tea would be very welcome, thank you.'

'When we've had tea, Mrs Waters will show you to your room. I suggest that we have an early dinner this evening – shall we say at seven – and then you can get a good night's rest.'

'That's very thoughtful of you, Mrs Osborne; thank you. I must admit, I do feel tired.'

As she finished speaking, Mrs Waters came in with a tray of tea and a plate of homemade cakes.

She rested it on the corner of a small occasional mahogany table inlaid with marble, which had been placed between the two armchairs. When she'd transferred the contents from the tray on to the table, she left the room.

Alice leaned slightly forward. 'I'll pour the tea, shall I?' she asked hesitantly. 'I've never been a companion before so I don't really know what to do.' She gave a nervous laugh.

Violet smiled at her. 'And I've never had a companion before, so I'm slightly unsure of what's expected of me. We'll work it out together, I'm sure. But do pour the tea, will you? I take milk and just one spoon of sugar, please. It's such a relief that sugar's no longer rationed, don't you think, even though John says it's very bad for one's teeth.'

'I'm sure that a little sugar wouldn't hurt anyone.'

Violet nodded. 'That's what I think.' She waited while Alice poured the tea into the white bone china cups, and added sugar to her cup.

Alice picked up a teaspoon, and suddenly paused, the spoon mid-air. 'Is it all right for me to stir your tea, Mrs Osborne, or would you prefer not?' she asked. 'At home, some people believe that if you stir another person's tea, you'll be stirring their troubles.'

Violet laughed. 'I'm quite happy for you to stir my tea, thank you, Mrs Linford,' she said.

Alice handed Violet her cup and offered her a cake. 'Perhaps the first thing to decide,' Violet said, taking the cup and a cake from the plate, 'is what we're to call each other. I'm hoping that we'll become friends during your time here, so would you mind if I called you Alice? It seems more friendly.'

'Not at all, Mrs Osborne. I'd like that.' She picked up her cup and sat back, trying to look more relaxed than she felt.

'And of course, you must call me Violet. So that's decided, then.'

'Thank you.'

'I realise that it must seem strange that I didn't ask you to attend for an interview,' Violet said, sipping her tea. 'But you live so far away, and as your background and references were superior to those of the other applicants, John and I felt confident in offering you the position without seeing you first. The initial contract is for six months only. If we find that we don't suit each other, I'm sure we'll be able to manage for what is a limited period of time, after all.'

'I hope you never have any reason to regret not interviewing me first,' Alice said.

'I'm certain I won't.'

They smiled at each other.

Feeling her tension gradually disappearing, Alice glanced around the room as they drank their tea, and then looked back at Violet. 'I hope you don't mind me saying so, but I think your house is really lovely. I haven't seen all of it yet, of course, but the hall and this room, they're beautiful.'

Violet beamed at her. 'Thank you, my dear. I'm glad you like it. I'm not sure that it would be to everyone's taste.'

'Well, it's certainly to mine. The pale walls and large windows make the room feel so light and airy.'

Violet nodded in satisfaction. 'That's my nephew's doing,' she said. 'John all but forced me to have the walls and ceiling lightened, and to replace some of the tiled areas with parquet flooring and rugs. This room is south-facing, you see, as are the breakfast room and living-room, so we benefit from a lot of natural light. According to John, walls that are pale in colour make the most of that light.'

'Looking at this room, he's certainly right.'

'And it's much more modern, he tells me, not to be too cluttered and ornate. But ornate or not, I insisted that the tiles in the entrance hall remain as they were. My late husband greatly admired them and I should be sorry to see them go.' She hesitated. 'Your interest in houses makes me wonder if you're connected to the Linford family, whose business is construction.'

Alice blushed. 'I was, but I'm not too sure now. I'm married to Thomas Linford, the youngest of the three Linford brothers. We had an argument last year which led to me going back to my family home in Waterfoot, and I don't know what my situation is now. I wrote to Thomas not long after I returned to the North, but I haven't heard from him, so I've no idea whether he's ended the marriage or not. If he hasn't, I don't know how he sees the future. It's something I hope to find out.'

'I'm so sorry, Alice. I had no intention of prying – really it's none of my business. I hope I haven't given offence.'

Alice shook her head. 'You haven't, and you weren't prying – it was a reasonable thing to wonder, given my name, and the fact that several Linfords live in this part of London. My mother suggested I revert to my maiden name, which is Foster, but I didn't want to. If I find out that Thomas has divorced me, then that's a different matter. But I've no idea if this is something he could do without me knowing.'

'It must all be very unsettling for you.'

'It is.' She smiled ruefully. 'But being married to a Linford has left me with an interest in houses, as you spotted. And because of Thomas's job, I think I've become particularly conscious of house interiors without realising it. Thomas chose the decorative detailing for inside the houses built by Linford & Sons, you see. And he was very good at it. Needless to say, the discussion on the few occasions that Thomas and I joined the family invariably turned to company matters at some point, even when the women were still at the table.'

'I'm afraid that I'm not very imaginative – I've always been guided by others. First it was by Leonard, my husband, and now it's by John. He's my late sister's son. But enough of that.' She put her cup down on the table. 'We'll have plenty of time in the future to talk. I can see that you've finished your tea and you must be wanting to freshen up and look around the rest of the house. I'll ring for Mrs Waters. She'll take you to your room and show you where everything is. I suggest you relax after your long journey, and come back down about half an hour before dinner, which we'll take at seven this evening, as I think I said.'

Alice stood up. She glanced down at the tea tray, and hesitated.

'Mrs Waters will take that away,' Violet said with a smile. 'You don't need to worry about it. Use the rest of the afternoon to become familiar with the house, and to have a rest. I, too, shall rest. Mrs Waters wheeled me into the garden this morning and encouraged me to take a short walk, so I feel I've done more than enough for today. Tomorrow, you and I will go into the garden together. I'm still not quite as strong as I was before my fall, so at present I tend to use a wheelchair for going outside, and then I do a little on foot.'

'Thank you, Mrs Osborne... Violet,' Alice said, her voice shaking slightly. 'You've been really kind. I'm very grateful to have been given such a warm welcome.'

* * *

Later that evening, after dinner, Alice stood at her bedroom window and stared out over the garden at the rear of the house.

The light from the living-room flooded on to the York stone terrace that ran along the back of the house, separating the house from the lawn. In one corner of the terrace, she could just about make out a white wrought-iron table and four chairs. But with the natural light of day fast fading into night, it was difficult to distinguish the different plants that formed the dark grey mass of foliage which proliferated between the lawn and the trees.

As she stood watching, everything before her melded into a dense charcoal grey.

Raising her eyes, she looked up at the star-studded sky.

This was the same sky that hung over the Linford family, she thought, gazing up at the pale moon, a crescent-shaped sliver of light surrounded by a halo of luminous grey. The same sky that hung above Thomas.

And they were breathing the same air.

An intense longing for him crept through her, and she rested her forehead against the cool window pane. In that moment, she felt closer to Thomas than she'd done since that day, almost a year ago, when she'd left London and headed north.

Oh, Thomas, she whispered. Do you ever think about me? Do you miss me? I've missed you. Or is it London I've missed? Well, I'm back now, and I'll soon be able to find the answer to my questions.

36

PRIMROSE HILL

That same evening

'Thomas! What a pleasant surprise!' Joseph exclaimed. 'I know we invited you to dinner this evening, along with Walter and Nellie, but when you didn't reply, we drew the obvious conclusion, and as Charles and Sarah are dining with friends, we looked like being very small in number.'

'A pleasant surprise, is it? Surprise, I can accept, Joseph. But don't you think that pleasant is rather overdoing it?' Thomas remarked, sitting on the chair that Mrs Morley had hastily pulled up to the table before going across to the sideboard, and opening one of the top drawers to take out another place setting. 'I admit that my decision to come was very last-minute. If my arrival means there's insufficient food, I should be happy to go without. Please note that, Mrs Morley,' he said, glancing towards her with a smile. He turned again to the table. 'After all, having been stuck in the trenches, I'm used to going without food.'

'As you know full well, Thomas, there'll always be sufficient for you,' Maud said smoothly, 'whether or not we're expecting you. You know you're welcome here at any time.'

He inclined his head towards Maud.

'It's good you've come, Thomas,' Walter said. 'In fact, I've been meaning to drop in on you and find out how you are.'

'Let me guess,' Thomas said. He exaggerated a thoughtful pose. 'Could it possibly be that you think I might want to talk about the new divorce bill? If you'll forgive me, that is, for raising the subject that you've all been assiduously avoiding for what must be a year by now.'

'Spot on, Thomas,' Walter said with a laugh. 'Well, if you want me to pop round, you only have to say.'

'I was reading about the bill in *The Times*,' Maud said. 'I'm delighted that it's rectified a situation that was most unfair to women.'

Walter nodded. 'That's right; that's what it does. It's only fair that women shouldn't have to prove rape, cruelty, incest, bestiality—'

'Walter! Nellie's in the room!' Maud exclaimed.

'Don't worry, Mother,' Nellie said brightly. 'Being married to a lawyer broadens your vocabulary. I believe that the last two are sodomy, and desertion for two years without good reason. Isn't that so, Walter?'

Joseph glanced at Thomas and chuckled.

'Indeed, it is, Nellie. You'll be stealing my clients if I don't look out,' Walter said in amusement. 'But if I may put myself at risk by correcting you, dear wife, you should have added that proving any one of those was in addition to proving adultery. All a man used to have to prove was that adultery had taken place. The new bill puts both parties on a level footing.'

'Possibly not the best choice of expression, Walter, if I may say,' Thomas commented, grinning at him.

Walter laughed. 'Shall we say in an equal position, then?'

'All I can say is, we've a lot to thank the Women's Equality Movement for,' Maud remarked. 'Now that women over thirty can vote, we're seeing a definite change in Parliament's attitude towards them.'

'That may be so,' Walter agreed, 'but I rather suspect that the current bill is less about ensuring gender equality, and more to do with what's been happening in the courts in recent years. Time and again, the courts have refused to reflect the severity of a law based on such obvious double standards, and there's now a great deal of confusion about the situation regarding divorce. It needed to be clarified.'

'Well, whatever the reason, the equality it brings is very welcome,' Maud said.

'Hearing your support for equality, Maud, you're raising my hopes,' Joseph said with a broad smile. 'I'm wondering if you're about to suggest that you go on site each day and tramp across the latest muddy field upon which we're building, while I stay at home and watch the maid flick a duster over the crystal or entertain my friends to tea or to a game of cards.'

They all laughed.

'It's suddenly occurred to me, Thomas, how did you get here?' Joseph asked. 'You obviously didn't ask Walter to pick you up.'

Thomas smiled. 'I've bought a car – a Ford Model T – and I've employed a driver. Mrs Morley is taking good care of him in the servants' quarters while I'm here. In addition to driving me wherever I want to go, George will keep an eye on my garden, such as it is, and do any other chores I ask of him when I don't require his services as a driver. I felt that it was about time I had some independence.'

'That's marvellous news, Uncle Thomas!' Nellie exclaimed.

'Camden Town isn't far from Kentish Town so I insist that you now visit us more often.'

'It *is* good news, Thomas,' Joseph said. 'We've never talked about what happened between you and Alice – that's *your* business – but we've all been concerned at you being on your own so much during the past year. I know it was out of choice – we've asked you to join us on countless occasions, and you've usually refused – but it can't be good, being such a recluse. Getting a car is the very best thing you could've done. I'm proud of you.'

Thomas nodded. 'Put it down to my new prosthesis. It's much more comfortable than the last. It's amazing the difference that's made.'

The door opened, and Mrs Morley and the housemaid entered. A plate of food was placed in front of each of them. Mrs Morley filled the wine glasses, then she and the housemaid left the room.

'Saunders at work was telling me that his wife buys potatoes in cans,' Joseph said, picking up his knife and fish fork, and starting on his poached salmon, 'even though it's hard work opening a can, and they don't taste anything like the real thing. And she uses Bird's Custard rather than the infinitely superior custard made by Cook,' he added. 'They just can't get domestic staff. No one seems to want such employment these days, and as his wife works in a shop, she doesn't have time to cook. I felt quite sorry for the man.'

'It *is* a problem getting staff now,' Maud said. 'All the more reason to ensure that our domestic help feels comfortable living with us. I'd hate Mrs Morley to leave. I sometimes worry about Charles and Sarah, though. Louisa is so very rude to everyone in the house, staff included. Charles and Sarah really should discipline her more. If she's like that at thirteen, what *will* she be like in a few more years?'

'I'm sure she'll grow out of it, Mother,' Nellie said. 'Aunt Sarah knows what she's doing. She'd never let Louisa go too far.'

'Well, I certainly hope you're right, Nellie. I find it hard to picture Sarah slipping into a wrap-around apron, picking up a broom and sweeping the floor,' Maud added drily.

Nellie laughed. 'Me, too.'

'You're fortunate that your Mrs Carmichael has a stout hide, Thomas,' Joseph remarked. 'I've heard the way you speak to her at times.'

Thomas grinned. 'We understand each other.'

'The divorce bill isn't the only Act that's recently come into effect,' Walter remarked. 'The Property Act I was telling you about a little while ago, Joseph, has now been passed. They're calling it the Chamberlain Act. As I thought, it's good news for private developers.'

Nellie gave a loud groan. 'Your choice of topics of conversation shows that you're getting as bad as Father, Walter. It must be catching.'

'In what way is it good for us?' Thomas asked.

Joseph put down his knife and fork, sat back and beamed at Thomas. 'First, a car, and now you've referred to yourself as part of Linford & Sons. You've never said that before. Despite the excellent work you do for us, Thomas, you've always seemed to distance yourself from the company.'

Thomas put up his hands in mock horror. 'You're scaring me, Joseph, with all this pleasantry and *bonhomie*. I feel disorientated, as if I'm in the wrong building.'

Joseph laughed. 'You're in the right place, for sure. To answer your question, if I remember correctly what Walter told me, provided that we build a house within certain dimensions, the Treasury will give us a cash subsidy for each house. That's for a period of up to twenty years. There are one or two other stipulations about the houses – there must be a fixed bath in a designated bathroom, for example – but that's the gist of it. Is that right, Walter?'

'It is, sir. What the Conservative Government has done is reverse the policy they adopted at the end of the War when they didn't trust private builders to be able to meet the huge demand for housing. Encouraging local authorities to move into the housing market, thinking they could become the major providers of working-class houses, rather than private enterprise, didn't work, and now, under the Chamberlain Act, they've reverted to supporting private business.'

Joseph nodded. 'I've never thought much of Chamberlain as a politician, but he's come through for us this time with flying colours.'

'What happens if there's a change in government after the next general election?' Thomas asked. 'More people are able to vote now, and membership of the Labour Party is soaring. The Liberal Party's in decline, and Labour's the most likely beneficiary of that. I can see the day when we actually have a Labour Government.'

'You're talking rubbish as usual, Thomas,' Joseph snapped.

'That's more like the Joseph I know and love. I *am* in the right house, after all,' Thomas said with a grin, and he leaned forward and clapped his brother on the shoulder.

* * *

'I'm glad you felt like another cognac after Nellie and Walter had left, and Maud had gone up to bed,' Joseph said, as he sat in his library opposite Thomas. He drew deeply on his cigar. 'I wanted to thank you, Thomas. You've had a very difficult year, and you've behaved with dignity throughout. You could have shamed

Charles before the family, but you didn't, and most of them have no idea of his involvement.'

Thomas made as if to speak.

'Don't worry, the only reason I know of the part that Charles played was because I once saw him with Alice. As I said before, I'm proud of you, Thomas. And I'm both relieved and delighted that you've started to look towards the future. If there's any way we can help you, you can be sure we will.'

Thomas nodded. 'I know that, Joseph.'

Joseph gave him a half-smile. 'Is that it? No biting comment? I keep waiting for you to accuse me of offering to help you out of guilt that you fought in the war and I didn't.'

'Alice told me I said it so often that it no longer had any effect,' he said with a smile. 'So, I've stopped. And also, I accept that David and I chose to go to war; you didn't make us.'

'You're still married to Alice, I know. On the only occasion that I spoke to you about her, I passed on what Walter had told me about possible changes in the divorce law in the future, and since then, I've been assuming that you were waiting for them to be in place before you did anything. If so, is it now decision time?'

'Not really. I don't feel in a hurry to do anything. After all, I've no intention of marrying again.'

'You might change your mind one day. You said that your leg was easier now.'

'It's all relative. I won't marry again. I'm not saying that I'm never lonely, because at times I am. But no amount of loneliness will push me into taking another wife. And marriage isn't necessarily a cure for loneliness, anyway. You can be just as lonely when you're with someone, as when you're not. More so sometimes.'

'Well, you know your own mind; you always did. But do think about bringing your marriage to an end, even if at the moment you don't think you want to marry again. For Alice's sake as well as for yours.'

'Funnily enough, doing what's good for Alice is not a priority of mine.'

Joseph swirled the cognac in his glass, and drew again on his pipe. 'Your unwillingness to bring the marriage to a legal end,' he said slowly, 'makes me wonder if you don't still have feelings for her.'

Thomas stared down into his glass. 'I certainly *do* have some! I still feel angry at what she did with my brother. And I feel humiliated, if you want to know. Those feelings are as real today as they were a year ago. But as for the sort of feelings you're hinting at, I don't think I do have any such feelings left. To be honest, I can't say that for certain, but if I *do*, they're not exactly pressing me to do anything about it.'

'I think it might be wise to find out what you *do* feel for her, if anything, and that means you would have to see her. After all, you were very much in love. If you didn't want to go up to Lancashire to talk to her—'

'I don't,' Thomas cut in.

'—you could write to her,' Joseph continued. 'You could invite her to come down to London. If she agreed, we could arrange for her to stay in a hotel for a couple of days, and I'd make sure that Charles and Sarah were out of town during the visit.'

'Thank you for the suggestion, but I prefer to leave things as they are. If it makes it inconvenient for Alice, that's tough luck. If she wants to marry again, she'll need a divorce, but she knows where she can find me. And that's the subject closed, Joseph.'

37

BELSIZE PARK

Beginning of August 1923

'Dr O'Neill, madam,' Daisy announced, coming into the living-room, where Violet and Alice had taken to sitting after breakfast.

Alice glanced in surprise at Violet, and lowered her hands around which was looped a skein of yellow wool which Violet had been rolling into a ball. 'I didn't know your doctor was visiting today,' she said, and she put the wool carefully on to the table next to her, and rose to her feet.

Violet laughed. 'There's no need for you to leave. That's my nephew,' she said. 'He works in a hospital not far from here, and he often pops in. Hello, John.' She held out her hand to the man who'd followed Daisy into the room.

He crossed the room quickly, took Violet's hand, and at the same time kissed her on the cheek.

Alice glanced at him. He was of medium build, with broad shoulders and dark brown hair. Probably in his thirties, she decided. He was the sort of man you'd notice, but not one you'd call strikingly good-looking. Not that he was unpleasant to look at. And judging from the delight on Violet's face as she beamed up at him, he was a kind man, and genuinely cared for his aunt.

He stepped back, held Violet at arm's length and studied her. 'You know, you look much better than you've done for a long time, even since before your fall.'

Violet's hand went to her chignon, and a pink flush spread across her cheeks.

Then he turned to Alice with a broad smile. His chestnut brown eyes were full of warmth, she noticed.

'The improvement in my aunt must be your doing, Mrs Linford,' he said, and he held out his hand to her. 'It's a pleasure to meet you in person.'

Frowning slightly in surprise, she shook his hand. 'What did you mean by in person?'

He laughed. 'I first met you on paper. My aunt and I went through the applications together, and we both felt that yours sounded the most suitable, partly because of your significant nursing experience. Obviously, my aunt is no longer in need of nursing care, but it's a relief for me to know that she has a companion who'd know what to do, should anything of concern arise.'

'Do sit down, John,' Violet said, indicating the chair opposite her. 'And you, too, Alice. We don't have to ring for coffee as, if I know Mrs Waters, she'll already have it under control. You couldn't have come at a better time, John. Poor Alice must be very ready for a break. You've been holding skeins of wool since breakfast this morning, haven't you, Alice? Your arms must be extremely tired by now.'

'Don't worry, they're fine. I'm glad to be of help. Winding wool is so much more easily done with two people.'

'It all looks very yellow,' John said, glancing from the skeins of knitting wool on the table next to Alice to the balls of wool in his aunt's lap.

'I'm knitting you a jumper in time for the cold weather,' Violet said with a smile. 'It's time you threw away that old brown jersey you're wearing. I can't see why you're so fond of it.'

'That's very kind of you, Aunt; thank you.' He looked at Alice. 'Are you a keen knitter, too, Mrs Linford?'

She shook her head. 'Not at all, I'm afraid. I can sew, of course. Where I come from, women have to learn how to sew as it's cheaper to make the family's clothes than to buy them. And I can darn just about anything. But I don't sew out of pleasure, and nor do I knit.'

Daisy appeared at the entrance to the living-room, a large tray in her hands, closely followed by Mrs Waters. While Daisy held the tray, Mrs Waters put the coffee down on a low glass-topped table in front of the armchairs. Then they left the room.

'Do you take sugar, Dr O'Neill?' Alice asked, getting up.

'Just a little milk, please,' he replied.

She poured a coffee for each of them and handed the cups around. Then she offered the plate of biscuits, and after that, sat down.

'Alice has been very flattering about the colours you chose for the rooms, John. It seems that like you, she has a dislike of dark, over-fussy rooms.'

'Then that shows her good taste,' he said cheerfully. 'These lighter rooms are so much more attractive than the overcrowded, ornate rooms that used to be popular, and still are with many people.' He glanced around at the pale walls and high white ceiling as he spoke.

'As I told your aunt, I think the house is quite beautiful, both inside and out,' Alice said. 'And the garden is superb.'

John nodded. 'I wholeheartedly agree.'

Alice took a sip of her coffee. 'I don't want to be presumptuous, Dr O'Neill,' she ventured, putting her cup down, 'but I was wondering if, even though I'm here as a companion and not as a nurse, you would consider it helpful for your aunt's recovery if each morning, I took her through a short exercise routine in order to strengthen her muscles. This was an important part of the patients' rehabilitation at Queen Mary's, so I'm completely familiar with such programmes.'

He smiled gratefully at her. 'I think that's an excellent idea. Don't you agree, Aunt?'

'I certainly do. Thank you, Alice. The sooner I can dispense with a wheelchair, the better.'

'I hope you didn't mind me asking Dr O'Neill without consulting you first,' Alice told Violet apologetically, 'but I wanted to make sure that this would be acceptable medically before I mentioned it to you.'

John smiled at her. 'And that was the right thing to do, Mrs Linford.'

Alice cleared her throat. 'If it's not inappropriate, Dr O'Neill, perhaps you would like to call me Alice, as your aunt does.'

'I doubt that it's inappropriate, as you put it, and I'd be happy to do so. It's so much less formal. And as my aunt has called me John several times since I arrived, I'm sure you know my name.'

'You can see how good Alice has been for me in the short amount of time she's been here, John. She's already proved a tremendous help, as well as being a very pleasant companion.' Violet smiled warmly at Alice.

'Just looking at you, Aunt, I can see the truth of that. We obviously chose well.' He stirred his coffee. 'I meant to introduce myself sooner than this, Alice,' he continued. 'I work in the Hampstead General and North-West London Hospital. It isn't far from here, and I'd intended to come over the morning after you arrived, just to check that there weren't any problems. But the best laid plans and all that. Well, you've worked in a hospital, so you know what it's like. You've settled in all right, I trust.'

Alice nodded. 'Everyone's been really kind. I feel tremendously lucky that my application caught your eye.'

'That's good.' He took a sip of his coffee. 'Have you been to Belsize Park before?'

'Yes, a few times. Usually on the way up to Hampstead Village or to the Heath. I used to live in Kentish Town.'

'Not far away, at all.'

'Before that, I worked at Queen Mary's in Roehampton, which you'll have seen from my application. Prior to that, I worked in the Pike Law Infirmary, not far from Waterfoot where I lived with my parents. That's the infirmary for Haslingden Workhouse. It became a military hospital during the war, and people started calling it Pike Law Hospital.'

He nodded. 'There've been similar name changes at many infirmaries. I believe it was felt that the word infirmary was an unpleasant link with the Poor Law and pauperism.'

'You'll stay to lunch, won't you, John?' Violet asked.

He raised his eyebrows in amusement. 'I do hope that the mention of pauperism didn't cause you to look at me, feel a mixture of compassion and horror at my jumper, and make your offer out of a sense of charity.'

Violet laughed. 'Not in the least. Even though you will persist in wearing that threadbare thing.'

Alice stood up. 'I should leave you two to talk, and to have lunch.'

'Please don't let me drive you away, Alice,' John said quickly, getting up. 'I'd be very happy for you to join us, and I suspect my aunt would, too.'

'Of course, you must stay, Alice. Do sit down again, won't you, dear?' Violet said. 'After lunch, I shall have a lie-down, and you're free to do as you wish for the rest of the day. You haven't had any real time to yourself since you arrived, and you're most definitely due some.'

John glanced at Alice, and visibly hesitated. 'Forgive me if I'm stepping out of line, but with my aunt saying that you're not needed this afternoon, it occurred to me that you might like to take a walk after lunch. We could perhaps go up Haverstock Hill, past the hospital where I work, and then down Pond Street to the southernmost part of the Heath. There's a shorter route to the Heath that one can take, but I thought you might enjoy seeing the centre of Belsize Park and also my hospital. Whichever route we take, once we get to the Heath, there's a very pleasant walk near the first of the three ponds.' He suddenly looked anxious. 'If I shouldn't have made such a suggestion, given your marital status, please forgive me.'

'I've no idea whether you should or shouldn't. But I know that being married, I don't need a chaperone, if such things matter these days. Where I come from that wouldn't be a consideration, but after living with the Linfords, I know that down here it *does* matter to some people,' Alice said. 'So if you really wouldn't mind, and have the time, I should love to go for a walk with you.'

38

THAT AFTERNOON

'I'm afraid there's not much you can see of the hospital, given the height of the wall round it. As you can probably tell, though, it's not a particularly old building, and it's not exactly attractive.'

Alice nodded. 'But at least it isn't overly ornate.'

They both laughed.

'The name's a bit of a mouthful, and people tend to call it the Hampstead General Hospital, which it was until it amalgamated with the North-West London Hospital almost twenty years ago,' John said as they walked down the narrow path between Hampstead Green on one side, and the wall surrounding the hospital on the other.

'How many beds does the hospital have?' Alice asked.

'A hundred and thirty-seven. There's talk of an extension in a few years' time, but that'll be mainly to house a new operating theatre, and a Casualty Department and Dispensary.'

'It's certainly in a lovely location, being this close to the Heath,' she remarked as they started walking down Pond Street.

'And in a very historical part of London. Do you know anything about the history of the area?'

She shook her head. 'Not really. I was once taken for tea at Jack Straw's Castle by my sister-in-law, and we had a look at Whitestone Pond. She told me a little about both places. And I've walked over parts of the Heath a few times, but that's all.'

'Then I'll fill you in with a little more local knowledge. Hampstead used to be called Hemstede, but by the time of the Domesday Book, it was known as the Manor of Hampstead and was owned by Westminster. It passed into private hands in the twelfth century, and the manorial rights to the land are still privately owned. In recent years, plots of land have been sold off for building development, but the Heath itself remains common land.'

'You're very keen on history, aren't you?' she said as they turned left at the bottom of Pond Street, and the edge of the Heath came in sight.

He nodded. 'If you live in a place – and I have a small house not far from here – it's fascinating to find out as much as possible about its past. What about you?'

'Before today, I've never really given any thought to learning about the area where I was living. But listening to you, I'm beginning to wish that I knew something about the history of Waterfoot. And about Kentish Town, too, though I'm not sure if there'd be much of historical interest in Kentish Town.'

'You might be surprised. Most parts of London have a rich history.'

'I suppose they must do.' The Heath opened out ahead of them. 'Did Violet often come here before her accident?' she asked.

'Yes, she did. But I can't see her being able to do so quite as easily in the future. She's very unlikely to be able to walk as far as she used to, so she'd have to use her wheelchair, whether or not we came in the car. And she hates being seen in a wheelchair.'

'Oh, that's a shame. I'd been thinking I could bring her here in the wheelchair.'

'It's a nice idea, but even if she'd agree, I think you might find it difficult to do. It would be quite a struggle to push the wheelchair up the hills, and it's a hilly area. And I don't think she *would* agree – she likes to feel she's independent.'

Alice nodded. 'I've seen that in the short time I've known her. She wants to do everything on her own. But that fall really shook her. She obviously listens to you – the colour of her walls are evidence of that – so if you stress the risk she'd put herself in if she tried to walk too far, she might agree to let me take her out in the wheelchair. Even if we went no further than Belsize Park, it would be good for her.'

'It's certainly worth a try.'

'I think she's the sort of person who'd recognise her limitations, and accept them. There are some people who are never reconciled to the fact that they can no longer do as much as they could before their disability, and their anger and resentment poisons them against everyone else,' Alice continued, warming to the subject. 'I don't think that applies to your aunt. She would never behave in such a way.'

John glanced at her quickly, and then looked back ahead.

'She'll certainly want to be brought here in April or May,' he remarked after a few minutes. 'Every year, we come to see the wild bluebells that grow in the areas of woodland, and also to visit the Hampstead Pergola. It's built on a hill with a wonderful view over the Heath. The wisteria that curls around the trellises in the spring is absolutely glorious. Mind you, the Heath is lovely in the autumn, too, especially when the sun's shining and the ground glistens with leaves that are a rich golden brown or red. In fact, no matter what time of year you come, this place is paradise.'

She turned to look at him, and smiled. 'You obviously love it here, John – that shines out of every word you say. I'm guessing you come from around here.'

'You're right – I was born in what's now called New End Hospital. And I later worked there for a while. It was originally the infirmary for the Hampstead workhouse, and its history isn't so different from that of your Pike Law Hospital. New End, too, became a military hospital during the war, and facilities were improved – X-ray apparatus and an operating theatre were installed. Surgical cases were thought to benefit from the pure air.'

'Why did you leave?'

'A vacancy came up at the Hampstead General, which was closer to my aunt. It meant I could see her more easily. My timing wasn't that good, though – I moved from New End just before they installed the wireless in all the wards, and repainted the walls in a modern pale green and cream,' he added with a wry grin.

Alice laughed. 'I'm sure that armed with a pot of cream paint, you're now working on the powers that be in the Hampstead General.'

'But, of course,' he said cheerfully.

* * *

A little while later, they sat across from each other in a café at the bottom of South End Road while a waitress clad in a black dress and frilly white apron brought them tea, and a tiered cake-stand piled high with pastries, which she placed in the centre of their table, next to a tiny vase of colourful flowers.

'Tell me to mind my own business,' John said, stirring the tea that Alice had poured for him, 'but a little while ago, when you talked about people adjusting to, or failing to adjust to, their disabilities, it sounded as if you were speaking from personal experience. I'd understood that you worked with the amputees in Queen Mary's, but that wouldn't mean you'd know how they coped after leaving the hospital. Or am I mistaken?'

She felt herself blushing. 'Not really. You're right, it *was* personal.' She gave an awkward laugh. 'I hadn't intended to do more than make a very general comment about people coming to terms with their limitations, or failing to do so. It seems to have been a bit more revealing than I meant.' She laughed again in discomfort.

He smiled at her. 'Then we'll forget you ever said it. You can tell me about Waterfoot, if you like.'

'It's very thoughtful of you to change the subject, but since I've rather hinted at my situation, although unintentionally, I think I should tell you at least as much as I've told Violet.'

He shook his head. 'There's really no need, Alice.'

'I think there is. After all, I'm still using my married name, though I'm obviously not with my husband. And I haven't said that I'm a widow, because I'm not. I think you and Violet have the right to know my position.'

'We rather assumed you weren't a widow.'

'I met my husband, Thomas, when I was working in Queen Mary's. His leg had been almost completely blown off when he was fighting in France, and also part of his right hand. We married at the end of the war, just before he left the hospital, and went to live in Kentish Town, across the yard from his family's business. As you may know, they're in the construction business, and very successful, too.'

'Linford is certainly a well-known name.'

'The early weeks of our marriage were really happy, but Thomas gradually changed from the amusing, lovely man that

I'd known in the hospital, to someone who was always miserable and bad-tempered. He was bitter about his disability, you see, and resentful, and everyone around him suffered as a result, including me.'

'It must've been extremely difficult for him to adjust to such altered circumstances.'

'It was. His brothers told me how adventurous and energetic he used to be before the war. For someone like that to have come back so badly wounded, it must have been devastating. But stupidly, I underestimated the time it would take him to adjust to his changed life at home. I became impatient with his moods, although, as a nurse, I should've known better.'

'Working in a hospital couldn't possibly prepare you for such a situation. You shouldn't be too hard on yourself.'

'Yes, I should,' she said firmly. 'We would still be together if I'd been more understanding. But all I could see was that Thomas didn't appear to be making an effort to feel better, and that he even seemed to revel in being really unpleasant to everyone.'

'That must've been difficult for you.'

She nodded. 'It was. Without going into details, we separated last June, and I don't know whether or not we're still married. I went straight back to Waterfoot and to my parents, and I haven't spoken to him since I left.'

'I take it you've come back to see him and find out where you stand.'

She nodded. 'Yes, I do need to know that. But that's not the only reason I've returned. I loved living in London, and I found it completely impossible to settle back in Waterfoot. I gave it almost a year, and that was more than enough to know I'd never want to live up there again.'

'Once you've got used to the variety offered by living in a large town, it's bound to be difficult to go back.'

'That's right,' she said. 'And if it turns out that Thomas doesn't want us to try and make a go of the marriage, I'd still rather be here than in Waterfoot. I'm sure I'll always be able to find work. Perhaps as a companion, rather than a nurse – I'm very much enjoying my work with Violet.'

'Have you arranged to see Thomas yet? You're still very young, and if things don't go the way you want with him – and I hope for your sake that they do – it'd be wiser to know that as soon as possible, wouldn't it? Suppose you wanted to remarry?'

She pulled a face. 'If Thomas divorces me, assuming he hasn't already, I'll never want to marry again. My first attempt was far too painful. As for contacting Thomas and arranging to see him, it's too soon. I'd rather leave it a little longer.'

'May I ask why?'

She shrugged. 'I don't know. I just would.'

He gave her a warm smile. 'Actually, I think I can answer my question. While you might be delaying your future happiness by not meeting him, at the same time you're not at risk of hearing anything you don't want to hear.'

'That's perceptive of you, and I'd say you were right if it weren't for the fact that I genuinely don't know what I feel about him, which means that I don't know what I want to hear from him.'

'Well, if there's ever anything I can do to help, be sure to let me know.'

'That's very kind of you; thank you.' She picked up her cup.

'And to answer the question you might want to ask out of general curiosity,' he said a few minutes later, breaking into the companionable silence that had fallen between them, 'but feel it would be inappropriate to do so, no, I'm not married. I should have married Beatrice, my fiancée, several years ago, but she was killed a few months before the war ended. A bomb fell on St Pancras Station, where she'd just got off a train after visiting her mother.'

She put her cup back on the table, and leaned forward. 'Oh, John, I'm so sorry.'

He nodded. 'So am I. Everyone in the country, one way or another, has paid a terrible price for our victory. Losing not only Beatrice, but also my parents, who were killed in a Zeppelin raid, was the price I paid. And Aunt Violet suffered, too – Mother was her only sister. Since then, I've thrown myself into my work, and because I enjoy what I do, it's helped me get through a very difficult time. I loved Beatrice deeply, and I think it unlikely that I'll ever feel that way again about anyone else. I suppose I could say that I'm now wedded to my work.'

'And I could say the same.'

They smiled at each other.

39

SEPTEMBER 1923

The afternoon that she and John had gone to the Heath together had been the first of many such afternoons, and the next few weeks sped by for Alice. Despite the fact that she was working for most of the week, and living in someone else's home, they were among the most enjoyable weeks she'd ever known.

At the start of each day, she took Violet through a series of exercises to strengthen her leg muscles, and both had the satisfaction of seeing the steady improvement in Violet's ability to walk, and her need for a wheelchair diminishing.

Appreciative of the help that Alice was giving her, and seeming genuinely to like her, Violet was a considerate, undemanding employer, who invariably treated Alice as a friend rather than as one of the staff. Hardly a day passed when Alice didn't tell herself how lucky she'd been to secure such a position, and in her letters home, she'd more than once thanked her mother for giving her *The Lady*.

On her free afternoons, of which there turned out to be many as Violet liked to rest after lunch, she'd nearly always go out. One of her favourite destinations was the Booklovers' Library in

Belsize Park, run by Boots the Chemist. Because Violet had a subscription, she was able to borrow books for both Violet and herself, and regularly did so.

Other times, she'd just wander up the wide, tree-lined pavement of Haverstock Hill, glancing in the shop windows as she passed. When she reached the large redbrick and stone Town Hall at the far end of the parade of shops, she would cross over the road, glance swiftly to her left towards the hospital in case there was any sign of John, and if there wasn't, she'd walk back down the road past the underground station.

If the weather was pleasant enough, she'd sometimes stop just before she reached the station and sit on one of the wooden benches, her back to the café and row of businesses that lined the pavement on that side of the road, and watch the cars and horse-drawn vehicles pass by.

On one afternoon, though, an unusual incident caught her attention as she was ambling back down Haverstock Hill, heading for the bench.

She'd been enjoying the beauty of the autumnal afternoon, when the strident clamour of men shouting angrily at each other burst forth from a room above one of the businesses on her left. She'd halted, startled, and raised her eyes to the windows, but there'd been nothing to see.

And then the yelling stopped. Before she could move, she heard a loud crash come from behind the narrow door between a glass-fronted office and the café, followed by a dull thud.

The door swung open.

Alarmed, she took a step back.

A small, dark-haired man was propelled out on to the ground, and several sheets of paper were thrown out after him. The man landed a short distance from where she was standing. She looked down at him in concern. One of the sheets of paper settled on top of the man, and before it was carried away by the breeze, she had time to see that it was a photograph.

She glanced back at the doorway. A man was coming out, his face red with rage. He must have been the one who did the pushing, she thought. She watched him visibly make an effort to compose himself, straightening the jacket of his suit, and smoothing down his lapels. Then he turned and made his way up the hill towards Hampstead Green.

She'd started to approach the man on the ground, wanting to help him if he was injured, but he struggled to his feet, and waved her away.

'Just part and parcel of the job, I'm afraid,' he said, rubbing the dust from the arm of his jacket.

Then, moving awkwardly as if in pain, he went back to the building, disappeared inside, and closed the door behind him.

There was a small plaque on the wall next to the narrow door, she noticed, and she'd been tempted to go up to it and see the nature of his business, but she was afraid that it would have looked either rude or nosy, or both, so she'd resisted the urge and carried on walking back to the house.

'What did he mean by saying what he did?' she asked John when she saw him a few days later on her day off, and recounted the incident as they passed the door on their way to the Heath.

'He's a private detective,' John said. 'People go to someone like that for all sorts of things. From what you've said, the man who attacked him was probably someone he'd been spying on. It's often about divorce. If a husband wants to divorce his wife, or the other way round, there must be evidence of the other's infidelity. That's where a private detective comes in.'

'In what way?'

John shrugged. 'I suppose it depends on which one wants the divorce. Of course, if they both want it, they can cook up something together. A colleague of mine took a woman to a hotel room, they got into bed, and a detective burst in as arranged and took photos. My colleague sent the receipt for the hotel bill to his wife, so they had two pieces of evidence of his adultery. But they must be careful to ensure that the evidence looks genuine. If the court thought there'd been collusion, the evidence would be rejected.'

She pulled a face. 'It sounds very complicated. But I can certainly see why the private detective found himself at the end of the other man's shoe.'

* * *

It wasn't just her free afternoons that they spent together, but also as many of Alice's days off as possible. Whenever he could, John would get away, too, and they'd go off together somewhere. Increasingly, she found herself looking forward with real anticipation to their time together as they got on so well.

Sometimes they'd just walk and see where they ended up, and sometimes they'd go further afield, either in his car, or by the underground train, or on a bus. If they went by bus, they tended to choose the new motorised buses rather than one drawn by horses.

'A number of bus companies have been started up by ex-servicemen who learned mechanics in the Army. This is a way of them using their skills to their advantage, and also to ours,' John told her on the first occasion that they climbed the narrow, winding stairs to the open upper deck of a motorised red bus. 'Sitting up here is a really pleasant way of seeing London. When the weather's good, that is,' he'd added with a laugh.

Under John's guidance, she went to a lot of places in London that she hadn't been able to visit when living with Thomas, and she learned a considerable amount about the history of the city.

They seemed to be able to talk about anything, and conversation flowed easily, whether they were sitting in one of their favourite cafés where they'd head when the weather was bad or if it was time for tea, or resting on a bench on the Heath or in one of the London parks, or strolling along the leafy lanes of Belsize Park, or winding their way through the cobbled back streets of Hampstead Village.

Over the weeks, John told her a little about his childhood, and how alone he used to feel, being an only child and left in the care of his nanny while his parents enjoyed a seemingly endless round of social activities. It wasn't that they were unkind to him, he told her – it was that they had a life that mattered to them, a life into which he didn't fit. His Aunt Violet and Uncle Leonard, who were childless and who didn't live far away, had come to feel more like parents to him than did his real parents.

Meeting Beatrice had given him the companionship of someone close to him in age, something for which he'd longed throughout most of his life, and he'd been beside himself with joy when Beatrice had agreed to marry him, and then completely devastated when he'd lost her so unexpectedly and in such tragic circumstances.

He talked also about his work at the hospital, and some of the patients for whom he was caring, and he said that one day he'd love to show Alice around his hospital, an offer she'd jumped at with enthusiasm.

On Alice's side, she reported on the progress of his aunt, and described to him the minutiae of his aunt's life, which she might not have done had she not been seeing John in person, and been so aware of the affection he felt for his aunt.

And she told him about her early years, about the hardships

endured by the women in the area she came from, who despite working long hours in the factories and mills, had insufficient money to support an easier life, but who had a strong sense of community.

She said that although she and her friend, May, had read all the magazines they'd been able to get hold of, she hadn't had any idea of just how poor they were, and how little by way of comfort they had, until she'd come south and seen the way people lived in places like Oxfordshire and London.

Perhaps it wasn't a bad thing, he'd said, that women who had so much less than others elsewhere were unaware of that. Such knowledge could be very unsettling. And also, he added, there were many areas of deprivation in the South, too, both in rural parts and in the towns. It was only because she had married into a family that was well off, and hadn't seen the deprived and impoverished areas, that she obviously hadn't realised that.

Although the weeks were passing very pleasantly, the situation with Thomas lurked constantly in the back of her mind, and as winter approached, she wondered if it wasn't time to contact him.

Her contract with Violet would finish at the end of January, and she really ought to find out her position regarding Thomas before then. After all, Violet might want her to stay on – she'd hinted as much several times. But if she and Thomas were to find that after everything that had happened, they still loved each other and wanted to be reconciled, she'd obviously return to Kentish Town. Although she would no longer work for Violet, she would hope that they could stay in contact as they had formed a strong bond.

However, whenever she went to put pen to paper to write to Thomas, something inside her invariably stopped her. She just wasn't ready, she told herself each time.

But ready for what, she was increasingly wondering in the dead of night.

And one single name kept rising to the top of her mind – John!

She'd been enjoying his company so much that it had taken away any sense of urgency about establishing where she stood with Thomas.

Also, in truth, as she was still no clearer as to what she wanted the outcome of her meeting with Thomas to be than she'd been when she'd first arrived in Belsize Park, it was better that she waited a little longer.

Therefore, until she understood herself better, her letter to Thomas must remain unwritten.

40

OCTOBER 1923

If it was difficult for Alice to know what she wanted from a meeting with Thomas, it was even more difficult for her to devise a way of getting her own back on Charles.

In July, when she'd started working for Violet, she'd been convinced that, if possible, Charles should be made to pay for the part he'd played in wrecking her marriage. But her mind had been blank as to what that payment should be, and as she'd been so happy in her work, and in the hours spent with John, she'd not given any serious thought to the subject.

But she really must decide what to do about Charles, if anything, she reminded herself as she dressed for dinner that Sunday, conscious of her delight that she and Violet would be joined by John that evening. He shouldn't be allowed to get away scot-free, to pursue his life as if nothing had happened.

It was a whole week since she'd seen John, and as the days wore on, she'd found herself really missing their walks and easy conversation. Her pleasure at the thought of seeing him that evening told her just how much she enjoyed his company, and it was gradually dawning on her that not only her paralysis about writing to Thomas, but also her failure to focus on finding a strategy to deal with Charles, could be put down to the effect John was having on her.

If that was so, she thought, pausing, her necklace in her hand, shouldn't she be asking herself the nature of that effect?

Was it possible that she was actually falling in love with John?

Or was she in danger of confusing what was no more than a liking for him with feelings of a more romantic nature?

She truly didn't know.

She shook herself mentally. It was time to clear her head.

She knew that she liked John enormously, and she was sure that it was mutual. But realistically, looking back at the way they were together, it didn't seem to be anything more than friendship on either side.

Despite the fact that she and John were usually alone when they went out, and were often in places where there weren't other people around, he'd never so much as once attempted to touch her, or kiss her, or behave in any way other than in a friendly, almost brotherly, manner.

And she'd never so much as once felt the desire to lie with her naked body next to his, as she had from the moment she set eyes on Thomas.

This clearly meant that what she felt for John was a strong liking, but not love, and that was surely true for both of them. Her feelings for Thomas had been different.

A burning desire to know if she'd still feel the same way about Thomas if she saw him again, and if he'd feel about her as he used to feel at the beginning of their marriage, swept through her. It suddenly felt more important than ever to know, and as there was only one way to find out, and that was by writing to him, she'd pen a letter the following day. She had put it off for far too long.

Smiling with relief at having finally settled on taking the first step towards clarifying her future, she raised her arms to fasten her necklace behind her neck. She stopped, her arms in mid-air.

Frowning, she bit her lip and lowered her arms. Having decided to approach Thomas, she should also determine whether to do anything about Charles, and if so, what.

For a long time now, she'd wondered if she should try to seek her revenge. But perhaps the fact that she'd pushed it to the back of her mind was telling her that she should abandon any such thought.

If she and Thomas were reunited, it would surely be better to start with a clean sheet, and to ensure that Thomas was the focus of her life. If she were to be planning revenge on Charles, he wouldn't be. And there was always a risk that Thomas might find out what she was doing. If that happened, it would remind him of her betrayal, and she'd be letting Charles effectively ruin her life for a second time.

And in truth, no one had forced her to open the door to Charles that day, no matter that he'd encouraged her to believe how much he loved her. So it could be said that she was harbouring a potentially destructive resentment towards a man who wasn't solely responsible for her misfortune. She, too, must take some responsibility for what happened.

To jeopardise her future happiness with Thomas in such a way would be utterly reckless, and she wasn't going to do so. She would abandon any idea of hurting Charles.

She took a deep breath, and smiling again, slid her hands around the back of her neck and fastened her necklace.

* * *

'You may leave the tureens, Mrs Waters, thank you,' Violet said. 'We'll serve ourselves.'

'Certainly, madam.' Mrs Waters placed the peas and carrots on the table, and left the dining-room.

John started to cut the slice of mutton on his plate.

'Before I forget, Alice,' he said, suddenly, 'this'll interest you.'

She glanced up from her plate, a half-smile on her lips. 'What will?'

'We had a Linford in the hospital for the first part of last week. A Mr Charles Linford. He's a banker apparently, not a builder, but I believe it's the same family.'

She felt her insides tighten. 'Yes, it is,' she said, hoping that neither John nor Violet had noticed her shock at hearing the mention of Charles's name, especially so soon after he'd been in her thoughts. 'He lives in Knightsbridge, so why would he be in a hospital here?'

'Apparently, he had a slight scare last weekend when he was visiting some of his family who live nearby, and he came to us complaining of shortness of breath, a pain in his chest and nausea. We suspected a heart attack—'

'A heart attack!'

'Don't worry, we soon downgraded it to an attack of extreme indigestion,' he said, and he laughed. 'His wife was very relieved, I can tell you. However, he insisted on staying in the hospital for a few days as a precaution. We suspect it was because he was enjoying the nurses' attention rather than out of any serious concern about his health. He's clearly a personable man, and there was always a steady stream of nurses vying to attend to him. Nurse Gardiner, in particular, was especially smitten, according to the hospital rumour-mongers.'

'His family must have been worried,' she said, feeling some

comment was needed, but somewhat stunned by the knowledge that Charles had been so close by.

'You can visit him tomorrow, Alice, if you'd like,' Violet said. 'What are the visiting hours, John?'

'From three to four in the afternoon, but I'm afraid he's already left. He wasn't my patient so I didn't know he'd been admitted until he was leaving. Had I known sooner, I'd have told you at once, Alice, so you could have visited him.'

'Please, don't worry about that,' she said quickly. 'I was never particularly close to Charles. As you say, he was a banker, so he hardly ever came to the building yard next to where we lived, and we went to very few family gatherings.'

'That occurs to me, Alice,' Violet said, 'and I should have said this much sooner. There might be members of the Linford family that you'd like to visit while you're here. Of course, you must go and see them. Or if you'd like to invite them here, that would be perfectly fine.'

'That's very kind of you, Violet; thank you. But they don't know I'm back, and I'd like to keep it that way for the moment.'

'Then if you won't be paying any social calls on your day off next week,' John said with a smile, 'would you like to come to the theatre Friday evening with me? You, too, Aunt Violet, of course,' he added quickly. 'Some of the doctors were saying that *The Beauty Prize* is great fun, with lots of catchy songs. It's on at The Winter Garden. Jack Hobbs and Leslie Henson are in it. I believe that the reviews are indifferent, but I prefer to go on word of mouth. Well, Aunt Violet, what do you think?'

'I'm not sure that I'm up to the lateness of the hour which that would entail, John, but thank you for the invitation. I think you'd enjoy it, though, Alice, wouldn't you?'

Alice looked hesitantly at John, and then back at Violet. 'I would, but it wouldn't feel right to go if you couldn't come, too.'

'I insist that you *do* go,' Violet said. 'I'm enjoying the latest book you got me from Boots, and I shall spend a most pleasant evening, reading.'

'That's decided then,' John said.

Both he and Alice were beaming as they turned their attention back to their food.

41

THREE WEEKS LATER

Early November 1923

Alice stamped her feet to keep warm as she stood at the back of the short queue of people in front of the newspaper kiosk by the entrance to Belsize Park underground station.

While awaiting her turn to be served, she glanced beyond the station entrance to the stall that the flower seller had set up, as he always did, on the opposite side of the entrance. The garden was fairly bare at the moment, and she'd buy a few cut flowers after getting Violet's newspaper, she decided.

A man with his back to her was buying some white flowers. Presumably for the woman standing next to him, she thought. The woman was wearing a short dark blue cape over a blue and white striped dress, and the starched white cap of a nurse. Alice gave an involuntary smile. She must be from John's hospital, and she possibly knew him.

With the bunch of flowers in his hand, the man turned and, with a flourish, offered them to the nurse.

It was Charles!

Alice gasped aloud. Her hand flew to her chest, and she took a step back, moving behind the large man in front of her, making sure he hid her from Charles's sight.

She felt sick.

In the moment that Charles had turned towards the nurse, she'd seen the expression in his eyes – it was that same expression with which he'd gazed at her on more occasions than she could count.

The bastard!

And the look on the nurse's face – one of utter devotion – was just as she, too, must have looked when she stared up at the man who'd professed to love her so dearly.

The man who lied.

The man who rejected her for the wife he'd said on so many occasions he no longer loved.

Her heart beating fast, she watched him walk a short distance up the hill in the direction of the hospital, the nurse at his side. But then, to her surprise, they crossed the road. He tucked the nurse's arm into his, and they turned left into Glenloch Road.

She frowned. So they weren't going to the hospital, then.

She hurriedly took the copy of *The Manchester Guardian* which the newspaper seller was holding out, paid for it, thanked him, and ran past the flower stall to a point a little way up the hill from where she'd be able to look along Glenloch Road.

To her annoyance, her view was temporarily blocked by passing cars and a horse-drawn bus going down Haverstock Hill. By the time the road was clear, Charles and the nurse had vanished.

Darn.

She began to walk back down towards the flower seller. As she did so, she glanced to her left. And stopped. She was in line with the narrow door through which she'd seen the private detective propelled a few weeks earlier.

Turning slightly, she stared hard at the door.

Although she'd rather abandoned any idea of making Charles suffer for the misery he'd brought upon her, the sight of him cheating again on Sarah altered things. And if she *did* now want to exact her revenge on him, this could be her chance to do so.

She had some money – not a lot, but it should be sufficient for what she was thinking of doing. It was the remainder of the money that Thomas had given her at the time of their parting. She'd had no need to break into it while at Violet's, and had, in fact, been able to add to it a little, even though she'd been regularly sending money home to her parents.

There couldn't be a better use for it, she decided, and she found herself drawn towards the private detective's office door. What's more, she had the strangest feeling that if Thomas knew that she was using his money to get back at Charles, he'd find it quite amusing. In a way, Thomas would be joining in the action she was about to take against his brother.

She went up to the door and pressed the bell. A few minutes later, it opened and a girl of about eighteen was standing in front of her.

'I'd like to see the private detective,' Alice said, trying not to sound as nervous as she felt.

'Have you got an appointment?'

'No, but I can make one, if necessary.'

'You really should have one, but he's here so I 'spect he'll see you. Close the door behind you and follow me.'

Alice did as she was told, and followed the girl up the stairs to the first floor. The girl pushed open a semi-glazed door, walked into the room, stood aside and held the door open for Alice to enter.

Looking around, Alice saw that apart from a littered desk and an untidy bookcase, there wasn't much else in what was a small room. The girl sat down behind the desk.

'What's your name?' she asked, picking up a pen.

Alice hesitated. Linford was a well-known name in the area.

'Alice Foster,' she said, and watched the girl record her name in a ledger.

'Wait here.' The girl stood up, went to a glazed door next to the bookcase, knocked on it and disappeared into another room. A moment later, she reappeared. 'Mr Williamson will see you now,' she said, and she held the door open for Alice to go into the private detective's office.

* * *

A half hour later, Alice left the office, having given the detective Charles's name and Knightsbridge address, and also the address of the house in Kentish Town which Charles had bought. And she'd given him the name of Nurse Gardiner, who, she'd said, was possibly the nurse with whom Charles was embroiled.

Walking back down the hill towards the underground station, she'd felt a sense of satisfaction. But not elation.

It wasn't a comfortable feeling to know that she'd just paid a man to spy on Charles, which was an unpleasant thing to do to anyone. And to take photographs of both Charles and the nurse. But the detective had made it clear that photographs were essential as there could be no disputing them. He had a Kodak Number Two Brownie box camera, he'd proudly told her, which allowed for a hundred exposures per roll, and he'd get her what she needed.

She'd agreed. She felt that she hadn't any choice in what she was doing, and it had been provoked by Charles, anyway.

Instead of being humbled by the fact that he'd come treacherously close to losing his marriage, as he surely must have done, and showing respect and gratitude for Sarah's forgiveness, he was betraying her yet again.

Sarah should know the truth.

And when the detective gave her the photographs and the details of Charles's assignations with the nurse, and perhaps with other women, too, she would ensure that Sarah was the first to know.

She liked Sarah, and hated to think of her being treated as a fool. Painful as it would be for her to discover that her husband was once again having an affair and deceiving her, she was a proud woman and would want to know the situation.

So she'd be doing Sarah a favour at the same time as getting satisfaction for what had happened to her.

She reached the flower seller, who greeted her with a smile.

'I saw you sell some lovely white carnations to a man who was here with a nurse a short while ago,' she said. 'The flowers looked so beautiful that I thought I'd get a few, too.'

'They were lovely, miss,' the old woman said. 'The man what you saw always gets his lady red or white flowers. It's cos she's a nurse, you see.'

'What a romantic idea,' Alice said, the words sticking in her throat. 'She's obviously a lucky woman.'

'She's that, all right. I've lost count of the flowers he's bought her in the last two or three weeks. They make a lovely couple. Is six stems enough, dear?'

Alice stared at the white flowers. Did she really want to have such a blatant reminder of the cheating Charles in Violet's house?

'I'm really sorry to mess you around,' she said apologetically, 'but I was so busy looking at the carnations that I missed the freesia. Their scent is heavenly – I can smell them from here. Could I change my mind and have a bunch of freesia, instead, please?'

'Of course, you can, miss,' the woman said, and she returned the carnations to their tall black container, picked up a bunch of the multi-coloured freesia, wrapped it and gave it to Alice.

She paid, and then continued walking back to the house, her heart beating fast as she wondered what was going to happen next.

42

KNIGHTSBRIDGE

End of November 1923

'I don't mind telling you, it's a source of real concern, Charles,' Joseph said, swirling the cognac in his snifter. 'Dorothy's stuck out there, in some little village called Rundheim, living God knows how with that German she married. She's only twenty-six. How on earth is she going to manage?'

'She's a sensible girl, Joseph. I'm sure there's no need to worry,' Charles assured him.

'Not worry! What *are* you talking about? Inflation's at its peak in the Weimar Republic. Germany's no longer able to pay the striking workers, so they're just printing more and more money. I can't imagine what her life must be like.'

'I think you'll find that the *Rentenmark*, which is what they're calling the new currency, will bring an end to the rapid inflation. And now that the Allies have agreed to look at reforming the unjust reparations heaped upon Germany, that should help, too.'

Joseph scowled. 'But not enough, I fear. I do wish she'd come home. But not that husband of hers. I wouldn't have him in the house.'

'What about her daughter? How old's the girl now?'

'About three and a half. It's just the one child, Elke – Dorothy's had a couple of miscarriages.'

'Have you told her she can come back?' Charles asked.

'I don't write to her, do I? Nellie does. We have this farcical situation where because I've said that Dorothy's no longer a part of this family, no one's supposed to be writing to her, so I'm not meant to know that Nellie and Dorothy correspond. But Nellie deliberately leaves Dorothy's letters out, knowing I'll see them, so she must know that I'm aware they're in touch.'

'Sounds somewhat familiar,' Charles said in amusement. 'Didn't you leave the first letter Dorothy wrote you from Germany on your desk so that Nellie would find it, copy the address and contact her?'

'That's different,' Joseph snapped. 'I needed to know that we could get in touch with Dorothy if necessary, or in an emergency. That was the easiest way to do it.'

'Of course it was,' Charles said. 'Much easier than you and she actually writing to each other.' He smiled at Joseph.

Joseph grunted.

'It's good that they're in contact. We both know how much Nellie misses her sister, despite the fact that Dorothy's five years older,' Charles went on. 'Sarah said that it's a huge regret of Nellie's that Dorothy's never met Emily, and probably never will. And that she's unlikely to meet Dorothy's children.'

'She certainly won't if I have any say in it!'

'To move on to something less stressful for you, which might even bring a smile to your face,' Charles continued, 'namely, Chamberlain's Housing Act, which you talked about a while ago.

The subsidies to private builders are surely having a positive effect on the business.'

'To a certain extent, that's true.'

Charles gave a theatrical sigh. 'There's no pleasing you today, is there?'

Joseph gave a grudging smile. 'You're right, it *is* good news. But – and this but is very important – a number of private companies have started building houses that are out of the financial reach of most people. If that continues, the government will reverse the Act and we'll be back with local governments being encouraged to become developers.'

'So that's quite a stressful topic, too. Well, on to something that will definitely be free from stress, Maud was looking lovely this evening.'

'Third time unlucky,' Joseph said with a grin. 'The cost of each small piece of material on Maud's back would be enough to make your eyes water. Now that I'm no longer supporting Nellie, who wants for nothing with her very clever, extremely successful husband, Maud has taken it upon herself to ensure that my wallet doesn't notice Nellie's absence.'

'It must be a relief, then, that Chamberlain's Act has come just in time to save you from dire poverty. Another cognac, Joseph? I see that your glass is empty.'

'I won't say no.'

Charles got up, went across to the mahogany drinks cabinet, picked up the decanter of cognac, came back and put it on the table next to Joseph, who immediately filled both their glasses.

'Tell me how you're feeling,' Joseph said, sitting back in the armchair. 'Have you recovered from your stay in the hospital?'

'You mean from the extreme humiliation of learning that it was nothing more momentous than indigestion?'

Joseph looked thoughtfully at him. 'You *would* tell me if it was anything more than that, wouldn't you?'

Charles gestured his surprise with the hand that wasn't holding the snifter. 'It was just indigestion.'

'According to Sarah, you've been back to the hospital for several check-ups in the past three weeks. That doesn't sound to me like indigestion.'

'Well, that's what it was.' Charles took another sip of his cognac. 'If I'm truly honest, though, the whole episode rather scared me. As you've implied, indigestion is usually a trivial thing. It's hard to believe that it can cause such agony, and such difficulty with breathing. I really thought I was going to suffocate. And so did poor Robert. What an end it was to the lovely lunch we'd had with him. I think it was such a shock that I found it hard to believe, even after they'd discharged me, that it wasn't anything more serious. I suppose I needed some reassurance, hence my visit to the hospital several times since for a check-up.'

Joseph nodded. 'I can understand that. It must've been frightening, and you're very wise to make sure that they made the correct diagnosis, and that it wasn't your heart, after all. Sarah and the children don't want to lose you yet. And nor does the rest of the family.'

'I'm not too sure about the children,' Charles said drily. 'Christopher's an easy lad. Louisa has always been difficult, but for the past year or so, she's surpassed herself and has been an absolute nightmare. The next few years don't bear thinking about.'

'She'll grow out of it.' Joseph glanced at his watch, and finished his cognac. 'It's later than I thought – Maud and I had better get off now. I must be on site early tomorrow morning. Thomas is coming with me as he needs to see the internal layout of the new houses. What about you? D'you want to join us? I could use some help with him. For all he's not as bad as he used to be, he can still be hard work.'

'He needs another woman. He should get a divorce and then look around.'

'Maybe. But it's not a subject I intend to raise with him. So what about tomorrow?'

Charles pulled a face. 'I've got a check-up, I'm afraid. Another time.'

Joseph shook his head. 'Well, they're certainly being thorough. Or, put another way, it's your money. If you want to continue indulging yourself, who are they to stop you?'

'So true,' Charles said, smiling into his glass.

* * *

Alice sat on her bed and stared at the envelope on her lap. She opened it and took out the photographs that she'd already looked at several times, the first time being in the detective's office. Slowly, she leafed through them again.

Each of the photos had a time and location recorded on the back. They showed Charles and Nurse Gardiner together on several different days, going to and from a house in Glenloch Road. Each time, a light went on in an upstairs room, and the curtains closed a short time after. They showed the curtains being opened again a couple of hours later, and in one of the photographs, a glimpse of the nurse could be seen, her shoulders bare. Other photos showed Charles and the nurse, fully dressed, walking to and from Haverstock Hill and the house.

They demonstrated clearly that Charles was cheating on his wife, something he may well have done with other women, too, since his affair with her. And he should be stopped. And he would be when she showed the photos to Sarah.

And then a memory struck her with force.

She put her hand to her mouth and drew in a deep breath. She mustn't ever tell Sarah.

She recalled Sarah's words several years earlier during their tea together in Jack Straw's Castle. Until that moment, she'd forgotten that Sarah had said that she'd prefer never to know if Charles was betraying her as she wouldn't be able to cope with it.

That being so, it would be unfair to tell Sarah. Or to tell her directly, in a way that might throw her into a state of utter distress and confusion.

She liked Sarah, and didn't want to heighten her anguish for something that wasn't her fault. She was a victim, too. She'd have to know the truth, of course, but it should be revealed in a gentler way than by sending her photographs of her cheating husband.

But she had to send the photographs to someone.

Charles shouldn't be allowed to continue as he'd been doing for goodness knows how long. That would wrong Sarah just as much as bluntly forcing her to confront the evidence of her husband's deception, if not more.

Perhaps she should send the photographs to Joseph, instead.

Yes, that's what she'd do. She felt a wave of relief. She'd send them anonymously to him, and let him decide upon the correct course of action to take. She'd send them to his Primrose Hill address, marked private, and not to the Kentish Town office.

The danger of sending them to the office was that his secretary might open the envelope, even if it was marked private. There would then be a risk of Thomas seeing them, too, and who knows how he'd react.

Also, there was a chance that Joseph might think that they'd come from Thomas, that it was Thomas who'd arranged to have Charles followed, and if so, he might be angry with Thomas for trying to stir things up. Whatever her thoughts about Thomas, that wouldn't be fair on him.

No, it would be safer to send them to Joseph's home.

She slid the photos into the clean envelope she'd taken earlier from the bureau, wrote Joseph's name and address on the front and slipped it into her bag.

Well, that was Charles dealt with, she thought in satisfaction.

It was now time she faced Thomas, and she would arrange to see him, but not until after Christmas. It was bound to be an emotional visit, whatever the outcome, and it would be better to leave such a mental upheaval until the new year.

But then she'd go.

43

FOUR DAYS LATER

Joseph stared at the envelope that had arrived that morning in the post, and at the word private. It filled him with a sense of foreboding, although he didn't quite know why. Perhaps it was the blankness of it – just a brown envelope with his name and address. Nothing else. And sent to his home address, too. And the word private had an ominous ring.

Whatever it was, he decided to finish his breakfast before opening the envelope.

Fortunately for him, Maud wouldn't be down for some time, so there was no one to prompt him to open an apparently personal letter, rather than one related to work, and he could leave it till later. He had the strongest of feelings that he'd enjoy his breakfast more if he remained ignorant of the contents of the envelope for as long as possible.

'That was delicious as always, Mrs Morley, thank you,' he remarked when the housekeeper came in to check if any of the buffet dishes on the sideboard needed refilling. 'I'll finish my coffee and then get off. Perhaps you would give me a few minutes to myself first, though, before you clear away – I've some items to read that look as if they'll require a degree of concentration, and as I'm settled comfortably here...' He smiled at her.

'Certainly, sir,' she said, and left the room.

He finished his coffee, picked up a silver paper knife, carefully slit open the envelope and took out the contents. Just photographs, no letter. He looked again inside the envelope, but there definitely was no accompanying message, and no indication of the sender.

Sitting back in his carver chair, he started going through the photographs, his irritation rising. And his contempt for Charles. So it wasn't hospital check-ups that were taking him to Belsize Park so frequently. It was a woman! After everything that had happened the previous year with Alice, he was again threatening his marriage by having another affair. Would he never learn to keep his trousers done up!

He studied the envelope again, but there was no way of identifying its origins, save that it was posted in north London.

Whoever sent it must have felt very strongly that they wanted Charles's cheating to be revealed to his family. The photographs had almost certainly been taken by a private detective, and over a number of days. The weather conditions, and the different clothes they were wearing, testified to that. As did the time, date and location that had been neatly printed on the back of each photo.

He looked again at the address on the envelope. He didn't recognise the handwriting. There was nothing striking about the formation of the letters – anyone could have written it.

So who had sufficient money to hire a private detective to watch Charles, and who hated him enough to spend their money in such a way? And what did that person hope to achieve? Were they trying to damage Charles, or was it Sarah they wanted to hurt? Had Sarah perhaps offended someone, unlikely though that seemed?

And who could have discovered in the first place that Charles was betraying Sarah? Unless they'd seen him, of course. Just as he had seen Charles with Alice over a year earlier.

In truth, anyone in the family could have afforded to hire a detective, but not everyone would have wanted to do so, or would have had a motive.

Thomas could be ruled out at once. If Thomas had discovered that Charles was cheating on Sarah again, he would have without doubt confronted Charles and taken the matter of informing Sarah into his own hands – he wouldn't have used Joseph as a go-between.

And Sarah could be ruled out, too. If she'd found out, Charles would already be prostrate on the pavement, his possessions scattered around him. From the little bits of information that Charles had dropped in the past year, Joseph knew that Sarah had forgiven him his dalliance with Alice, but had made it clear that she'd never again forgive him if he cheated on her. He'd thought that Charles had believed her when she'd said that.

Apparently not.

If he had, he was behaving unbelievably stupidly and recklessly.

Alice was another possibility.

She would have been more than peeved if she'd discovered that Charles was again having an affair, which could end with another woman being treated in the same shabby way as he'd treated her. She would have wanted to see justice done. But she was miles away – no one had seen or heard from her since she'd been sent from Thomas's house, apart from the one letter that Thomas had told him she'd written not long after returning to the North, but which he'd ignored.

He rested his elbow on the arm of his chair, and stroked his jaw, mulling over the situation.

Could the sender have been Nellie?

She wouldn't have known for certain that Charles had betrayed Sarah with Alice, but she might have guessed.

She was the only other person he could think of who'd have been so appalled, and so angry with Charles for hurting Sarah, that she might have been moved to make his actions known, believing she would be acting in Sarah's best interests.

But Nellie would surely have gone straight to Sarah, and not sent him the photographs.

And if she'd been uncertain about what to do with the photographs, she'd never have sent them to her father for him to decide – not independent, impulsive Nellie – she'd have asked Walter for advice. Walter would almost certainly have advised her to speak to her father, but he would never have encouraged her to send him the photos anonymously.

So if it wasn't Nellie, either, who could it be?

And did it actually matter who sent them?

Perhaps it would be more sensible and constructive to ask himself what the sender had hoped to achieve by letting him have the photos, and then decide if he agreed.

They would have wanted Sarah to see the photos, of that he was sure. They wouldn't have sent them directly to her as there'd have been a risk, albeit a slight one, that they might have fallen into Charles's hands or, God forbid, into one of the children's. But the intent must have been to end Charles's marriage.

He sat back in his chair. So, did he agree that they *should* go to Sarah? It wasn't a decision to be made in a rush.

Over the years, Sarah had contributed generously to Linford & Sons, and he wouldn't want to see an end to that generosity or even, a considerably more worrying thought, to find himself obliged to offer to return a part of her investment in the business, most of which had already been converted into bricks and mortar.

In addition, there was bound to be a divorce, and despite the fact that divorce wasn't the rarity that it used to be, it still carried a stigma. As chairman of the company and head of the family, he ought to do everything in his power to protect his family's name, and not risk damaging it. Sarah, Louisa and Christopher would suffer as much from a divorce as would Charles.

Upon reflection, therefore, it might be better to keep the photographs to himself and not pass them on, and to do his best to ensure that neither Sarah nor Charles learned of their existence.

For the moment, anyway.

A smile hovered across his lips. Yes, that wasn't a bad idea. And there was one other reason, too, why it might be prudent to keep his knowledge of the private detective's findings to himself.

A few years earlier, he'd needed Charles's help with something he'd wanted to do. Charles had been reluctant to give him that help, and he'd had to apply what some might term a form of blackmail in order to persuade Charles to go along with his plan.

There could well be a time in the future when he again needed Charles's help, and in the face of any opposition from Charles, the photographs would undoubtedly be useful as ammunition.

With a broad smile, he slid the photographs back into the envelope, added the date, stood up and went out of the room and across the hall to his library. There he opened the safe and put the envelope inside. He closed the safe door, locked it with a secret combination, stood back and stared at it.

The next time he saw Charles, he'd definitely say something to him about his frequency in going to Belsize Park, and tell him what a suspicious person might deduce. He might even mention Glenloch Road. Charles would be smart enough to realise what Joseph was telling him, and that should be sufficient to throw him into a state of panic and make him end the liaison at once.

After all, the most desirable outcome was that Charles ceased his extra-marital liaisons, not that Sarah found out about his adultery.

There was no need for Charles to know at this point in time that there was photographic proof of his infidelity. Or possibly ever to know.

If the person who sent the photographs became concerned that everything in Knightsbridge seemed to be carrying on as normal, they'd have to identify themselves, one way or the other, if they wanted the matter to become public knowledge. If they did that, he'd deal with it then, but for the moment, he had both the photographs and Charles exactly where he wanted them.

44

THE BEGINNING OF DECEMBER 1923

'Just before you brave the freezing cold outside to get a breath of fresh air, Alice, John agrees with me that we should invite you to stay here longer, if you wish. Isn't that so, John?'

'It definitely is.' He smiled at Alice.

'Of course, if you prefer to leave at the end of January when the contract is up,' Violet continued, 'you know that we'll wish you well in whatever you do.'

'Thank you,' Alice said.

'The only reason I've raised the subject at what might seem an unusually early time,' Violet went on, 'is because you've told us that you'd like to stay with us for Christmas, rather than return to your family for a few days. With all the snow we've been having, that's probably a wise decision, although it can't have been an easy one, and we thought it might make Christmas more enjoyable for you if you knew how happy we'd be if you were to stay on after January. It might encourage you to look upon us as something closer to family, and not just employers.'

'That's really kind of you.' Tears sprang to Alice's eyes.

'Anyway, that's something for you to think about.' Violet

glanced through the French windows at the large soft flakes of snow that were drifting down from a slate-coloured sky and covering the garden in a mantle of white. 'Be careful when you go into the garden, Alice, won't you? The snow hasn't let up all morning. Much as I'd like to go outside with you, I know you're both right – I mustn't risk falling again, not when my leg has only just healed.'

'You mustn't put yourself at risk of falling again at any time, Aunt,' John said firmly. 'And *you* should be careful, too, Alice. It's easy to have an accident when the ground is so slippery.'

'I promise I'll be careful,' she said with mock meekness.

Violet smiled at her. 'I think I'll go into the next room and play Patience till you feel you've had your fill of fresh air, or it's getting too chilly. It's a game for one person only, so why don't you go outside, too, John. We'll play Old Maid when you come back in.'

John rose to his feet with alacrity. 'I'll just get my coat and see you in the garden, Alice. Be careful now.'

The cold hit Alice full in the face as she stepped out into the garden. She stopped in her tracks, tugged her hat more firmly on her head and pulled the collar of her black woollen coat tightly around her neck. While waiting for John to join her on the snow-covered terrace, she stared at the scene in front of her.

The pond in the far corner of the garden was a smudge of grey and white. The snowflakes that were falling steadily on to the sheen of ice that covered the frozen water, lingered a moment, and then dissolved into a watery nothingness. Beyond the pool and at the back of the garden, now-skeletal trees reached up out of the hard, snow-covered earth, each dark brown branch lined with a thick strip of white, and stood stark against the pale grey sky. Enclosing them, the garden wall was topped with a glittering white crust.

The windows behind her clicked shut as John came out of the house and stood next to her. She glanced at him. There was already a dusting of snow on the hair that was visible beneath his brown trilby, and fresh snow was rapidly settling on his hair and his hat.

'You'll soon resemble a giant white gnome!' she exclaimed.

Laughing, he brushed the snow from his clothes with his gloved hands, turning towards her as he did so. His face was alive with pleasure at the freshness of the air and his eyes were creased with laughter. His whole person conveyed his sheer enjoyment of life.

Her heart gave a sudden lurch, and she felt a thump deep in her chest, as if someone had reached into the core of her being and squeezed the air from her lungs.

Oh, no, it can't be, she cried inwardly.

All the time she'd been pondering over her feelings for Thomas, John had been imperceptibly creeping into her heart, a man who regarded her in a sisterly way, but as no more than that.

And she hadn't even realised it. Not till that moment.

If she stayed on at the house, as she'd dearly love to, her feelings for John would only deepen, and at some point in the future she'd be exposed to an unbearable intensity of pain when eventually he took a wife, as he surely would.

She hadn't a choice – she'd had too much grief in her life to be able to cope with any more. She must get as far away from him as possible, and hope that the feelings she'd developed for him could be checked before they consumed her whole being.

'Snow makes everything so beautiful,' he said, looking back at the garden.

'This garden doesn't need any help – I've never seen it look anything but beautiful,' she said shakily, her insides in a turmoil. She heard the tremor in her voice, and cleared her throat.

'Very true.' He clapped his hands together. 'It certainly is a cold day,' he added, his breath forming puffs of white mist in front of him.

She nodded.

He glanced at her. 'You look a bit down,' he said, his voice taking on a note of anxiety. 'Is this about what Aunt Violet said just now about you staying longer? It can't have come as a surprise. Or did it?'

She shook her head. 'No, it didn't.'

'Despite being over the effects of her fall, it's clear she's going to be far more restricted in what she can do than before the accident, particularly in going out. It means she'll be on her own in the house a lot more. Having someone like you with her is the ideal. No,' he corrected himself. 'It's having *you* living with her that's the ideal. That's why she'd like you to stay on. And so would I.'

She stared at the ground. 'I think I ought to leave,' she said at last, her voice a whisper.

'Why?'

The word hung between them.

'Let's go back inside,' he said, with a touch of desperation. 'My aunt's in the next room so we can talk freely, and it'll be easier when we're not at risk of slipping over.'

He put his hand under her elbow, and guided her back through the French windows.

When he'd closed the windows behind them, he knelt down, unlaced her boots and pulled them off for her. His hand brushed against her leg. Her breath quickened, and she sat heavily on the nearest chair. He sat down on the chair closest to her.

'What's wrong, Alice?' he asked quietly.

'Nothing,' she said. 'Really, there's nothing wrong.'

'But there *is*.' He looked down at his hands. 'Is it me? Is it something I've done?'

'How could it be you, John? You've been nothing but kindness itself.'

'You say that, but I'm wondering if you've realised how I've come to feel about you, and out of kindness, you're trying to spare me from ever having to know that you could never feel the same.'

A small seed of hope sprang up within her.

'What are you saying?' She held her breath.

He raised his head and stared into her face. 'I've tried so hard to prevent my feelings from showing, and I really thought I'd succeeded. I didn't want you to stop coming out with me. But the truth is, I've fallen in love with you, Alice. I know I shouldn't have done, but you're so beautiful, and such a lovely person, and such fun to be with – how could I have prevented myself from loving you?'

She released her breath.

'Oh, John.' Filled with a sense of wonder, and of joy, she met his eyes, eyes that shone with love.

'When I wake in the morning,' he said, 'you're the first person I think about, and when I go to bed at night, I look at the pillow next to me and wish that your head was on it.' He gave a slight laugh. 'Aunt Violet must know the way I feel – I've never visited her as much as I have since your arrival. She wants you to stay because she likes you and you're a tremendous help to her. But most of all, I know her well enough to realise that she wants to give me the best chance possible of winning your love.'

Struck silent by an inrush of overwhelming happiness, she stared at him, her eyes slowly tracing the familiar planes of his face.

'Say something, dear Alice,' he said after a few moments.

'Even if it's only to tell me that you won't leave, or not so soon. I couldn't bear it. Please, tell me what you're thinking.'

'I'm thinking that I love you so very much, John, and that I could never have believed that anyone could be as happy as I am at the moment,' she said, her voice trembling.

'Oh, Alice,' he breathed in rapture.

'And I'm thinking I ought to write to Thomas and make an arrangement to see him. But before anything else, there's something I must tell you. You deserve to be told the truth about what happened between Thomas and me.'

He shook his head. 'There's no need for you to tell me.'

'Yes, there is. I don't want there to be any secrets between us – I've had enough secrets to last me a lifetime. You need to know the sort of person I am.'

And her voice low, her eyes on her lap, she told John everything that had happened between her, Charles and Thomas. When she finished speaking, she sat still, her head bowed, and waited.

'Everyone makes a mistake at some point in their life,' he said. 'We would all want to be forgiven for it, and allowed to bury it. What you did behind Thomas's back doesn't reflect the person you are today. It shows what can happen to someone at a time of great difficulty and misery. I love the Alice that you are today, the Alice who was honest enough to tell me something she hadn't needed to. What you've told me doesn't alter a thing – I love you far more than I can say.'

She gave him a long slow smile, and stood up. 'May I borrow your pen, please?' she asked.

45

FEBRUARY 1924

Thomas sat across from Alice in his small sitting-room. Perched on the edge of her seat by the fire, she stared at him, her nervousness growing.

'You've been here for about forty minutes,' he said, 'and you've had tea. You could have had tea in any one of the cafés near the station, but you didn't. I'm assuming this wasn't out of appreciation for the quality of my tea, nor for the purpose of eliciting from me a compliment on your appearance more than a year after I last had the misfortune to set eyes upon you. I'm wondering, therefore, what the purpose of this visit could be.'

She gave him a wry smile. 'You're right, it wasn't either of your suggestions,' she said, 'although the tea was very good as usual, and a compliment never goes amiss. Guess again.'

He gave a theatrical sigh. 'Then it must be one of two things. You want to know if we're still married, and if we are, either you want me to fall in love with you all over again and urge you back into my bed, or you'd like me to bring the marriage to an end. If we're not married any longer, the permutations are obvious –

either you're hoping we'll remarry, or you'll promptly be leaving with a smile on your face.'

She hesitated. 'What would you like it to be?'

He raised his hands and put them, palm to palm, in front of his mouth. 'Now, let me think.'

'I would've thought it a very easy question to answer.'

'You're right, it is. Well, then, let's take the first of the two. I should like to ask you something.'

'What?'

'You slept with someone else when we were married. Why wouldn't I think you might do it again? Not with Charles, of course – I'm sure that the very mention of your name would shrivel every part of his anatomy – but with another man?'

'To play your game, we'll assume that I want you to take me back. So to answer your question, you were bad-tempered all the time we were together, and you stopped sleeping with me. But just by looking at you now, I can tell you've changed. You're more like the Thomas I fell in love with. That being so, why should I be drawn to anyone else?'

'You're right, I *have* changed in the past year. It just shows that you should've been prepared to wait a little longer for full marital bliss, Alice. You were too impatient. With a new leg that's so much better than the old, I'm different from the person I was when you left. I'm almost back to being the old me again.'

'When you threw me out, you mean.'

'If you want to put it that way.'

'But not everyone returns to normal, you know. You showed no sign of your mood improving over the four years I was with you; in fact, it got even worse. Try to imagine what it was like for me, bearing the brunt of your temper every single day for four years. I'm not a saint.'

'No, you're certainly not that! Not when you gave in to your carnal desires with my wicked brother – and not just once, but again, and again, and again. There's a word for a person like that, dear Alice.'

'Believe it or not, Thomas, when you told me to leave, I was distraught.' He raised his eyebrows and stared at her in exaggerated disbelief. 'But I admit that it was only when faced with the reality that I might end up living with Charles, and not with you, that I realised how much I loved you.'

He shook his head. 'If that's the genuine reason why you're here, you're going to be disappointed. I'm sorry, Alice, but we're finished, you and I. Which brings us rather neatly to the part about bringing our marriage to an end, I believe.'

'That's right. As I'm the one who was at fault, would you please divorce me?'

He grinned at her. 'What's his name?'

'I don't know what you mean.'

'Of course, you do. You showed no concern when I said we were finished. And there's a glow in your eyes that I know well. You've the look of a cat that's got the cream. Cat's a pretty good fit for you, but I'm hoping for your sake that he merits being seen as the cream. What did you say his name was?'

She laughed. 'I obviously can't get a thing past you, can I?' He opened his mouth, and she quickly raised her hands to stop him from speaking. 'No, don't make the obvious comment. Let's leave all that in the past. His name's John O'Neill. He's a doctor. And he knows what happened between us, so if you're thinking of telling him out of spite, don't bother.'

'Well, I hope for the benefit of his future happiness that he's whole in body and that he doesn't have a brother.'

'He is and he doesn't,' she said cheerfully.

'Knowing that he's without a brother must be a relief for him.'

She stood up. 'Meeting you again, Thomas, has shown me

very clearly that despite your cruel tongue, which you used against me on many occasions in the past, I do like you, and I think I always will. It'll never again be anything more than that, though. That's obviously more than you feel for me, but I hope that nevertheless, you'll consider my request for a divorce.' She turned and took a step as if to go towards the door.

'Sit down,' he ordered, and he gestured with his hand towards her chair.

Puzzled, she sat again.

'You're not the only one who's been doing some thinking since you left. I have, too. And despite what I've said about where the responsibility for your action lies, I *do* see myself as partly to blame for us drifting apart.' She stared at him in amazement. 'I wouldn't have wanted to be living with the person I became in the years immediately after Queen Mary's. And Charles, too, must take a share of the guilt. He took advantage of the way I made you feel.'

She swallowed hard. 'Thank you, Thomas. You didn't have to say that, but I'm really grateful that you did.'

'It doesn't mean that I want you back, because as I said, I don't. Even though I can see that you've grown up, and that the spirited part of you I so liked, but rarely saw, has come to the fore. But it *does* mean that I've come to feel about you as you seem to feel about me. To my surprise, I find that I do, indeed, like you – like, not love – and I'm going to give you your freedom. I'll have a word with Walter about the best way of doing this.'

Relief flooded through her, and her eyes brimmed with tears.

'Thank you,' she repeated shakily. 'You've been more generous than I deserve.'

'Haven't I just?' he said, and he grinned at her.

* * *

As she made her way back to Kentish Town Station beneath a pewter sky that was packed with snow, her heart felt light. Thomas no longer had any romantic feelings for her, and she had confirmed in herself that she no longer felt any romantic attachment to him.

But they liked each other.

A year and a half of wondering what she felt about him, and he about her, had been brought to a close, and it was the right resolution. The deep happiness she felt told her that.

Taking care where she walked to avoid slipping, she stared ahead of her, the cold wind sending flurries of snow into her face, and she smiled. John had told her that he'd be spending the day with Violet, and he'd be wondering how it had gone. Well, she'd soon be able to tell him.

She'd been right not to let him drive her to Thomas's, which he'd offered to do, even though he'd promised to remain outside. She'd wanted to feel entirely free of anything that might influence her when she confronted Thomas, and had John been waiting outside, it could have felt to her as if she'd already given her heart to him. And she hadn't wanted that.

Much as she hated to acknowledge it, there'd still been a small, niggling part of her that had wondered how she'd feel when she saw Thomas after so long.

Now she knew.

She liked him, but it was John she loved wholeheartedly. And she couldn't wait to see him.

She hugged her coat more tightly around her, and walked as quickly as she dared along the snow-covered pavement.

* * *

Long after Alice had left, Thomas sat in his chair facing the window, staring with unseeing eyes at the people who hastened by, their faces pinched with cold, their heads bowed low against the ice-cold wind.

For Alice to have come across London to see him on such a day, with the air so chill and with snow blanketing the ground, it must mean that she'd truly fallen in love again.

How did that genuinely make him feel?

Over a year ago, in the aftermath of telling her to leave, his pain had been so sharp, and his hurt and humiliation so great, that he'd scarcely known what he felt. It had been all he could do to get to the end of each day.

But as the days had turned into months, he'd found himself missing her.

He'd remembered how patient she'd been with him, and the way she'd sponge his forehead to calm him down when he'd lain in bed in the dead of night, sweating and shaking, caught in the thrall of a nightmare.

And how she used to brush stray tendrils of hair behind her ears, without realising she was doing so, and how lovely she looked as she went about her daily tasks. He'd remembered also how she'd kneel beside him in the evening, helping him to remove his prosthesis, and how she'd often rest her cheek against his good leg and stay there without moving.

And he'd remembered the joy he'd felt in their early days together each time that he'd seen her face, and seen the love that had sprung from her eyes as she looked at him. And the desire. He had to be honest with himself – he'd seen desire, too.

Despite his ravaged body, she'd wanted him.

But he'd driven her away.

How could he have been so stupid, he'd repeatedly asked himself in the months immediately after she'd gone.

But the searing pain at her absence from his life, and his acute sense of missing her, had gradually settled into a dull ache, which was slowly fading. At times he'd wondered idly what he'd feel if he saw her again, but not knowing what she now felt about him, and fearful of being hurt again if his emotions were rekindled in vain, he'd avoided any contact with her.

Well, now he had his answer.

He liked her, as he'd told her, but he no longer felt the passion for her that had overwhelmed him in their early months together.

It had been a huge relief to realise that. Such a passion could have exposed him again and left him vulnerable, and he'd already had more than enough hurt and pain to last him a lifetime. The way he now felt about her was altogether easier to live with. And it left him free to think clearly, for the first time, about what he wanted to do with his future.

Basically, did he want to marry again?

The answer was no.

It was true that he was different from the person he'd been when she'd left him, but it wasn't true that he was back to being the man she'd met – the man he'd been before he'd left hospital. Despite what he'd said to Alice, he knew that the old Thomas had gone forever, and that although he was no longer as caustic and nasty to everyone in the family, he could still be quite tetchy.

In fact, he thought, smiling to himself, he rather relished the sarcasm and brutal honesty that he frequently employed when talking to people, and he'd be most reluctant if he had to mince his words in order to please a wife.

Also, he knew himself well enough to know by now that he was never going to come to terms with his body. And if *he* couldn't, he would never be able to believe that a woman could.

But as long as he was on his own, that didn't matter.

If he had a wife, it would.

His way of thanking Alice for not causing any unwelcome stirrings in his groin, and for showing him with clarity the future he wanted, was that he would give her a divorce as quickly as it could be arranged.

46

BELSIZE PARK

An hour later

By the time that Alice neared Violet's house, she was half-running, careless of what she looked like to passers-by, careless of her safety on pavements that were icy in patches. She just couldn't wait to get back to the house. To get back to John.

As soon as she reached the house, Mrs Waters materialised as if she'd been waiting for her, and took Alice's coat, hat and gloves. Smoothing down her hair, she hurried across the entrance hall to the living-room.

The first person she saw when she walked into the room was John. He was sitting on the opposite side of the baize-topped card-table from Violet. There were cards in their hands and on the table between them.

He saw her come in, dropped his cards and rose to his feet.

Her cheeks smarting from her dash through the chill air, she went across to the card-table, and stopped inches away from it. Breathing heavily from her haste to get back, she glanced down at the pairs face-up on the table.

'You need to check that your aunt's not cheating, John,' she said, when at last she was able to speak.

Violet laughed. 'I'm afraid that John isn't considerate enough to let me win by anything other than honest means.'

Alice looked up at John's face. Their eyes met, and held.

Violet glanced up at Alice. Alice's eyes were on John's face. Her gaze moved from Alice to John. John's eyes were on Alice's face.

'I need to have a word with Mrs Waters,' she said, standing up.

Alice made a move to help her, and John began to stand up. Violet waved them away, and took firm hold of her walking stick.

'Alice had better play my hand, John, as I might be gone a while,' she said, starting to walk away from the table. 'As you can see, we're playing Old Maid, Alice.' She paused parallel with John. Leaning on her stick, she looked down at him with eyes that were full of love.

'Play your hand well, dear John. I very much hope you win.'

Turning slightly, she smiled at Alice with warmth and affection, and then she made her way out of the room.

A lump in her throat, Alice sat in Violet's chair. She looked down at the table. The cards in front of her blurred.

'My aunt isn't the most subtle of people,' he said quietly. 'She must have sensed that I've been counting the minutes till your return.' He looked at her in sudden alarm. 'Oh, no, you're crying. Is it bad news? Don't tell me it is.' He put his hands to his head. 'He won't let you go. Is that it? Of course it is. He would have been mad to do so.'

Shaking her head, she wiped her eyes on the sleeve of her dress, reached out and caught his hand.

'They're tears of happiness,' she said, her voice catching in a sob. 'I can't remember when I last felt so happy. Thomas was actually pleasant, and the afternoon went better than I'd dared hope. We agreed that we like each other, but that neither of us feels any more than that. I'm free, John, or I soon will be. Thomas is giving me a divorce.'

He caught her other hand, and held it tightly.

'Then I can ask you what I've wanted to ask you for so long! I love you, Alice Linford. And nothing, but nothing, could bring me greater joy than if you'd agree to be my wife. Please, dearest Alice, marry me?'

'Of course, I will,' she cried. 'There's nothing I want more, I love you so much.'

He released her hands, and both stood at the same moment. Instinctively, they stepped to the side of the table, stopped and faced each other.

For a long moment, neither spoke. Then he held out his arms to her.

Smiling through her tears, she moved forward, slid her hands around his back and rested her head against his chest. She felt his arms enfold her.

'How I love you, John,' she breathed, and she raised her mouth to meet his.

* * *

MORE FROM LIZ HARRIS

ACKNOWLEDGEMENTS

A huge thank you to the brilliant Jane Dixon-Smith for another wonderful cover. The cover's the first thing to strike the eye of a reader, and my cover is certainly striking.

A massive thank you, also, to my terrific editor, Emma Beswetherick, and the absolutely fantastic team at Boldwood Books for bringing *A Wife's Betrayal* to a brand new readership.

Thanks are also due to my Friend in the North, Stella, and to fellow authors Charlotte Betts, Carol McGrath, Jenny Barden, Janet Gover, Henriette/Ella Gyland and Deborah Swift for their unfailing support, helpful advice and friendship. The friendship among writers helps to make the writing process such a hugely enjoyable one.

In looking back at Alice Linford's early years, I've presented a somewhat negative picture of Waterfoot, the mill town in which Alice was born. My heartfelt apologies to the residents of Waterfoot for dragging up such negative aspects of its past. It's a town I know well and always enjoy visiting.

I drew on many books for research, too numerous to list in full. I must mention, however, *A Social History of Housing, 1815–1970*, by John Burnett, which has helped me greatly with my understanding of the day-to-day work of Linford & Sons and with the history of housing in England, *We Danced All Night: A Social History of Britain Between the Wars*, by Martin Pugh, and the Bacup historical archives.

Last, but not least, a big thank you to my husband, Richard, for making it possible for me to bury myself in my study and write, and to you, my readers, for reading the novels that emerge from my study and go out into the world.

ABOUT THE AUTHOR

Liz Harris was born in London and studied law, before moving to California and working a variety of professions. Six years later she returned to London, completed a degree in English and became a secondary school teacher. Liz now lives in Windsor, and has written a great number of historical novels and short stories.

Download your exclusive bonus content from Liz Harris here:

Visit Liz Harris' website: www.lizharrisauthor.com

Follow Liz Harris on social media here:

- facebook.com/lizharrisauthor
- x.com/lizharrisauthor
- instagram.com/liz.harris.52206
- bookbub.com/authors/liz-harris

ALSO BY LIZ HARRIS

Linford Saga Series

A Daughter's Courage

A Wife's Betrayal

A Sister's Hope